Forever, Montana

Forever, Montana

Deb Martin-Webster

Cover Design & Photo: Deb Martin-Webster

Published 2016 by Shorehouse Books
Printed in the United States of America

ISBN 0-9980899-1-5
EAN-13 978-0-9980899-1-1

For Honey

Dedicated to my talented father C. Theodore Simpson, 1919-2015

Acknowledgments

Heartfelt thanks to my sister Marlene, my adoring husband Pete, publisher extraordinaire Donna Cavanagh for believing in me during those moments when I want to throw in my tattered writer's towel, Jim "Catfish" Curry for your contribution, dearest friends Sheila and Murph, my daughter Miasha and wonderful grandkids, Jeremiah and Samaya, my amazing extended family Lynn, Tim and Suelin, countless friends and loyal fans who encourage me to continue this series. Without this legion of supporters I'd probably be living in a cheap motel, with a half dozen cats, eating Oreos for breakfast.

Introduction

"My greatest lament in life is not bein' born in the cowboy era I love so much. Now I know a fella can't pick when and where he's born. But livin' here in Montana with Montana blood runnin' though my veins makes it easy to picture myself in some old western town sittin' in a noisy saloon, having a shot of redeye with an old prospector who's been searchin' for that elusive deposit of gold. For that reason, like any good fiction writer, I live vicariously through my western characters instead."
– Lash Jackson Montana (Montana Joe)

Prologue

"Hello and welcome to Big Sky Western Writers Magazine Weekly Radio Show. I'm your host, Jaycia Derasen, and today I'll be interviewing one of my favorite cowboys, renowned western writer and Big Sky native, Lash Jackson Montana; or, as he's better known to his millions of fans, *Montana Joe*."

"Welcome Mr. Montana. It's such a pleasure to meet you. I would . . ."

Lash: Whoa, let me stop you right there darlin'. Please, call me Joe – everybody else does.

Jaycia: [chuckles]

Jaycia: Okay, welcome to our program Joe. We talked extensively prior to the interview, so I'll get right to my first question. How do you begin writing your novels? Honestly, I don't know how one individual is capable of creating so many charismatic characters and believable storylines. What's your process?

Joe: *Ha, never thought about the process darlin'. But there are times I have to remind myself that I'm a fiction writer and these characters are basically, well . . . they're all ME. I believe writin' novels takes teamwork. The team consists of the author, the characters, the editors, the publishers and the most important team is the readers. The readers are the glue that holds the teams together.*

Jaycia: I bet all of those teams keep you awake at night. Am I right Joe?

Joe: *Yep, darlin they do . . . and, with that bein' said, I'd be kindly beholdin' if someone could bring this tire ol' fiction writer a cup of coffee – brewed, no instant please.*

Chapter 1

Potatoes, onions, sugar, milk, sweet feed, horse wormers, three boxes of horseshoe nails, barn door hinges, Jack Daniels, four pounds of coffee and two daffodils for my beautiful Rose Darlin' .

I miss being called Rose Darlin'. Lash's death was devastating to an entire generation of loyal Cowboy and Western Fiction fans, especially those in the Cowboy Writers Community. They're still mourning his death. Many readers knew him only by his nom de plume of Montana Joe. I know some fans that took his death harder than I did. One particularly overzealous woman named Mona Moon Rae. I swear I received at least forty sympathy cards from her, but that's another story in itself.

Our marriage was short lived; however, the union created a lifetime of memories and a beautiful daughter. I know Joe wouldn't want me living in the past. As difficult as it was, I had to move on with my life.

I'm now married to Paul Saxton. I remember Lash telling me what a fine man Paul is and if anything were to happen to him, Paul was someone I could depend on. His work ethic impressed Lash, as did his great sense of humor. Lash would say, "He's one dang entertaining bloke." He never knew what Paul was talking about. British slang wasn't Joe's forte. I'm beginning to pick up some of his expressions. His accent still throws me a bit. He calls me, Poppet – it means sweetie. When Lash and I first met, he gave me the nickname of "Rose" and it stuck. So much so I rarely answer to my given name of Amelia. Our housekeeper Cecilia always addresses me as Amelia. It took her two years to stop calling me, Miss Amelia. In some ways she's like a second mother to me. She stayed on at the ranch after Lash died and remains in charge of the family menus, shopping, and offers a steady shoulder to cry on when needed. I don't know what I'd do without her.

On occasion Lash and his cowboy persona Montana Joe would drive into town to pick up a few odds-and-ends and mail autographed copies of his books to special fans. He enjoyed chatting with the locals at the post office and swapping tall tales about his travels at the High Ground Cafe coffee shop where he was a regular. The locals swore that Joe singlehandedly kept the shop in business.

I remember one old fellow saying, "I ain't ever seen one man drink so much dang coffee in my life! I bet he pisses dark roast." They always had a good laugh at his expense. He loved sitting at the counter eavesdropping on their cowboy history conversations. Despite his being a world renowned author, the townies, our friends, and family never treated him as such. To us he was Good Ol' Lash the western writer or simply, Joe.

I read the creased-worn shopping list a few more times before tucking it back into the pocket of his old ranch jacket. I don't know why I went through the pockets of that particular jacket. It had been hanging in the attic since before his death; however, today I felt as though he wanted me to find it. Maybe it was divine intervention on his part; especially today. Paul and I are celebrating our wedding anniversary. I read the list of things aloud and chuckled. I thought, no matter what I'd jot down, he'd always add two daffodils to the list. It was his way of telling me he was thinking of me. I miss them. I tried planting them but they didn't do very well in Montana – too cold I suppose.

I also noticed a couple of old emails I'd printed and saved. They were always signed, your cowboy Joe or Love, Joe. Sometimes I believed he was Montana Joe. So much so I rarely called him Lash. The puzzling subject titles were his assurance that I'd open them. Funny, this particular email subject title stated it was part one of two; however, I never received part two of two. But that was Joe. I never knew what he was thinking. I started reading it aloud.

To: Rose
Fr: Montana Joe
*Subject: **Vincent Van Gogh Lends an Ear – Part 1 of 2***
Evenin' Rose Darlin'

I'm just about to check into my hotel room in Jackson Hole and of course my thoughts drift back to you and how much fun we had at this same old hotel. Sayin' I love you is the same as sayin' I love breathin'. You know my heart girl and I know yours. I can be away from you for days and when I see you it's like I never left. What a pair we are, darlin'. The other night we had some serious talk about how quickly we fell in love...and how things could have gone drastically different if you hadn't taken that trip out west or if I hadn't taken that last minute book signing gig in Currysville. Life has a way of working out the way it's supposed to darlin'. We are a perfect example of that. You brighten this ol' cowboy's life and I'll always be beholdin' to you for puttin' up with me. Bein' the peculiar ol' cowboy writer that I am!

Speakin' of peculiar, here's the perfect example. I remember our visit to the museum to see the Van Gogh Exhibit. Here's me, not knowin' the difference between a Monet and a Matisse and you the smart and sexy art critic tryin' to bring a little culture into this old cowboy's life. I was askin' you all kinds of silly questions about Van Gogh's work. And, you were tryin' not to laugh when I took off my cowboy hat and had that bandage stuck to my ear. Any other woman would have been embarrassed beyond words and walked out – but not my Rose darlin'. You just looked at me and said, "Do you know that Van Gogh had an extra testicle." The folks around us were so outraged but we laughed so hard they kicked us out. I tell ya' darlin', that was one of the best days of my life. You're a crazy girl and I'm crazy in love with ya', more than I've ever loved any woman, much more than I deserve. Keep on lovin' me girl. We can only get better. Goodnight darlin'.

'Ears to you darlin', your artistically challenged cowboy, Joe

I loved receiving his emails and, honestly, there are times I miss them. Nonetheless, the past is the past. I'm with Paul now and we're very happy. I tucked the email back in the box and closed the lid.

Jannine's yelling from the bottom of the attic steps jolts me out of my daydream or evening dream since it was nearly 8:00 PM.

"Amelia 'Rose' Montana-Saxton, are you coming down for dinner or are you going to stay in that attic until your next wedding anniversary? Get your narrow ass down here because I'm out of breath calling you by your entire name."

Glancing down at my watch I realize I've been sifting through Joe's effects for more than an hour with the champagne glasses still in the box sitting beside me. I can't believe this is all that's left of him. I put the spurs, chaps and envelopes of old manuscripts back in their final resting places. Wiping the dust from my hands I dabbed my eyes with my sleeve. Joe, I hope you're happy for me. Paul is a *wonderful husband and has been such a great father figure for Charlotte.*

"I'm on my way, Jannine and please tell Paul I found the champagne glass. They were exactly where he said they would be."

I hate to admit it but Paul's memory is much better than mine. He says he vividly remembers what I was wearing when we first met. I barely remember to brush my teeth, yet his photographic memory for retaining complex information astounds me. Numbers and routes all tucked away in his mind. I guess it's his CDL training or just a natural born gift.

That's why I find it so odd that he didn't remember his previous marriage. When we first met he said he'd never been married. He later admitted the union was so short-lived that it wasn't a marriage – more like a drunken mistake; nothing memorable. I left it at that. Still, I never understood the reasoning behind his omission. A marriage is a marriage no matter how short or insignificant. Perhaps I'm overthinking the subject.

Another odd omission on Joe's mother's part was finding out that Joe wasn't born in June, but his actual birth date was in August. I suppose Charlotte didn't want him to know he was Jameson's twin brother. I wonder what other quirky facts will be brought to light? Oh well, I'd better head downstairs and join our guests.

Paul's brother Thom and his wife Maggie flew in from England. Their British accent is much thicker than his. There are times I have to ask them to repeat themselves. They laugh and say that it's me who has the accent and not them. Keough wouldn't stand a change. I can barely understand him so I can only imagine their inability to understand him with his thick western drawl. All in all, I enjoy my ever growing eclectic family and friends.

I took one last glance and turned off the attic light. It took two tries to get the door to close properly. It needs new hinges. Keough said he would fix it. I know I'll have to ask Paul to do it if I want it done before our next anniversary. Keough has his hands full with ranch work. Running a ranch as large as Casa Montana is no easy task and Keough isn't getting any younger. Eventually, I'll need to hire additional ranch hands. However, tonight was not the time to worry about ranch duties; it was our anniversary and time to celebrate.

Paul had the first bottle of champagne open and another chilling. The family was mingling in the family room and kitchen. It seems we always end up in the kitchen. I put the glasses in the sink to rinse them off. Paul came up behind me kissing me on my cheek.

"Are you okay Poppet? You were gone for quite a while and you seem a bit quiet tonight." I told him of my experience in the attic, rummaging through a lifetime of memories.

"Paul, you know how much I love you?"

He nodded and said, "Yes I do and I know how much you still love Joe – am I right?"

I nodded. He continued to explain how a person can love two people with the same intensity. In his own way, he loved Joe as much as I did. "Joe was an amazing fellow. He had an allegiance of loyal fans that still refer to him as the best cowboy fiction writer of the twenty-first century. I know I will never replace him or compare to him, so I love him – just as you do. We shall always love Joe and that's what makes us so unique. Two people who were brought together by one incredible and extremely bizarre human being – Lash Jackson Montana."

I kissed Paul on both cheeks and thought, how lucky am I to be loved by such incredible men and not to mention very handsome men.

To say Paul is a brilliant, sexy and kind man was like saying the Aurora Borealis is a bunch of pretty lights in the sky. Not many women can say they've found the love of their life twice. We kissed again and joined our guests in the family room. Paul made a toast to another brilliant year of marriage and to friends and family past and present. I swear I felt Joe's presence standing next to us. In that same moment Paul turned toward me, kissed my palm and winked, ". . . and that is from Joe."

Chapter 2

Rose peeped into Charlotte's room – she was still sleeping. *I swear that girl could sleep through a twenty-one-gun salute with jets flying over the ranch.* Her daughter was in her final weeks of fourth grade. Her birthday was six-months away and the only threat Rose felt was not getting the present Charlotte had been subtly hinting for – a canopy bedroom set. The young girl requested that she and Rose paint her room turquoise, orange and white. Rose was considering it. They already agreed on the solid orange; however, she stubbornly insisted on orange trim. Granted her room still has toys from her nursery days—mostly stuffed animals from Paul and Joe. However, the addition of pop singers and cute actor posters were rapidly covering her walls.

Charlotte hadn't even entered her teen years yet, and Rose was already experiencing the Montana defiance. *As much as we love each other she's as strong willed as I am, not to mention having her daddy's tenacity.*

Charlotte zipped up her backpack and slung it onto her shoulder. Her walk to the truck was hesitant. She threw the bag into the back and plopped into the passenger seat. Rose glanced over at her half-closed eyes and said good morning. What came back was a garbled good morning reply.

"Well that was more or less audibly articulate and good morning to you too."

She glanced over to Rose and gave a sarcastic grin. It's the same shit-eating-grin her father flashed so often. Her mother asked her if there was something bothering her. She didn't answer. Rose asked again.

"Mama, nothing's wrong, I'm just tired."

She's been going to bed on time and Lord knows she's getting enough to eat. Cecilia still can't cook less than a banquet for dinner.

The ride was awkwardly silent. The school was only twenty minutes from the ranch entrance. However, they wouldn't allow the school buses to pick her up stating they'd need to refuel midway to reach their front door.

The school's entrance was coming up fast. Before they reached her drop-off area, Rose stopped the truck.

"What's the matter Mama? Why are we stopping?"

Rose took a deep breath and asked her what was going on? "What's wrong baby girl? You've not been yourself for weeks. Is it something I've done to upset you?"

She looked at Rose, her eyes tearing. "I'm just tired Mama. Tired of everyone telling me how sorry they are about Daddy's death and how wonderful he was. I know he was a famous western writer and a celebrity . . . but, I'm not him! To be honest, I never knew him at all. He died minutes after I was born. Everyone expects me to be like him. I'm not a writer and I'm not famous; in fact, I failed my writing test."

Charlotte pulled out a paper sporting a circled red F. "The teacher wants you to sign it. Can you imagine how embarrassing it is to get an F when you're the daughter of the famous Montana Joe and Amelia Montana? They expect me to be like you and Daddy, but I'm not – I'm me and I'll never be as talented at you or Daddy."

Rose leaned over to give her a hug but she pulled away. "I let you and Daddy down. I'm sorry Mama, I'm sorry to disappoint you."

Rose could feel her heart breaking into a million pieces. How did she not know how she was feeling? "Come over here baby. Look at me. First of all, you are the most amazing young lady I know. You are sweet, caring, tough and not to mention beautiful. Secondly, you could never disappoint us – ever!"

Charlotte leaned over and hugged her mother. Rose could see she was upset for the both of them. She never realized how tough it must be to be the daughter of Lash Jackson Montana. Rose took the paper and signed it then gave her another hug.

"Charlotte, you know you can always come to me, Pap-Pap, Morgan, Raymond or Paul—especially Paul anytime you're feeling overwhelmed. We love you and would never judge you or your feelings."

I remember how Paul was my rock all through Joe's illness and death. I never thought I'd care for another man, however, his love and kindness supported me through the most dreadful time of my life. Rose asked her if she was okay to go inside

"Yes, and thanks Mama, I love you."

"I love you too, Baby Girl." She kissed Rose on her cheek and stepped out of the truck. She was about to drive away when Charlotte ran back over to the passenger-side window. "What's the matter did you forget something?"

"No, but I need a huge favor Mama and don't get mad, okay."

"I promise I won't – what do you need?"

"When we're at school can you PLEASE not call me, *Baby Girl*? I'm almost a teenager for goodness sakes."

"I'll try to remember."

"I love you Mama. Bye-bye." She flashed her father's shit-eating-grin and ran to meet up with her friends. *Joe our girl is growing up way too fast. I'll have to practice calling her Charlotte as well. Where had the time gone? She was only 2-years-old a week ago; now she's almost a teen.* Charlotte gazed back one more time, flashed another grin and disappeared into a crowd of noisy kids.

On the drive home, Rose thought how strong her daughter had been through all of the Montana drama: Keough discovering he had another son, Meryl's husband dying, Jameson's decision to resign from the Montford-Wellesley Corporation, Meryl appointing a new CEO and she and Jameson deciding to remain board members and backing away from the daily operations. Meryl and Keough have become close friends, refusing to call themselves a couple; however, everyone knew they were friends with benefits. Paul and Kurt have taken over much of the daily ranch work leaving Keough and Meryl to travel. They took a trip to Fiji, and then decided to go to Tahiti. Rose still laughs out loud at the photographs of him in a flowered shirt and cargo shorts. A New York Yankee's baseball cap replaced his trusty black Resistol. It's still hanging on the bunkhouse hat rack. As much as Rose misses the banter and petty arguments, he deserved his downtime. Meryl gave him a fancy cell phone for his birthday and he's slowly learning how to operate it. Although he still thinks the term app is slang for appetite.

Morgan and Jannine decided to elope and married in Las Vegas. Rose agreed to give them a proper reception as a belated wedding gift. Planning the festivities was the only thing keeping her focused. She has been thumbing through party magazines and catering websites bookmarking sites she thought Jannine would like to view. Rose and her dog Lou have become serious homebodies. While the pooch is getting visibly older, he never turns down a walk in the pasture or a swim in the pond with Rose.

Joe's emails were slowly diminishing. As strange as it must seem, Rose still found herself checking and hoping to see one of his nonsensical titles in the email queue. His long-time friend and faithful lawyer, Canton Parker called last month to inform Rose of his upcoming retirement.

Parker, as Joe referred to him, mentioned that he turned the entire legal portfolio over to his Junior Partner, Maxwell Laurence. "He's up to speed on Joe's affairs and . . . eh, his unique emails. He's a huge Montana Joe fan and he's eager to meet you."

Rose thought to herself, *Maxwell, I hope you know what you're getting in to. My husband was strange and unusual to say the least. And I must stop calling him "my husband." Paul is my husband now and he makes me extremely happy.*

Walking over to the door, Rose whistled for Lou. It was a beautiful day to go for a walk. A long walk would clear the fuzziness in her head. Reviewing the morning conversation she had with Charlotte, Rose realized she was not the person her young daughter confided in anymore. Her best friends Juliana and Corey are her new confidants both of whom have been in her class since her days at the Early Childhood Center. To Rose, Charlotte was still that bossy little toddler ordering Corey around. Time is flying by and still Rose could not help but feel stuck in the past. *Joe, these are the memories we were supposed to share. But I know you're looking down at us smiling, chest puffed at how proud you are of our daughter. And to make matters worse an invitation was sent to the house from the school announcing an upcoming Father-Daughter Dance in October. Charlotte refuses to go. I tried to explain that Paul, Keough, Morgan and even Raymond would be honored to escort her. In fact, all four would love to take her. But that didn't sit very well with her. She still has the Hottie Photo of Joe propped on her bureau. It was though he was close by and still watching over her. I totally understand her feelings of emptiness. Not having a daddy around, like the rest of her classmates, is a heavy burden for a child—especially a girl. It's an emptiness I can't hug or kiss away. But Charlotte has Montana blood coursing through her veins. I know eventually she will be able to handle his death. When you live on a ranch you grow up fast and you get used to injury and death. Horses go lame, cattle is hauled off to market for slaughter, ranchers constantly get hurt stringing barbed wire, toes get crushed beneath tractor wheels – the list goes on.*

A child shouldn't have to grow up this fast. I miss that little girl who would run down the hall with her Little Lou stuffed dog clutched in her arms at the first clap of thunder. And the times she'd come into the kitchen to steal a handful of animal crackers when she thought Cecilia and I weren't looking. She was growing up before my eyes and I was missing it because I was stuck in the past. In my mind I heard Joe's voice saying, Rose darlin', it's time you moved on and said adios to this ol' cowboy's memory. I took a deep breath and said aloud, "I'll try."

Chapter 3

The event took place in Fort Worth, Texas – circa 1959. "Welcome to the Eight Second Ride Café, I'm Sylvie, what are y'all havin' today?" She tossed a gravy-stained menu onto the table in front of each cowboy. Sylvia Awenita Harris, or Sylvie as she preferred to be called, was one of the original waitresses at the ESR café. Her middle name was given to her by her grandmother. It's a Native American name meaning *fawn*. She remembers her grandmother saying that her big dark brown eyes reminded her of a deer. Everybody in town knew her and knew not to piss her off. She was well-known for grabbing cowboys by the back of their shirt and flinging them out the door if they got too rowdy. At nineteen years old and the petite height of five foot two she had the nerves of a bullrider and the strength of a calf roper. Her temper was legendary amongst the saddle bums and drifters.

After receiving one of Sylvie's infamous ass-kicking, one old cowpoke recollects, "Sylvie's like ball lightning. She'll strike you so quick you don't know what hit ya' until ya' realize you're flat out on your back." He lifted his cowboy hat to show a crescent-shaped scar. "She threw a horseshoe at me for not scrapin' the cow shit of my boots before comin' into the café. I never saw it comin'. I woke up in jail with a boulder-sized knot on my forehead. I tell ya', after that episode she sure-as-hell earned my respect."

Originally from Oklahoma, Sylvie's family moved from Tulsa to Fort Worth, Texas. Good jobs were hard to come by. Being part Cherokee and black, Sylvie's smooth dark-skin was uncommon to the early Fort Worth rodeo folks. Cowboys would whisper derogatory remarks about her until she finally stood her ground threatening to butt-brand anyone who continued their insults. A young cowhand challenged her by calling her a nasty black heifer. Sylvie walked out the back door, over to the blacksmith's shop. She returned with red-hot branding iron and jabbed him firmly on his ass. He ran towards the door hollering with his pants smoldering.

An unfamiliar drifter stuck his foot out causing him to trip and landing face down on the floor. He stood over him, grabbed the back of his belt and dragged him back to apologize.

The drifter bent down and whispered, "Now, how about tellin' that lovely young lady you're sorry, that you're an ignorant piece of horse shit, give her a huge tip and maybe . . . just MAYBE, I'll let you live long enough to ride out of town and never come back – deal?"

The cowhand nodded and did everything the drifter said. Sylvie accepted his forced apology then walked behind the counter and poured a pitcher of water on his pants.

She snickered, "Okay, I feel much better. NOW you can leave. Oh, and by the way, you owe me ten bucks for ruining my new boots." She reached in the fellow's singed pocket and took the last of his cash. Sylvie wiped her hands and shouted, "That's what you get when you sit on your ass and plot evil, you ignorant son-of-a-bitch!"

The drifter walked over to Sylvie and handed her the cash for his drinks. "Sorry, for the commotion ma'am. Some fella's ain't got no dang manners – none at all."

Sylvie crammed the money into her back pocket. "You're a fine gentleman my friend and I thank you. If you don't mind my asking, what's your name? You're not from here 'cause I'd remember a handsome fella' like yourself."

He removed his hat and tucked it under his arm. "The name is, eh . . . Keough, Keough Teal ma'am, but my friends call me, KT and since we're now friends that's what you can call me."

Sylvie extended her hand, "Well, thank you KT, I appreciate your help and quick action. Your money's no good here – drinks are on me."

By his third shot of on-the-house whiskey they were swapping lies and stories like long-lost rodeo pals. She matched him drink-for-drink and then some. By closing time both of them were so drunk they didn't remember walking back to Sylvie's place. The next morning KT was gone and three months later Sylvie found herself pregnant with no clue where Keough Teal lived or where he was headed. Sylvie thought Teal might be his last name. She asked around town but no one knew him or his whereabouts and if they did they weren't talking. Rodeo men were a tight-knit bunch and offered her no information – a rodeo brotherhood code of sorts.

Six months later, Sylvie had her baby; a beautiful little girl with striking bluish-gray eyes that set off her fair-toned skin and wavy brown hair. She named her Annabella Teal. Sylvie never saw KT again. It was for the best. As kind as he was, Sylvie knew he was probably a saddlebum and she didn't want Annabella around him. From time-to-time Annabella would ask about her father. Sylvie was determined to keep his identity a secret, telling her he died soon after her birth in a rodeo accident. To seal her secret Sylvie and Annabella left Fort Worth and moved to Los Angeles, California.

While Annabella was in school, Sylvie attended classes at the local community college. She earned her Associates Degree and accepted a position at the University of California Los Angeles insuring free college tuition for Annabella. Sylvie also changed her surname to Harrison. *A new name for a new life,* she thought.

Annabella had to grow up fast. Being an only child they were more like sisters than mother and daughter. There were times people mistook them as friends because of the drastic difference in their complexions. They enjoyed making up stories about their relationship. Whatever people asked them they would agree. An older white woman asked if Sylvie was Annabella's nanny. Another black woman asked if Annabella was blind because her eyes were so different. They would laugh about the outrageous comments people would make and their response over dinner. It was part of their nightly routine that kept them entertained.

Once Annabella was tucked in for the night, Sylvie would read the local rodeo newspapers. As much as she hated herself for getting pregnant at nineteen by a rodeo bum she often wondered where Keough Teal was and if he thought about her. Both were too drunk to remember much of anything; still she searched the listings for rodeo events hoping to see his name amongst the Gold Buckle competitors.

I don't know if I'd remember him if I saw him, but I'd surely remember his eyes. Those beautiful blue-gray eyes – like my Annabella's eyes. Okay Sylvie, it's bed time, morning comes early in the Harrison house.

She tossed the newspaper on the floor beside her bed and turned out the light.

Chapter 4

"Can someone *PLEASE* answer the phone? I'm up to my elbows in biscuit dough!"

Charlotte ran from her bedroom and grabbed the phone mid ring. "Hello, Montana Ranch and Nuthouse, Charlotte Montana speaking."

A man's voice answered, "Well hey there darlin', this is your Uncle Kurt. How is the most beautiful girl in Montana?"

Charlotte giggled, "Hi Uncle Kurt, I'm doing well but I can't say the same for Mama. She looks like the Pillsbury Doughboy in jeans."

Kurt laughed, "Uh oh, is she trying to bake again? Because if I remember the last time she made biscuits I used one of 'em to plug up a hole in the horse trough. But don't tell her because I don't want to get her all riled up. I've got some good news for her." Rose peeped around the corner from the kitchen to see why Charlotte was laughing so hard.

Rose yelled, "Charlotte who is on the phone!"

"It's Uncle Kurt and he said you make the best biscuits in Montana and to save him some."

Rose could hear Kurt hollering from the kitchen. Charlotte thrust the phone into my hand and dashed back to her bedroom.

"Hello Kurt, it's good to hear from you. How've you been?"

"I'm good darlin'," Kurt replied. Rose asked if he'd heard from that ugly brother of his.

"Yeah, he called me yesterday. He's at some island resort with Meryl learning to do the hula or some other weird island dance. I swear he must love that woman more than his prize saddle because nobody else could get him to do the crap he does for her. But I'm truly happy for my brother. He's earned the right to be happy and I'm happy for him."

"So am I Kurt. He's come a long way from the man I threatened to castrate if he didn't make peace with his son. Don't tell him I said that. He may think I've gone soft and actually care about him."

They both had a good laugh at Keough's expense.

"So Kurt, what's this good news you have for me?"

Kurt explained he'd found a buyer for Bailey, Joe's roping horse. We'd been trying to sell him for a year. He's a lot of horse for a novice rider. Kurt went on to say that he contacted one of Keough's old roping buddies who said he knew of a young calf roper who competes in the rodeo circuit. "His horse is getting older and slower. Bailey would be perfect for him."

"That's great news Kurt. As sad as I am to see Bailey go, I know Joe would want him to go with someone who knows how to ride him. He's one powerful horse; much too powerful for me and Charlotte. Daisy and Daisy Deuce are plenty of horse for us. Plus, I wouldn't want to risk Keough attempting to ride him again. Meryl would never forgive me if he broke something important."

Kurt chuckled, "Yeah, he may injure the only working brain cell he's got left."

Rose laughed at Kurt's remark. "I'll be home all day tomorrow, so stop by whenever it's convenient for you."

"Okay Rose, I'll come over and pick up Bailey in the morning. And, I have another surprise for you and Charlotte, Adios darlin'."

"Wait, what other surprise?" But Kurt had already hung up. *Hm. What on earth could he be bringing us? It's not like we need anything. We have everything we want and then some. Guess we'll find out tomorrow.*

Rose walked back toward the kitchen when she heard a familiar knock at the front door. Like clockwork, Raymond dropped by for his afternoon chat and coffee. Rose knew it was his way of checking up on herself and Paul. Nonetheless, she played along with his kind gesture. It's not like the ranch is close by. In fact, it was exactly 46.5 miles from Raymond's place and that's only to the ranch entrance. It's another two miles to the front door. Raymond is no spring chicken and Rose worried about his driving—especially at night. He failed his eye test and was told he needs reading glasses. At first he resisted, however, he knew they were right. He finally gave in, was fitted for glasses and in the end passed his driving test. Rose told him he looked like a Blackfoot professor – quite studious.

He knew the door was unlocked, but out of respect he always knocked. "Hello, are my two favorite Montana ladies at home? Mmmm, something smells good – who's baking?"

Charlotte ran out of her room laughing, "Hi Raymond! Mama's trying to make biscuits again. Don't say I didn't warn you."

Raymond laughed at Charlotte's honesty. "Not to worry Nadie. Remember, I keep my friendly neighborhood Shaman on speed dial just for your Mama's cooking."

He grabbed a cup from the rack and poured some coffee. Rose offered him a biscuit. He declined saying he was watching his carbs. We heard Charlotte giggling in the hallway and talking under her breath, "Sure Raymond, watching your carbs, hah that's a good one!"

The two friends chatted about ranch business for an hour or so, but somehow the conversation drifted back to Joe and how both still missed him and how much his presence was alive in the house. Both were careful never to compare him to Paul. Raymond liked Paul and liked seeing Rose happy again.

"Rose, I know I'm getting older and that you don't need my counsel anymore, but I'm happy you listened to me and moved on with your life. Joe is proud of you. And, he is proud how you've become a true Montana."

Rose quickly reminded Raymond that legally she was a Saxton as she decided to take Paul's surname.

Raymond was quick to respond, "My dear beautiful Amelia Rose, you will forever be a Montana no matter who you marry. It's not just a name, it's a legacy and Montana will be your legacy to pass on to Charlotte and her children's children. That half-wit prairie buzzard did one smart thing, well two smart things in his life – marrying you and bringing Charlotte into this world. Not too bad for a mangy prairie lunatic."

Rose agreed with his humorous backhanded compliment. Raymond had a way of cheering Rose up – all the while playfully insulting Joe. She asked him if he'd been to any drum circles. He replied that the drum circle was the reason he stopped by.

"It's been a while since we've attended one and I thought perhaps Paul might like to come with us. I'd love to hear what his ancestors have to say." He chuckled. "Thinking of spirits with British accents tickles my warped sense of humor. I can just hear them, 'Hello old chap! So, how goes your day and would you like a spot of tea before you zone out.'"

Raymond's attempt at an English accent had Rose laughing to the point of tears. She loved Raymond and loved the fact he still cared about her and Charlotte. He was the dearest friend she had not counting Jannine, who Rose had not heard from in weeks. *Something's up, I can feel it.*

At that same moment Raymond asked about her. "And before I forget . . . how's Jannine doing? Now that girl could be related to Joe. She's as fruity as a Christmas fruitcake! But in a lovable sort of way."

Rose nodded. "I promise I'll check in on her and let you know if we have anything to worry about." Then she remembered they were still in Japan visiting her parents. I thought, *knowing Jannine she has Morgan at some country-western Karaoke bar in Tokyo singing Shania Twain songs.*

Rose took their cups over to the sink and walked Raymond to the door. "Thanks Rose for the coffee. And, I'm happy yours isn't as strong as that stuff Joe brewed. Good Lord, you could tar the barn roof with it! Maybe that's why he was so weird. His strong brew rotted his brain, huh?" Rose laughed and kissed him on the cheek; and, as always told him to drive safely. "I will Rose and I'll let you know when the next drum circle will be. To be honest I miss spending time with you. And, I know this will sound odd, but, I always feel Joe's presence when we're together. I miss him. I miss YOU Rose."

She gave Raymond a hug and clearly noticed his eyes welling with tears. "I know wherever he is he misses you. And, I miss you too Raymond. You know you don't need a reason to stop by the ranch. Come by anytime—and I mean anytime—understand?"

He nodded. "I promise I will Rose. Tell Nadie I said goodbye and to stay sweet."

Before Rose closed the door, Charlotte darted out of her room and ran over to Raymond. "Were you going to leave without saying bye to me?" He scooped her up in his arms and gave her a huge hug.

"I thought you were too old for my bear hugs and I wouldn't want to embarrass you, now that you're a young lady."

Charlotte kissed him on his cheek and said, "I'm never too old for your hugs Raymond! Plus, I want to tell you something." She whispered in his ear, *Mvto*. "It's a Blackfoot word isn't it? Did I say the word correctly Raymond?"

For a second Raymond was taken aback. "YES, yes you did Nadie! I'm surprised you pronounced it correctly – *Mad Oh*. Who is teaching to speak Blackfoot?"

"Nobody's teaching me. Daddy told it to me in a dream and said remember to say it to Raymond the next time you see him. So I did."

Rose thought, *Charlotte never mentioned anything about this dream to me.*

"When did you have this dream?" her mother asked.

"I don't remember the exact night Mama but it was sometime last week. Yeah, last week because I was looking at daddy's hottie photo on my bureau before I went to bed." She gave him another hug and went back to her bedroom.

Raymond was visibly shaken by the whole incident. He sat on the front step completely dazed.

"What's the matter Raymond? What does the word mean?"

Without looking up he mumbled, "It's not a word Rose, it's a phrase . . . it means, *see you later*. Joe's telling me he'll see me later. Holy Jesus Rose, see me later! Am I going to die? Or is he being his usual asshole self and trying to scare the shit out of me? Leave it to him to say *he'll see me later* with no explanation. I swear on every one of my dead ancestors' spirit . . . THE MAN WON'T DIE!"

Raymond tried to laugh it off, but he was clearly rattled by Charlotte's dream. He gave Rose a hug and said he'd come back tomorrow – if he was still breathing. She waved goodbye and watched Raymond's truck disappear into the thickets. Then, Rose walked into Charlotte's room and asked her to tell me more about her dream.

"It was just a silly dream Mama. I usually don't remember them but this time he told me to write down that word and say it to Raymond. He said it would make him crap his pants and that it would be funny. Was it funny Mama or is Raymond pissed?"

"No, he's not pissed—surprised—but not pissed. It's just like your daddy to aggravate Raymond even if it was by way of a dream."

Rose asked if she'd dreamt about her daddy often. She shook her head, "No Mama not a lot. It's mostly when I look at his photo or read one of his books before I go to bed – strange huh? I guess it's a subconscious psychological thing."

Rose grinned at her usage of such complex words. "Oh, it's a psychological thing, hmm? Okay then let's get this room tidied up like I asked you to do last week; it's just a psychological thing of course."

She smiled and stuck her tongue at her mother. "I love you Mama."

"I love you too Baby Girl. Now quit stalling and get this room clean or no dessert."

She paused for a second then asked, "Did you make the dessert Mama?"

"No, Cecilia made it. And, it's your favorite–peach cobbler."

She wiped her brow. "Whew, for a minute I thought you'd made it. Okay, my room will be clean before dinner – I promise."

She's becoming a true Montana smart ass like the rest of the family.

Chapter 5

It was early afternoon when Keough called asking if he and Meryl could drop by before they headed to Rock Springs for The Wyoming's Big Show Sweetwater County Fair. Keough's become quite the globetrotter thanks to Meryl. Rose thought how good it will be to see him. His hair had turned completely white and so had his beard. But it suited him. Rose would even use the word handsome. *I wonder if Joe would have looked as handsome as Keough and Kurt at their age. I'll never know.*

Joe's fraternal twin brother Jameson's hair was just beginning to show a little white at the temples. He's turned out to be quite a reliable guy and a great brother-in-law. He's even learned to help around the ranch. Who would have thought a New York CEO could shovel horseshit with the best of them? Rose credited Raymond for his transformation. He believed in him when no one else did. Rose could not believe less than four years ago she couldn't stand being in the same room with him. Time and sobriety heals all.

Forgiving Jameson had Rose thinking about her own family. Specifically, how she didn't keep in touch with them or attempt to reach out to her brother in California. Perhaps it was because they'd never understand her current lifestyle. *I know my sisters wouldn't. They think I sold out by not marrying a rich black man. However, I don't see them turning their new rhinoplasty, restructured noses up at the hefty Christmas gift checks I send. There are times I wish I had a local sister-in-law I could chat with on a daily basis. Someone who understands me and would never judge me for living my life the way I want to. Joe's sisters keep in touch, however they have their own busy lives to live.*

Lou walked over and sat by Rose's feet. She stroked his head thinking about everything she had survived. "Lou, you would never judge me would you boy?" He raised his huge head as if to say, *NEVER!* A few minutes later his ears perked and he ran to the front door. Rose glanced at her watch and realized that it was almost 4 o'clock. Paul texted her saying he would be home by 4:00 PM. Lou heard the rumble of his rig before Rose did. She could see the dust billowing in the distance. He's been on the road for two weeks. And, she hadn't thought about what they were having for dinner. Cecilia offered to drop Charlotte off at her friend's house to spend the night. Cecilia also took the evening off. Not being around when Paul returned from his OTR trips was her idea, saying "a husband and wife needed privacy – if you catch my drift." She'd wink and chuckle and Rose would blush at her statement.

Ten minutes later, Paul pulled up to the house and parked the rig in its usual place beside the barn. At first, Rose didn't recognize him. His hair was pulled back in a short ponytail and his beard was much longer than she'd ever seen it. She didn't know anyone whose hair grew as fast as his. She'd kill to have hair that grew so quickly. But then again she'd have to spend twice as much at the salon. *Speaking of which that reminds me, I need to make an appointment with Le'Roy, our local ranch plumber turned hairstylist.*

Rose ran over to hug him and he abruptly stopped her with an extended arm. "Trust me, you DO NOT want to be near me until I've had a proper shave and shower. I smell putrid!" At first she told him that she didn't care because she missed him so much.

"Oh trust me Poppet you would. So stand down wind until I get to the front door!"

He bolted by her and one quick sniff told her he was right. He was a bit ripe. *He stinks like he's getting paid to stink!*

"Eww, you've convinced me. I'll wait until it's safe to hug you. And, don't skimp on the soap and hot water."

An hour and a half later he emerged from the bathroom clean shaven and minus the ponytail. Still wrapped in a towel he royally announced, "Now, you may hug and kiss me as much as you like – please, carry on."

"And what makes you think I WANT to hug you after I was so rudely rejected."

He walked over to me and dropped his towel on the bed exposing his aroused penis. "Is this rude enough for you?"

"You are one horny dude Paul Saxton!"

"Yes, I know Poppet, but you still haven't answered my question. How about we get rid of it together – yes?" Paul was an amazingly talented lover. He had a way of engulfing her entire body with his body. His kisses were warm, tender, and very sexy. And his British accent melted her heart. After an hour of welcome home lovemaking the two talked about his travels and how, someday, she would like to ride along with him.

"Maybe we could head to California," Rose suggested. "I miss San Francisco and Los Angeles."

He laughed, "So you want to leave the ranch and travel in a stuffy old truck cab? I'd give you two days before you rip your hair out. My truck stop food flatulence alone would be grounds for divorce. Not to mention the lack of room for all of your makeup; which you don't need. You're just as beautiful without it. I love you Amelia Montana."

"You mean Amelia Montana-Saxton." Paul looked surprised. "So, you've decided to add my last name to the famous Amelia Montana. Why now? What changed your mind?"

"Because you are my husband and I love you. I'm proud of the Saxton name. I'm proud of you. And, it's time I let go of Joe's ghost. I know he'd want me to move on with my life and I can't do that if people continue to referring to me as Mrs. Montana. He'll always be a part of me, but I need to acknowledge my new life as a Saxton."

Paul rubbed his chin. "Okay, if that's what you fancy. I'd be proud to have my last name attached to Montana. On second thought, perhaps I should add Montana to my name. Just think of the royalty money I'd accrue! Paul Saxton-Montana. Has a bit of a nice ring to it – wouldn't you agree?"

Rose rolled her eyes and laughed. "Paul Saxton will do just fine. Plus, I don't need another long-lost Montana family member showing up on our doorstep. Finding out I have a twin brother-in-law is enough of a shock."

Chapter 6

"Mama, Uncle Kurt's here." Charlotte ran to the end of the walkway and waved. He parked his truck beside the barn. A man with a young boy in the passenger's seat followed behind him. They were towing a large horse trailer. *They must be Bailey's new owners.*

Charlotte ran over to Kurt giving him a big hug. "Hi Uncle Kurt, are they taking Bailey to his new home?"

"Well hey there beautiful! How's my favorite niece? Are you getting taller or am I shrinking?"

Charlotte laughed. "I'm getting taller. Mama had to get me new jeans last week because my ankles were showing. So answer my question. Are they going to take Bailey?"

"Yes, Bailey is going with this gentleman," Kurt smiled. "He's a championship roper from Billings and Bailey's gonna enjoy being his new roping horse. Come over and meet him."

Charlotte seemed more interested in his son. "Charlotte this is Josh T McCabe – JT to his friends. He's one of the best calf ropers in Montana and this handsome young fella is his son, Sawyer." Both took their hats off and said hello. Charlotte said hello to JT but continued to stare at Sawyer. Sawyer put his hand out and said, "Howdy Miss Charlotte. I really like your boots!"

Charlotte blushed and shook his hand, "Thank you, my Pap-pap brought them for my birthday."

Sawyer smiled, "Well he's got *damn* good taste!" JT nudged Sawyer. "Oh, I'm sorry, I mean he's got *very* good taste – sorry ma'am."

Kurt told them to run in the house and get some carrots for Bailey. Kurt and JT walked over to the barn.

"Mama, Uncle Kurt and Mister JT are going to load Bailey and he told me and Sawyer to get carrots." Rose stopped both of them before they opened the refrigerator.

"Whoa slow down. First things first, before you go in the fridge wash your hands and second aren't you going to introduce me to this handsome young man?"

Sawyer took his hat off again and introduced himself. "Hello, I'm Sawyer . . . eh, very nice to meet you."

Rose shook his hand. "It's very nice to meet you too Sawyer. My daughter seems to be more interested in carrots than introductions."

Charlotte rolled her eyes and whispered, "Mama, you're embarrassing me! Anyway, Uncle Kurt said to come over to the barn – they're loading Bailey."

Rose put on her barn boots and walked over with Charlotte and Sawyer. Kurt and JT had already loaded Bailey, along with his tack and saddle.

Kurt started the introduction. "Rose this is Josh T McCabe. He's the best cattle roper in the state of Montana."

Rose smiled, "I know exactly who he is Kurt – what a surprise! You won the World Series of Team Roping in Las Vegas last year!"

"Why thank you ma'am. I have to admit I'm surprised you know so much about the rodeo circuit. Did you ride?"

"The only thing Rose ever roped was my nephew. She's from New York City." Kurt snickered. I laughed,

"Yep, the only thing I'd ride was a yellow cab and the subway; however, I've become quite the horsewoman. I had to learn quickly. My husband was the horseman in the family. He taught me everything I know about horses."

JT paused, "I'm sorry for your loss Miss Rose. I had the pleasure of meeting Mister Montana at a book signing in Las Vegas. He was a fine man and a talented novelist. In fact, I just finished the, *Outlaws of Burnt Canyon Crossing* series. I heard they're making it into a miniseries." Rose nodded, "Yep, in fact it should be airing next month."

Sawyer and Charlotte came running into the barn almost knocking me over. "Hey slow down you two!"

"Mama, can Sawyer come over sometime? He can help me groom Daisy and Daisy Deuce – please?" Rose looked at JT and he said it was okay with him as long as Sawyer did his chores at home. He promised he would.

"Then it's okay with me JT. It'll be fun having two kids running round the ranch. It's been way too quiet for my taste." Rose winked at both Charlotte and Sawyer who had huge smiles on their face.

Sawyer extended his hand, "Thank you Miss Rose. It's been real nice meeting you." Rose shook his hand and told him he was very welcome."

Rose also thanked Kurt for his help in finding Bailey a new home and joining him up such a famous new owner and JT for introducing Sawyer to Charlotte. "She doesn't have many friends and hasn't been interested in doing so since I remarried. Can you imagine how awkward she feels when everyone in the world knows the great Lash Jackson Montana and she never got to meet him. It breaks my heart."

JT understood. "I'm happy she's taken such a shining to Sawyer. In a way he has the same problem. Being the son of a famous rodeo star; he has no interest in roping. Actually, he loves to read and write. He's written a few short stories."

Rose told him that she'd be happy to give him some writing advice if he's interested.

"Thanks Miss Rose I'm sure he'd appreciate it."

"My friends call me Rose and you and your son are friends."

He smiled, "Okay Rose. Again, thanks for your hospitality and I know Bailey will be just fine as my new roping horse." JT motioned for Sawyer. He extended his hand again. "It was very nice to meet you and Charlotte."

"It's my pleasure, Sawyer and I hope to see you back at our ranch soon." He glanced over at Charlotte. "I'll come back soon, I promise. Bye Charlotte.

"Goodbye Sawyer and don't forget to call me, okay."

Hmm, call me? She's getting calls from boys already Joe. Lord, help me!

Kurt had started walking towards his truck when Rose remembered he said that he had some sort of surprise for them. "Hey, hold on Kurt. You mentions a surprise – was it meeting Josh T McCabe?"

Kurt grinned, "Well that's part of it." He reached into his truck and handed her an envelope. She opened it and inside was a generous check for Bailey and tickets to this year's World Series of

Team Roping in Las Vegas. "He's hoping you all will come out and watch him ride Bailey. Ya' know, to cheer him on."

It was a huge surprise. Rose had always watched the event on television but never attended. *I'll have to call and thank him for his generosity.*

Paul was on his way home from running errands in town when he passed JT's horse trailer and Kurt's truck leaving the ranch. He thought, *Oh no, I've forgotten they were coming for Bailey today. Rose must be going mad. Good thing I bought her favorite chocolates. They might smooth things a bit.*

Rose glanced out of the living room window and saw Paul parking the truck. *Hmm, looks like he bought out the store.* She went outside to help him with the bags when he motioned for her to take the small one hanging from his wrist.

"I bought you a little something. Consider it a peace offering because I totally forgot Kurt was coming over to help load Bailey today. Forgive me?"

Rose pretended to be upset; however, when she looked inside his bag she couldn't stop smiling. *How does he know these are my favorite chocolate? I never mentioned them because I'm trying to lose the ten pounds I gained when Joe died.*

Rose grabbed his arm and asked, "Okay, how did you know these are my favorite? I don't remember mentioning them to you – so fess up. Who told you?"

Paul glanced at the bag then said, "I must confess it was purely coincidental. I happen to like these and thought you'd like them too." He thought, *I can't admit I found the sweet wrapper in her truck – many wrappers. And with her trying so hard to lose weight, I can't upset her. That would cause her to eat more!*

"What an amazing coincidence! I'll take a few to nibble on in the truck and put the rest in the refrigerator until I lose a few more pounds."

Paul took a deep breath. *You truly wiggled out of that one Paul.* While they were putting the groceries away Paul asked me how the transfer of Bailey went. "Was he difficult to load?"

"No, not at all, he was very willing to go. It bet it was the scent of their mare lingering in the trailer."

He kissed her on her cheek, "Again, my sincerest apologies Poppet for not being here. I'll call Kurt later tonight and thank him for his help."

Rose told him he also missed Kurt's surprise. "You'll never guess who purchased Bailey?

"Let me guess. Was it perhaps the Queen or maybe George Strait? I don't bloody know who purchased him; however, did they leave the check? I'd like us to start saving for Charlotte's college fund."

Rose gave him a blank stare. "Paul, I know you didn't come from a wealthy family, however, Joe left us well off. So you needn't worry about money – we're financially solid."

"I understand Poppet, but there are times I feel as though I'm living off of you. I know I bring in my own income but that's just sitting in my account and I haven't used any of it in years. So forgive me for wanting to provide for my wife and daughter."

It was the first time Rose heard Paul refer to them as HIS wife and daughter.

She walked over to him and put her arms around his waist. "Paul we are a family now. You aren't living off of me no more than I'm living off of you. We are equals and I respect you as such. And, if I've made you feel less than that, I'm sorry."

He smiled, but pulled away from her embrace. "No need to apologize Poppet. Well, I'd better go check on the horses."

Rose watched him disappear into the barn. *He seems distant and worried about something. I just can't put my finger on what it could be.*

Chapter 7

Los Angeles Metro Hospital was bustling. Saturday nights are always a busy time in Emergency. Annabella had been on call for eighteen hours and was ready to go home for a bath and shot of whiskey. She was seriously considering the position of Chief of Surgery. However, with her focus in Oncology, she didn't have enough time for herself, let alone a running a team of surgeons. She glanced down at her watch. It was almost 5 o'clock in the morning. Things were starting to calm down so she called it a night, or day. By the time she gathered her things from her office, it was dawn. The sun felt good on her face and there was a mild breeze blowing on her neck. She thought, *why the hell am I considering the COS position. I guess I'm a freakin' sucker for punishment! I could have had a cushy administrative position, but no I had to go and put my hat in the ring to become the next head honcho. Maybe it's not too late to change my mind. But then I'd have to hear my mother bitching at me through eternity.*

"What a mess you've gotten yourself into Annabella Teal." she muttered.

She threw her backpack in the backseat of the car and headed for home. She made her morning stop at the local coffee café and ordered *the usual* – black with one sugar. The barista knew her well and had it ready.

"Here ya' go Annie. Damn girl, you look like someone shot your hair stylist." She reached under the counter and handed her a mirror. She ran her hands through her hair.

"Sophie, I'm too tired to give a shit. May I just have my coffee, please?" Sophie smiled and handed her the coffee with a croissant.

"The croissant is on the house Annie. When was the last time you ate? Sweetie, if you get any thinner I can use you as a bookmark."

Annie picked up the book Sophie had laid on the counter, "Hmm, *Lost Trails of Sweet Grass Canyon* by, Montana Joe. When did you start reading westerns? I pegged you as a trashy mommy porn type of gal."

Sophie snatched the book from Annabella. "So I like cowboys, you got a problem with that? Hell, I was even thinking of taking a vacation to Texas, maybe find a cowboy boyfriend. Hey, why don't you and I take a road trip? See the country. It'll do you good to get out of LA for a while. When was the last time you took off from work?"

Annabella took a quick sip of her coffee. "I can't remember Sophie and I'm too tired to think right now."

"Probably when Bush was in the White House – am I right?" Sophie chided. "And if you want my advice . . ."

Annabella took a deep breath and mumbled, "And if I didn't want your advice you would still give it, wouldn't you?"

"Annie, you need to take your name out of the hat for this COS position before it's too late. As it is you have no life and its making you look older than you are. I never met your Mom but I bet she'd agree with me."

She ripped off a piece of croissant and popped it in her mouth. "She probably would agree with you Sophie. Mom was a no-nonsense-woman; made her own rules and lived by them. She taught me to do the same. When did I become such a workaholic asshole? Jesus Christ, I'm in my forties and all I do is work! I suppose it's an inherited behavior. Mom and I always worked hard and saved our money for a rainy day."

Sophie handed her another cup of coffee and shook her head. "Well, sister, if you haven't noticed it ain't rainin' and hasn't rained in LA for over two months; so you must have a shit load of money saved! Annie, your Mom and Dad would be so proud of who you've become. A bigwig doctor making the big bucks – am I right?"

"You're half right Sophie. I never knew my Dad, and Mom never talked about him. I was what you would call a *wham-bam-thank you-ma'am* baby. Mom got pregnant by some saddlebum in Texas and had me. The only thing he left her was half of this rodeo heart charm. Who the hell knows where the other half is? Probably left it with another woman in some other rodeo town I suppose. However, she did say I look very much like him. Problem is, I've never seen him. She once told me that he was dead, but later said she lied to keep me from searching for him. For all I know he could be dead or worse a Republican."

Sophie cringed, "A Republican – God forbid! I can picture you trying to have bipartisan Health Care debates with him. Maybe it's best you don't know him." They shared a good laugh as Annabella finished her second coffee.

Sophie excused herself to take care of the growing line of customers. Annie picked up the book Sophie was reading and browsed through the pages reading a paragraph or two just to pass the time. *Montana Joe huh, I never heard of the guy. But then again I don't read westerns.* She flipped to the back and started reading his author biography. About half way through she froze. She knew she stopped breathing for a second and then read the paragraph out loud:

"Renowned award-winning western writer, Lash Jackson Montana or Montana Joe to his fans, is the talented son of retired Rodeo Champion, Keough Teal Montana and Charlotte Montana . . ."

Sophie asked a co-worker to take over the line and walked over to her favorite doctor. "Annie, are you okay? You look like you've seen a ghost…no, many ghosts with a couple of zombies thrown in the mix. What's wrong?"

For a minute she couldn't respond to Sophie's question. she was still in shock by the fact she'd found Keough Teal. She and her mom always thought Teal was his last name. Now she came to find out his actual surname is Montana. Not to mention that he's also the father of this renowned hotshot western writer.

When she was finally able to speak, she stammered, "Sophie, I . . . I think I may have found my father. This writer's father may actually be MY father! Oh my God, look at the author's photo. He has the same color eyes as I do. Those gray-blue eyes. In fact, his features are unbelievably similar to mine. Well, except he's white and I'm . . . I think I need something stronger than coffee."

Sophie ran to the back and returned with a mini bottle of Jack Daniels and poured it into Annie's empty coffee cup then topped it off with a little bit of coffee. "Hey, it's my emergency stash – don't judge me!"

Annie took a swig of the spiked coffee. "All this time, all these years of being a Harris/Harrison only to discover I could be a

Montana! What the hell do I do Sophie? Should I look up these people, ring their door bell and say, 'Howdy guys, I'm the bastard child of Keough Montana – where's Pops?'"

Sophie grabbed Annie's coffee and took a swig. "Jeez, Annie I don't know what to tell ya'. But if I were you, I'd at least scope them out; maybe they're decent people. I'd be willing to go with you. In fact, we can take along my roommates Joel and Ginger if you want."

Annie knew Sophie meant well, but if she were going to meet her long-lost daddy she'd like to do it alone. She didn't want to scare him off by bringing an entourage of eccentric Los Angeles weirdoes. No offense to her friends but Joel had part of his head shaved with piercings on the other side and Ginger, well let's just say she had trouble separating reality from fantasy. She liked to tell people that she was a companion of Doctor Who and lived on Gallifrey.

"Thanks, Sophie but I think this is something I need to do on my own. Can I borrow this book? Maybe I should read it before I introduce myself to the family – an icebreaker of sorts."

"Of course Annie; keep it if you like. Just let me know how you make out. Look at this as divine intervention. Your decision is being made for you not to take this shitty COS position."

Annie hugged Sophie and drove home. After taking a very long shower she did some research on the Montanas. Sadly, she found out that Lash had died a few year ago, leaving a wife and young daughter. There were no photographs of them. *I guess Lash liked to keep his private life private.* Keough had three other grown children. *I bet they don't know they have a half-sister. And, I bet it'll be even more of a surprise that their dad has another kid by a black woman. She* fell asleep with the book still in her hand.

The next morning, Annie packed her bags and headed to work. She wanted to let them know that she had a family emergency and needed a few weeks off. She didn't want to get into details – *none of their business.* One of her colleagues said he would take over her patients while she was away. *I owe him big time.* Plus, there was less of a chance for her to chicken out if she departed directly from the hospital.

Annie left Los Angeles midmorning. The traffic wasn't too backed up; just a half dozen accidents to avoid. Not bad for LA.

Once she was off the freeways and on the interstate, she ran different scenarios in her head on how she would approach these people. None seemed genuine. Others were trite and sarcastic to be exact. *Hey there white folk. I'm the caramel kid you never knew – surprise!* The image of them standing lifeless, mouths a gasped, grabbing their chests, a la' Fred Sanford gave her a quick and much needed chuckle. On the other hand, maybe they're really cool people. *I guess I'll find out soon enough.* About the time she reached Utah, she began to question her decision to make such a trip; her life without a father, her life with a father or how her life might have turned out differently if she were raised by Mom and Keough.

Annie pulled the car over at a gas station to refocus and to take a quick bathroom break. While she was in the bathroom stall it finally dawned on her, *Oh My God, if Lash was his son and he's older than me, he must have been married when I was born! Mom had a one-night-stand with a married man.* Annie tried to rationalize that perhaps Keough wasn't married to Lash's mother when she was conceived or maybe they'd separated.

As she came out of the stall, Annie bumped into a startled woman clutching her young daughter. They stared at her as if she'd lost her mind. She must have been talking out loud in the stall. They continued to stare as she washed her hands and left the area. Annie figured she probably would have stared too if she overheard some lunatic babbling to herself in a toilet stall.

She filled up her Audi then stopped in the connecting Quik Market Shop for a cup of coffee. She never liked coffee very much, however for some reason she instinctively craved it just like her mother did. She always had a pot brewing for those long work days. The guy in front of her had two large cups of coffee, a burrito and a bag of pork rinds. *What an odd combination; must be a Utah thing.* While the cashier rang up his items they began to chat.

"So Paul, where ya' headed today? I think I see you more than I see my wife. It can't be the coffee because it really sucks – if I'm being honest."

Paul grinned, "Oh it's not that bloody awful. I'd drink old engine oil if it had enough sugar in it." Both men laughed and continued their friendly conversation.

Annie was surprised to hear a British accent coming from what looked to be a Utah cowboy. He was decked out in western jeans, boots and a cowboy hat. He went on to tell the cashier that he was on his way home to Montana from Las Vegas.

"And with that being said, you may not see very much of me. I'm thinking about quitting this over-the-road driving. Now that I'm a married bloke I really miss the wife and Bab'bee. I promised Lash I'd take care of his family and I intend to keep that promise. And now that Rose and I are married it's doubly important that I keep my word."

His statement stunned Annie. *Lash? Did he say Lash? Could he be referring to Lash Montana?* "NO WAY!" Again, she realized that she was talking out loud again. The cashier and the truck driver stopped talking and turned their attention toward her.

Paul asked, "Pardon me, but . . . no way? No way what? Were you addressing me? Are you okay Luv? *C'mon, Annabella think fast.*

She mumbled, "Sorry, I'm just surprised to hear an English accent in Utah. You are British, right? I have friends in England."

Paul smiled, "Yes I am, Birmingham to be precise. And, where might you be from Luv?" She choked out Los Angeles. Paul laughed. "And are all the people in Los Angeles amazed by British accents?"

The cashier chuckled at Paul's attempt to be funny. She was about to answer him when the bathroom lady and her daughter walked in. The mother pointed at me and quickly left the store. Paul looked confused. He asked if Annie knew them. She told Paul no but they also heard her talking to herself in the rest room.

"I guess I must have spooked them too. Well, it's been nice chatting with you two gentlemen, however, I'd better get going or I'll never get to Malta."

Paul turned around and asked, "Are you going to Malta . . . Malta, Montana?" she nodded, "Yes, I'm looking for my . . ." she stopped midsentence. *If this guy knows Malta then he may know my father and I wasn't ready to share any information – not yet.*

"I'm looking for a nice place to vacation, you know, to relax. I'm a doctor and my life is extremely stressful, so I decided to take a few weeks off."

Paul and the cashier simultaneously rubbed their chin. Paul replied, "Hmm, Malta is a small town but Billings might be a better place to vacation – lots of restaurants, theaters and such."

The cashier agreed. Annie thanked both men for their help and for not calling the local psychiatric hospital to report her external-internal chatting episode.

"Not a problem Luv, you take care of yourself and if you decide to visit Malta feel free to stop by the Montana ranch. I'd like my wife to meet someone who talks to herself more than she does. She's a writer and she's always talking to herself while she's writing. In fact, in some way you remind me of her."

Annie thanked him for his generous offer and left the store. Paul waved goodbye as his big rig kicked up the parking area gravel and headed back toward the interstate. She smiled and waved back at him. After putting the key into the ignition, she sat for a minute to process what had just happened. What are the odds of running into a person from England, who not only knows the Montanas, and just happens to be married to one? She looked at the half heart rodeo charm hanging around her neck. *Mom, if you have something to do with this you could have at least given me a heads up!*

Chapter 8

Kurt took off his hat, reached in his back pocket for his bandana and wiped his forehead. *I can feel the change in the season in my bones. Autumn is an unpredictable month in Montana. One day it's sunny and the next day you've got a blizzard bearing down on you. Add to that running a ranch as large as the Montana ranch and you've got yourself one hell of a job!* Kurt brushed the corral dust off of his hat and headed back to the barn. He gathered all of the summer horse tack, blankets and saddles and took them to the tack room. He hung the blankets over the stall doors to air out before storing them. Kurt sat the saddles on their saddle stands. "I'd better start cleaning and oiling them." He glanced at his reflection in the horses' water bucket. "Damn I'm getting grayer by the day. Must run in the Montana family I suppose. Now that Bailey's gone there's more room to store saddles. I swear that horse was crazier than snot – high strung son of a bitch. The only three people who could ride him were Lash, Keough and his new owner, JT McCabe. Not even our seasoned ranch hands would try to mount him." *That reminds me, I need to hire two more ranch hands before November. As wild as he was, I'm glad Bailey went to someone who needs a fast roping horse, but there are still two horses that need stalls cleaned and haying. Thank goodness Paul is bringing enough hay to get them through the winter months. Speaking of Paul, where the heck is he? I hope he didn't get delayed behind some pile up on the interstate.* "Oh well, I'd better get to work." Kurt started cleaning Keough's saddle. He unbuckled his saddlebags to oil the flaps and found an old photograph of Keough and him sitting in a bar in Texas. It brought a smile to his face. *This must have been taken after Keough's first professional Bronc Riding Competition.* "Dang, we look soused and young." Kurt grinned and ran his finger over the photo's weather-worn creases. "What a pair of drunken assholes. He stuffed it into his shirt pocket and thought, *I'm happy for you brother, but I gotta admit I really miss talkin' to ya'. What I wouldn't give to have one of our weekly brotherly arguments over stupid shit.* He ripped the string from the bag of horse feed and topped off the winter grain barrel. The sound brought Daisy and Daisy Duce trotting over to their feed bowls. He grabbed a handful and let them nibble it out of his hand. "Sure do miss ya' brother. Maybe someday I'll find someone like Meryl and possibly settle down. I'm too damn old to start a family. I would have loved to have had a kid or two of my own, but I guess it just wasn't in the cards for me." He dabbed his eyes with his shirt sleeve. *Must be the prairie dust makin' 'em water.*

Reflecting on his own life, Kurt wondered how it might have been different if he'd stayed in Texas. He loved Montana, but Texas had a special meaning for him – especially one young lady. He smiled thinking, *what a spitfire she was; she sure as hell stole my heart. Well, I guess I'll never know.*

He felt something vibrating in his jacket pocket – it was his cell phone. He took his work gloves off and tried to press the answer button. *Damn, I really hate these things!*

"Hello." There was a moment of silence, then a barely audible reply.

"Hello, Kurt is that you?"

He pulled the phone away from his ear and stared at it, then placed it back to his ear. "Of course this is Kurt! Who else would be answering my damn phone! Who the hell is this?"

"It's Meryl, Meryl Wellesley and how-the-hell are you, Kurt?"

"Oh Jeez, I'm sorry! Hello Miss Meryl, I didn't recognize the phone number. Thought it was one of them pain-in-the-ass telemarketing folks. I'm good, and how is that jack ass brother of mine?"

"That's why I'm calling. We want to come to Malta and spend the holidays with the family. It's been far too long since we've visited and to be honest I think Keough is feeling a bit homesick. We want it to be a surprise for Rose and Charlotte so keep it between us, okay?"

"Sure thing Miss Meryl, however, I'll have to let Cecilia know so that she can prepare for y'all. She'd tan my hide if I didn't tell her we're having company and she didn't prepare enough food. Like that would ever happen. She cooks enough for the entire county." They chuckled knowing how true his statement was about her unintentional leftovers.

"I totally understand Kurt. I love Cecilia's cooking. I always overeat when she cooks. And, let's drop the 'Miss' title, Meryl will do just fine. Plus, you're family. Hold on, Keough wants to say hello."

"Hey there big brother, damn I've missed you. How've you been?"

Kurt wiped my eyes, "I'm finer than frogs hair, I've missed you too brother. It's sure good to hear your voice. I hate to admit it, but I've missed our daily banter about who was the better driver, swapping rodeo stories and seeing that ugly face of yours strolling into the barn, grumbling about something or other."

Keough chuckled, "You do realize we're identical twins, right? So, if I'm ugly – well, you catch my drift. " We both laughed. "You have a point there little brother. Meryl says you all are coming to Montana for the holidays?" Keough whispered, "Yep, we want to be with our family when I tell everybody we're married. It's a surprise so keep your big mouth shut okay."

Kurt was pleasantly taken aback. "Well, butter my butt and call me toast – congratulations! Yes, I'll keep my pie-hole shut, but I've gotta tell ya', this is the best news I've heard all week. I'm happy for ya' both!"

Keough also mentioned that they were seriously thinking of moving back to Montana.

"Meryl is retiring and to be honest she's beginning to hate New York City – too many city folk she says. And those are her words. Personally, I think she just misses all of you especially Jameson, Rose and Charlotte. And, as quiet as it's kept, so do I."

He wiped his eyes again. "Brother, we'd better hang up or I'm going to be a bawlin' like a baby from all this good news. Please give Meryl my love and we'll see you in a few weeks." The conversation ended with the twins wishing each other well.

Taking a deep breath, Kurt thought, *it's times like this I wish I'd kept in touch with that sweet gal from Texas. She was a beauty. I guess the Montana apple doesn't fall too far from the tree. My nephew Lash married a beauty too. Oh well, my loss I suppose.*

I'd better get these stalls cleaned or Rose will have my ass in a sling." Kurt brushed the hay off his pants; put his bandana over his nose and mouth. *How can two horses produce so much SHIT!*

He heard footsteps coming through the barn door – it was Charlotte. "Hi Uncle Kurt, need some help?" She handed him a travel mug of coffee. "Here, it's from Mama. She said it might light a fire under your butt to get these stalls mucked."

Kurt laughed out loud. "Oh, she did – did she? Well yes you can help me and yes I needed coffee. I swear sometimes I think your Mama is a psychic."

Charlotte put on her barn boots and grabbed a rake. "Good grief Daisy Duce, you sure poop a lot! You're just one big fat poop machine."

Kurt chuckled at her declaration and agreed. He grabbed Keough's hat off the hook and plopped it onto Charlottes head. "Now you look like a real cowgirl."

She smiled, "Yep, just like my Mama." Kurt thought back to how Rose was like a fish out of water when she first arrived at the ranch. Not knowing a heifer from a steer. She's become an honest to goodness Montana cowgirl. Lash would be proud.

Kurt could hear Rose bellowing from the front door. "Charlotte Rose Montana, get back in this house and finish your homework!"

Kurt glanced over at Charlotte and said, "Oh so that's why you came out to help me. And here I thought you just wanted to help an old man."

"I hate math Uncle Kurt! Mama says she'd help me but I'm just no good at figures. Maybe it's because both my parents are writers. I wish I was related to Einstein and then this math stuff would come easier to me." She frowned.

He pushed the cowboy hat back on her head and gave her a kiss on the forehead. "I don't care if you're no good at math. But I do care about you minding your Mama. So you better get going." She hopped up on a hay bale and kissed his cheek. Charlotte gave him a quick hug, then ran back to the house. She whipped around and said, "I love you Uncle Kurt." He waved goodbye and watched her bolt pass Rose through the front door and disappear into the house.

Kurt thought how much Charlotte was starting to bear a striking resemblance to her grandmother. *She was one fine looking woman. Way too good lookin' for that saddlebum brother of mine. However, if it weren't for him, I wouldn't have Lash, his sisters, Morgan, Rose and Charlotte in my life. Lash and Keough didn't waste any time sowing their oats, that's for sure.*

Kurt's phone vibrated again – it was Rose. Before he could say hello Rose hollered, "Get your butt up to the house right now, or I'm giving your supper to Lou." The abrupt click on the other end was his signal to head over to the bunkhouse and get cleaned up.

He thought, *I hate to admit it but I kinda' like being bossed around by a woman; especially one as intelligent and good looking as Rose.* "I'd better get goin' before Rose comes up here with a bull whip."

For a moment his thoughts drifted back to the pretty young lady he once knew. *Why can't I remember exactly where I met her? I know it was Texas, but where? Was it Dallas, Houston or Fort Worth? Maybe if I stop thinkin' so hard I'll remember. But rest assured if we ever meet again I hope she'll find it in her heart to forgive me for leaving without saying goodbye. I'm embarrassed to say I don't even remember her name, but I'll always remember that sweet face – such a beautiful face. Her skin was so soft and she smelled of honeysuckle. Stop it Kurt. You're getting' all hot and bothered over someone you met decades ago!* He stripped off his dirty work clothes and headed for the shower. *This hot water feels good on my old bones.* He let the water run over his head hoping it would jog his memory, but he still couldn't remember her name. Kurt turned the water off and grabbed a towel. It felt good to be clean of all those bits of hay and dust. He opened the closet. *Now, let's see if I can find a clean shirt. I really need to do my laundry.* He sat on the edge of the bunk to put on his boots and saw something shiny wedged between the bunk and wall. *Hmm, it's that spur I've been looking for. It vanished weeks ago. Just goes to show how messy I am. And they say Keough is the slob of the family.* Kurt was about to stand up when something else caught his eye. It was a gold necklace. *Dang, I thought I'd misplaced this years ago. It must have fallen out of a box when I moved into the bunkhouse.* He put it back into the small wooden box with his bolo ties clips and took one last look in the mirror, "Not too bad lookin' for an old geezer. Hell, at least I still have hair and my own teeth. I wonder what that lil' gal looks like now or if she's still around." He buttoned his shirt and put his hat on. Before closing the bunkhouse door, he looked up at the early evening sky. The sun had already set behind the thickets and the stars were just starting becoming visible. Kurt thought *it just doesn't get much better than this.*

Rose met him at the kitchen door. "You sure do clean up well Kurt. I swear you look so much like your brother. It's amazing how identical you two are. So much so I have to remember not to insult you like I insult Keough."

"Why thank you Rose. I think I'll take that as a compliment." Rose handed him a hot cup of coffee and a cinnamon roll. "And before you ask, no, I did not bake them – Cecilia did. But she promised to teach me how to bake. My cooking has improved, right?"

Kurt hesitated. "Which answer won't get me shot?"

Rose threw a dishtowel at him and said, "You know Kurt, I used to like you more than Keough, but now . . . I'm not so sure?"

"Rose, you know I'm only teasin' ya'. You're becoming a pretty good cook. That instant oatmeal you made me for breakfast last week was delicious. However, I didn't know what those little brown things were – any idea?"

"I was wondering the same thing? I found a half-eaten box of them in Charlotte's school book bag. I thought they'd add flavor to your morning meal . . . I'm kidding! They were organic raisins. They're healthy for you!"

"Huh, okay Rose, if'n you say so. But, I prefer my oatmeal plain. Sometimes I fancy it up with a bit of butter and sugar. However, I'll eat anything put in front of me."

"Thank you Kurt, that's good to know. Hey, maybe I'll attempt homemade oatmeal from scratch. Do I have to boil it in water or can I put it in the oven."

Kurt shook his head. "Rose, I think I hear someone calling me. I'd better get back to the barn."

Rose looked around. "There's nobody here but me and Charlotte – nice try Kurt. I swear you are just like your brother – a genuine smart ass. And, I wouldn't have it any other way. I really miss that old coot."

Kurt almost let Keough's and Meryl's surprise slip. *They'd kill me if I told her that they will be coming back to Montana for the holidays.* He quickly agreed that he missed her too.

Rose gave him two more of Cecilia's cinnamon rolls in case he got peckish later on. Peckish is a word Paul uses when he's hungry. *Funny, our grandpap used to say the same thing when he was hungry?* Kurt and Keough's parents died of pneumonia not long after the twins finished grammar school. They moved in with their grandparents. Grandpap Geoffrey came over to the states from England with Grandma Gretta. She raised them and kept them in line. Taking care of two rowdy twin boys was no easy job. At the age of eighteen Keough and Kurt moved out, each going their separate ways. That's when Keough decided to rodeo for a living. Kurt wasn't really interested in rodeo, so he became a saddle maker.

He stopped for a moment and sat on the bunkhouse steps. He hadn't thought about their upbringing in years. *I reckon gettin' older makes a fella start taking stock of his life and where he came from. Maybe I should write all of this stuff down and pass it on to Charlotte. She deserves to know where her kinfolk came from.*

He thought to himself, *maybe I should take my own advice and try to find that gal. I just wish I could remember her name. Oh well, I guess it's for the best. She probably wouldn't remember me either.*

Chapter 9

"Will you please hurry Chinchilla? We're going to be late! I've never missed a Montana Joe event and if we miss his induction into the Western Writers Museum I'm going to shave your head."

Chinchilla scuffled to pull up her pants and jumped into the passenger seat of the car. The two had been driving for more than nine hours from Wyoming and Chinchilla desperately need a restroom break. "Mona Moon Rae, I swear I will never travel with you again. You are a freaking maniac! Why on earth do we need to be on time for a dead writer? He is dead, right? I'm sure he won't notice if we're a few hours late!"

Mona Moon Rae gave Chinchilla a frigid stare, threw the car into drive and sped off. About twenty minutes into the drive she finally explained to Chinchilla that Lash Jackson Montana was a western icon. "His books are legendary and if you'd met him you would understand how amazing a man he was. I met him once when I worked at the Billings Logan Airport gift shop. He was so friendly and handsome. And his wife Rose is beautiful. At first I was jealous, but when I saw how much he loved her it was like a western fairy tale romance come true. There was another time I met his entire family at a restaurant. I was a part-time waitress. I was about to quit when I saw them walk in. Talk about right place at the right time! They were very cordial, but seemed kind of nervous. But like I said they were always nice to me."

Chinchilla shrugged her shoulders. "Well, that sounds fabulously boring. I can't believe how star struck you are when it comes to this guy. He's just a writer Mona. It's not like he's a movie or television celebrity. I've never seen him at the Oscars or on the red carpet with Julia Roberts. How famous can he be?" Mona gave Chinchilla her infamous Mona Moon-Rae stink-eye glare. It took all of her self-control not to bitch slap her traveling companion.

"Chin', because I'm in such a great mood I will ignore that comment and let you live. But I'm warning you, never dis' the great

Montana Joe again – understand?" Chinchilla mumbled something under her breath, crossed her arms and stared out the window.

Hours later they finally arrived in Billings– tired, but unscathed. Mona shook Chinchilla. "Hey, wake up, we're here."

She rubbed her eyes. "Oh shit, I thought I was dreaming. You mean we really are in Montana? I was hoping to wake up in San Diego, San Jose or San Francesco, or any place warm and sandy. This is what my nightmares are made of – waking up in Montana or Utah. I hate you Mona!"

"Oh for God's sake Chinchilla will you shut up! It's not like you have anything else to do? You are a Certified Nurse's Assistant, single-with-no-life, hypochondriac lunatic. What else would you be doing? Wait . . . let me guess, surfing the internet. Reading about symptoms of diseases you may or may not have? Anyway, the fresh Montana air will do you good."

"Mona, I'm tired, I need something to eat, a shower and, more importantly . . . I need to pee! Can we table this conversation until after I've peed?"

Mona sighed, "Okay, okay. Go pee. I'll park the car, bring the luggage and check us in. Chinchilla hopped out the car and headed toward the entrance of the hotel. Mona hollered, "I think there's a restroom in the lobby."

Chinchilla swung around. "Jesus Christ Mona! Why don't you tell the whole world I have a weak bladder"

Chinchilla ran through the lobby to the restroom unzipping her pants even before she opened the restroom door. Of course all of the stalls were occupied. *Never again in LIFE will I drink a Big Sip soda and travel with Mona!* She mumbled. As one woman exited the stall she jumped in before the door shut. *Ah, sweet relief.* She was still in the stall when two other women walked in. They were excited and chatting about Montana Joe. Chinchilla sat quietly, listening to their conversation. She tried to understand what all the fuss was about. *For goodness sakes he's just some hick cowboy writer!* One woman started by gushing, "He was such a handsome man. I always loved cowboys! The character Montana Joe was my secret crush. I used to think he was real person. Well, in a way he was: Lash was Joe. But when he married *that woman* it broke my heart."

The other woman agreed saying, "It's not like he didn't have his choice of women. I would have cheated on my husband for one night of sex with him." They chuckled at each other's confession. As Chinchilla was about to flush one of the women made a disturbing comment? "I know that Rose gal is beautiful, but you'd think he could have found a white woman to marry. I mean, come on . . . really? And, did you know his illegitimate son is half Mexican?" Before the other woman could answer, Chinchilla flung the stall door open, scaring the shit out of both women.

She walked up to both women, looked them up and down and said, "You know something, my friend and I have traveled hundreds of miles to attend Montana Joe's induction. I never understood my friend's obsession with the man, but there is one thing I know about his wife. She loved him unconditionally. Unlike you two ignorant box-colored, red-headed, skinny bitches. And, you wonder WHY he married a beautiful woman of color? I'll give you two scary reasons." She turned both of them towards the mirror. "That's why! Oh and by the way, my father was Spanish and my mother is Irish, however my great-grandfather was black. That combination of genes makes me want to kick your asses into next year!" She gave them the finger and wished them a pleasant day.

Mona was pacing in front of the check in desk. "Damn Chinchilla, I thought you'd flushed yourself down the toilet. What took you so long?"

The two woman from the restroom raced past Mona and Chinchilla without making eye contact. "I had some other shit to take care of."

Mona rolled her eyes at Chinchilla. "You know . . . sometimes, I really worry about you, Chin'."

Chinchilla thought, *I can't tell Mona what happened in the restroom. She'd skin those two bitches with her bare hands.* The two took the elevator to the 8th floor and searched for room 817. The room was spacious with a sunken tub. Mona claimed first soak. "My bones ache from all of that driving. Plus, I want to look my best for Montana Joe at his induction ceremony." Chinchilla let the absurd comment pass. She thought, *looking good for a dead man would typically launch me into a tirade of ridicule over Mona's Montana Joe obsession. But tonight I'll let her enjoy her fantasy relationship with the only man she's ever loved. He must have been one hell-of-a-man . . . one hell of an amazing man.*

The induction ceremony started at 8'oclock in the evening. It was half-past seven. Mona was dressed and ready to leave when she noticed Chinchilla was still getting dressed.

"Chinchilla please hurry! I don't want to miss one minute of the ceremony. His wife Rose will be accepting the Western Writers award for him and rumor has it that Tim McGraw will be singing! I'm dying here; I'm so excited!"

"Mona, if you don't calm the hell down I'm going to slip a tranquilizer into your bottled water – chill out woman! Now if you don't mind, I'd like to finish getting dressed."

"Well, hurry up or I'm going to leave you and head down to the banquet hall without you. Lord, sometimes I think you'd be late for your own funeral – cliché yes, but so true."

Chinchilla rushed out of the room with her blouse partially buttoned. "I'm ready. Jeez, let me button my shirt for Christ sake."

They hurried to the elevator and pushed the button for the lobby. The doors opened and Chinchilla noticed the same two women from the bathroom were also in the elevator. They saw her and immediately walked out. Mona looked at Chinchilla with her usual bewildered Chinchilla stare. "Okay Chin', how and when did you piss those two women off? They looked at you as if you were Satan's bastard zombie child." She just smiled and changed the subject. *Chinchilla doesn't smile very often but when she does, it usually means she's up to no good or she's done something so bizarre it can't be explained.*

The lobby was packed. So many people loved Montana Joe. Mona felt honored to be in a room with so many like-minded people. She remembered the first Montana Joe novel she read. It was the first book in his, *Outlaws of Burnt Canyon Crossing* series. It's been rumored that the Wild West Channel wants to make it into a miniseries. An announcement came over the lobby speakers that the program was about to begin. Mona grabbed Chinchilla and dashed down the aisle.

"I want to be up front and close to the stage. Oh, Chinchilla, I'm so excited! Look at me I'm tearing up. Why did he have to die so soon?" Chinchilla was about to say something when the lights dimmed and a spotlight came on. Lash's publicist, Hanna Vagando walked onto the stage. She was acting Master of Ceremonies for the induction. Behind her was a photograph of Lash dressed up like his alter-ego Montana Joe, donning his signature gray Stetson. It was the first time Chinchilla had seen him in his cowboy attire. She leaned over and whispered, *He's not bad looking Mona, and not generally my type . . . but I'd do him.* Mona rolled my eyes at her and told her to remain silent.

Once the applause stopped, Hanna addressed the audience, "Thank you all for coming to Billings, Montana to honor one of the world's most renowned western writers of the twenty-first- century, Lash Jackson Montana or as most of you know him as the witty and always charming cowboy, *Montana Joe.* I had the privilege of being his publicist, confidant, at time disciplinarian, but most of the time I was honored to call him a dear friend. Many of you may know that Lash wrote over a hundred novels, twenty-five series; one of which I'm happy to announce will be adapted into a miniseries!" The audience exploded in applause. "Tonight, I have the esteemed pleasure of inducting Lash Jackson Montana into the Western Writers Hall of Fame. But before we do, I'd like to introduce an amazing woman, an accomplished writer herself, and, the only woman who was brave enough to rope and marry this rambunctious Wild West writer. Please welcome, the very talented and beautiful Amelia Montana-Saxton or as she's better known as the woman who roped Joe's heart, Rose." The audience was on their feet applauding for over two minutes.

Chinchilla whispered, *so this is the legendary Rose Montana. Now I understand why so many people are jealous of her . . . she's freaking beautiful!* Mona held her finger to her friend's lips, "Shush Chinchilla! I'm trying to concentrate on her speech." The room began to quiet down as Rose started to speak.

"I would like to thank all of you for coming tonight and for such a warm welcome. I haven't spoken to this many of Lash's fans in years. I'd almost forgotten how loyal you are and it humbles me. Lash . . . Joe was an amazing writer. He wrote about the west as if he knew it firsthand. I frequently told him that he was just a reincarnated trail boss, an outlaw, gentleman cowboy like Brett Maverick. However, he likened himself to the Gary Cooper character, Will Kane in High Noon. He told me if you understand him, you'll understand Lash Jackson Montana. I'd agree with him because if I didn't, I knew I'd get a lecture and be made to watch the film for the umpteenth time. Did you know if you start watching the film at 10:45 AM, it'll be twelve noon when the film reaches twelve noon? Okay, now that I've bored you to tears, Lash was a stickler for authenticity. He'd travel to every little hole-in-the-wall town listening to the locals and their stories. I remember him telling me a story about a rodeo bar in Fort Worth called the Eight Second Café where his father, my father-in-law, Keough Montana would frequent. Before Lash died they would talk for hours about the old rodeo cowboys and their antics.

Rose's speech went on for another fifteen minutes captivating the audience with her Montana Joe stories. She wrapped up her presentation with a quote from Lash.

"Lash had a favorite quote and tonight I'd like to leave you with it. It's one he loved to use at the end of his book signings and radio interviews."

"When a barn door swings shut and smacks you in the ass, it's tellin' you to get out there and do the best you can . . . even with a sore ass. Life's filled with sore ass moments. Don't let them cripple you pard'. Cowboy up and keep on ridin'."

Before Mona realized it, she had jumped out of her seat and started applauding and hollering yeehaw. She scared Chinchilla so badly, she fell off her chair.

"For God's sake Mona, can you at least give me a heads up when you're going to do something weird – ya' freakin' nut job!"

"Sorry Chin' but I just love Montana Joe so much I tend to lose my mind when it comes to him." Chinchilla dusted off her pants and thought *you'd have to have a mind to lose.*

They started to walk toward the exit when Chinchilla came to a sudden halt and said, "Wait, you aren't going to try to talk to Rose? I mean . . . come on, you've talked about these people for years and now you're just going to leave without trying to say hello or howdy in the vernacular of the cowboy you love so much."

Mona was shocked that Chin' wanted her to do something odd that might embarrass her, but she was right. She would at least have to try to say hello again. She grabbed Chinchilla's arm and they made their way back through the exiting crowd. Rose was collecting her papers from the podium and heading backstage when the two called her. She saw them and looked a bit nervous. Mona smiled and waved. She waved back but still looked uneasy. At this point Mona thought she'd better reintroduce myself.

"Hello Miss Rose. You may or may not remember me but my name is . . . before I could finish she stopped me."

"Hello, I know exactly who you are. You're the . . . eh, lovely fan who we met at the airport and the restaurant."

Chinchilla was surprised that she actually remembered Mona and she introduced herself. "Hello, I'm Mona's best friend Chinchilla. It's a pleasure to meet you. Mona talks about Montana Joe all of the time and I now understand why she loves him and his writing – he's amazing! Oh, and so are you ma'am."

Rose's nervousness began to subside. She asked them how they'd been. The two told her how much his fans missed Joe and, as much as Rose loved him, they were happy to hear that she remarried. "That Paul fellow is one lucky guy. He's British isn't he?"

Rose nodded, "And he's waiting for me, so I'd better get going. It's been a pleasure chatting with you both, and keep reading those Montana Joe novels!" She gave them a quick smile and left by the side door.

Chinchilla and Mona were just about to leave when she came back in waving for us to come back – very odd. Rose walked over to us and handed us his last two novels; both autographed by Lash.

"I couldn't let Montana Joe's biggest fans leave without something special. And this is for you Mona. I'm sure he's want you to have it." She handed her the gray Stetson Lash wore at his last book signing. "It's been in my car since he died and I didn't have the heart to get rid of it. But, it's yours now. I know Lash would want you to have it."

Mona couldn't feel her body. She was in shock! *Was she really giving me one of Lash's treasured gray Stetsons?*

Mona said something to the effect of, *I'll always treasure it until I bite the dust or something like that.*

Rose waved goodbye again and disappeared through the door. Chinchilla was standing beside her friend with her mouth hanging open. "Did she just give you his hat? Did she just come back in and hand you his hat! Oh my God! That was freaking unbelievable Mona!"

Mona was still in a daze. She could hear Chin' talking to her but all she could hear was Rose saying *I know Lash would want you to have this.* Chinchilla shook her arm. "Mona, snap out of it! Are you okay? Can you walk or am I going to have to ask the front desk for a wheel chair!"

"I'm okay Chin'. Never in a million years did I expect what just happened." "I know that I can be a little overzealous when it comes to Montana Joe; and, when I first met him I think he thought I was just another crazed fan. But this is too unbelievable for words." "I'll never forget this day – ever!"

Chinchilla smiled then nodded. I don't think she'd ever heard Mona sound so sincere. "Mona, you are a weird one that's for sure, but you've always had a kind heart and that's what Rose sees and Joe saw in you. And, you've always been tolerant of me and that's not an easy job."

Mona gave Chin a hug. "Chin' you are my best friend and I don't know what I'd do without you and I'm sorry I get irritated with you so easily. Can you forgive me?"

Chinchilla punched on her arm. "Okay, Mona now you're just sounding goofy. Let's get out of here and get a drink. I don't know about you but I could use beer, but first I really need to piss. I swear my bladder must be the size of a kidney bean. See what I did there Mona?

Mona stared at her for a second. "Chin', what the hell are you babbling about?" "Mona don't you get it, kidney, bladder . . . oh, never mind."

Chapter 10

"Damn it, I missed my exit!" *There won't be another for thirty miles. I guess I'm overly tired from driving all night. I've got to get some rest or I'll end up in Canada.* Annie pulled over to check her GPS. "Hmm, looks like there's a hotel at the next exit. I think I'll crash there for the night. It was only 10 o'clock in the morning but it felt like midnight. *Maybe this was a bad idea? Oh well, it's too late to turn back now. I'm only 50-miles from Malt; 80-miles since I missed my exit.*

Annie thought about her life with her mom and how she would think she was insane trying to track down her dad. *Why on earth would he want to meet me now that I'm an adult? It's not like he'd recognize me. Hell, he doesn't even know that I exist.* She put the car in drive and headed for the next exit. Thirty minutes later she was able to turn around and head back to the exit. The last thing she wanted to do is get lost in Montana. She saw a sign for Malta and continued driving, and about an hour later she had to make a rest stop. She pulled into what looked like a small grocery store or gas station. It looked like it was closed however, as Annie approached the door an old fellow was coming out. He tipped his hat and held the door for me. *This wouldn't happen in Los Angeles. They'd brush by me without a hello.* The clerk was stocking motor oil. Without turning around, he said hello and would help her in a minute. "No problem, please take your time. However, would you happen to have a rest room I can use? "

He pointed toward the back of the store. "It's in the back to your left." It was clean and tidy unlike the restrooms along the turnpikes. It smelled of some sort of flowery air freshener. *Much better than the industrial bleach they use in the turnpike toilets*

She washed her hands and walked back toward the front. He handed her a cup of coffee. "So, am I safe to assume that you're not from around these parts? I took the liberty of brewing a fresh pot of coffee. Looks like you could use it."

"Yes, I could and thank you. I appreciate it more than you can ever imagine." He asked her where she was from and how long she'd been traveling. Not to volunteer too much information she simple said that she had family in the Malta area and was visiting her father. He rubbed his chin and squinted.

"I reckon I know every family in Malta and I can't rightly place you. Did you grow up in Malta?" Annie shook her head. "No, but I believe my father did." He walked back behind the counter and brought out the local phone book. *I can't remember the last time I used a phone book.* He thumbed through a few pages.

"It would help if I knew your last name, if'n you don't mind." She instinctively said Harrison. He continued to look. "Hmm, I don't see a Harrison listed in Malta. Is that your married name?" She told him it was her mother's maiden name – they never married. He looked over the top of his glasses. She knew the look. *Oh, I see you're a bastard child, poor girl.* But surprisingly he was very nonchalant about it. "Hey, I'm not judging you. Heck my dad never married my Mama. He was a rodeo man. Not the kind of fella that would ever settle down with one gal if you catch my drift."

He offered to heat up her coffee and refilled it half way. "Most folks around here are sons or daughters of rodeo men and most had a gal in every town. They never stayed long enough to plant roots."

Annie felt her face flushing from his comment and the coffee; which she had to admit was pretty good roadside brew.

"Now, how about you give me the real name you're looking for." Annie paused and whispered *Montana.* He looked up and paused for a moment. "You're related to the Montanas? Well I'll be – I knew it! You look just like Rose Montana except for those beautiful blue gray eyes. I tell ya', she's one gorgeous gal. Lash Montana was one lucky man – God rest his soul. You could be her younger sister!"

Annie felt her face flush again. He noticed her blushing and smiled. He brought out a map from under the counter and showed me the ranch location. I studied it for a minute and thanked him for his help.

"You might as well keep it. I wouldn't want you to get lost again. Rose would kill me." Annie asked him if he knew her well. He said she would stop in from time-to-time for horse supplies and coffee. "As you can see I double as a small grocery store, that's why

I stock coffee and such. I swear those Montanas sure love their coffee. I try to keep extra on hand just for them. Oh, and by the way my name is Jimmy. A few years ago I helped a lost fella who was looking for the ranch. I believe his name was Jameson. Come to find out he was a long lost Montana too – crazy huh?"

Neither of them knew what to say so Annie broke the silence and asked him if there was a hotel nearby.

"Yep, there's one a few miles down the road on the other side of the interstate. It ain't much but it's clean and the folks are friendly. How about I call ahead and let them know you're coming?"

"Thanks Jimmy, I'd appreciate it. I think I'll call it a day. I can use a good night's sleep and a hot meal. Does it have a restaurant?"

He chuckled, "If you call the owner's kitchen a restaurant – then yes. The food is hot and filling. I think you'll enjoy it."

"Thanks Jimmy, and again you're hospitality is appreciated." Annie walked over and extended her hand.

"My pleasure ma'am." She walked towards the door and he stopped her, "By the way, you still haven't told me your name?"

She smiled and said, "Annabella . . . Annabella Teal Harrison." He smiled and told her to have a good day. "Hope I see you again Annabella. You take care, and no more getting' lost, okay?"

"I won't Jimmy, I promise."

Annie approached the exit ramp and saw the hotel in the distance. Jimmy was right, it was a small hotel; more of a motel with a balcony. It was rustic; reminiscent of something out of an old western film. She expected Clint Eastwood to walk out the front dragging some shiftless outlaw and threatening to send him to meet his maker. *Oh my God, I'm starting to sound like a cheesy cowboy movie!* Realizing her fuel was low, she made a mental note of a gas station she saw down the road from the hotel. She was too tired to pump gas and what she wanted now was a hot shower, something to eat and a comfortable bed. She popped the trunk and grabbed her carry on that held her toothbrush and a change of clothes. A young man saw her walking towards the hotel door and quickly turned back around. *What the hell's wrong with him? And why is he smiling?* As she got closer he smiled again and opened the door for her. She thought *this would NEVER happen in Los Angeles. They'd open the door for you, and then snatch your purse!* She thanked him and reached in her pocket for a tip. He shook his head.

"No need ma'am. Y'all have a good day." He tipped his cowboy hat and walked away. *Now I know I'm not in Los Angeles! These people are way too polite.*

The lobby was beautiful. Large fireplaces, huge overstuffed chairs and couches and dozens of dead animal heads mounted on the walls. Creepy, yet welcoming. She noticed there wasn't an elevator, but the hotel was only two floors. Once settled in her room, she called about food. A sweet woman answered the phone.

"Ah, hello, I notice there's no room service menu. Can I pick one up in the lobby or would someone bring one up to my room?" There was silence, then a muffled chuckle.

"What do you have a taste for darlin'?" She replied. "I can whip up whatever you want, as long as it's nothing too fancy."

For a moment Annie was taken aback. *Whip up?* She asked for an omelet with cheddar, spinach and mushroom, rye toast with butter and coffee.

"Okay, that's breakfast. Now, what would you like for dinner?"

Annie didn't know what to say. After an 18-hour shift at the hospital that WAS her typical dinner. She asked the woman to surprise her.

"Do you eat meat?" Annie said yes.

"Okay, I'll call you when your surprise dinner is ready Miss Annabella."

She hung up the phone and thought *I've driven into a parallel universe. Who surprises you with dinner unless it's someone trying to hit on you for a date?*

About twenty minutes later there was a knock at the door. It was a young man wearing a cowboy hat carrying a tray of something that smelled like heaven. "Hello ma'am, Jenny said you ordered dinner." He paused for a second then asked me my name.

"Annabella – it's Annabella."

He smiled and said, "Then this must be for you. Enjoy your dinner Miss Annabella." She asked him to wait so that she could give him a tip. He looked confused. She tried to hand it to him when he said, "Ma'am, now why would you want to give me a tip for doing my job. It's my pleasure!" He tipped his hat, said goodnight and left.

She placed the tray on the small table by the bed. *Hmm, if all the Malta guys are like this, I may need to move to Montana.* She cut into what she thought was a breaded chicken cutlet covered in a white sauce but to her surprise, she tasted steak. There was also some sort of baked beans and two hot rolls with gobs of butter. *I can feel my arteries collapsing.* She believed that this was the best meal she had in a long time and she would be happy to work it off at the gym when she got home. With her guilt abated, she finished the entire meal. *Guess I was hungrier than I thought.*

Trying not to fall asleep on a full stomach, she sat on the bed and started reading one of the local magazines someone left on the night stand. There was an article about Lash Montana and his latest Montana Joe series. There was a headshot of him wearing what they called his signature Stetson. "Holy shit, he's freaking drop-dead handsome; much better looking than the photograph on his book cover!" Then it dawned on her, "What am I thinking. This man could be my brother or at least older half-brother. And I'm saying he's hot? Eww, that's just creepy! Why is my world so freaking weird? Maybe things will make more sense in the morning." She burrowed underneath the thick comforter and turned the light off.

Chapter 11

"Good morning, Montana-Saxton residence, Cecilia speaking."

"Hello, Cecilia, it's Keough, how the heck are you darlin' or as they say in Hawaii, Aloha!"

"Hello Keough! I can't tell you how much I've missed you. There's nobody to eat all of my leftovers. How's Meryl?"

"She's great. We miss all of ya' so if you don't mind we'd like to stay a couple of days, if'n that's okay with you and the lady of the house. Speaking of which, where is Rose?"

"She's feeding the horses. Hold on, I think I see her walking back to the house. Don't tell her I said anything but she really misses you more than she'll admit. We all do. Rose walked into the house and Cecilia handed the phone over to her without telling her who was on the other end.

"Hello, Rose Montana-Saxton speaking."

Keough cleared his throat first then politely said, "Well howdy darlin' still trying to make biscuits or did you finally give up makin' them hockey pucks."

"KEOUGH, how are ya' you old crippled up rodeo has-been! How's life going for you and Meryl? Are you coming to the ranch? Where are you guys?"

He took a deep breath. "If'n you'd let me get a word in edgewise, I'd tell ya'." Me and Meryl are about fifty miles away from the ranch and wanted to drop by for a few days, if that's okay with you – Surprise!"

Rose almost dropped the phone "Oh my God YES, of course it is, this is still your home Keough."

"Good, because Meryl and I have some great news for ya' but you'll have to wait until we see ya. How's the baby doing? We brought her something back from Hawaii and can't wait for her to see it."

"She's doing fine and she'll be excited to see you too. We love and miss you so much Keough."

"Okay, let's not get crazy Rose. I get suspicious when you're too nice – it makes me nervous."

"Hah, that's very funny – not! But seriously, I can't wait to see you. I'll ask Cecilia to make your favorite meal. You know . . . food, any food as long as it's hot."

"Oh, now who's tryin' to be funny? But you know I'd eat anything Cecilia cooked. Even rawhide if it had enough gravy on it." "Well darlin', I'd better let you get going before we start swapping recipes and singing Kumbaya."

She laughed. "Hah, okay. Take care Keough and I'll see you two soon, bye-bye."

Keough hung up the phone and thought how proud he was of his boy Lash. "You really loved that gal. Son, you done good – real good. I'm happy to call her my daughter-in-law. I hope she'll be just as happy when I tell her that Meryl and I got married. Imagine me married to a highfalutin' gal like Meryl. Not too bad for an old rodeo drunk."

The old man walked back into the hotel and went to his room. Meryl was still sleeping. He remembered to bring his new bride a cup of coffee from the hotel kitchen. "Meryl, wake up darlin' I brought you something hot and sweet, oh, and some coffee."

She stretched and rubbed her eyes. "Thank you so much. Oh Keough, what time is it? Did I oversleep? Is it already afternoon? I wanted to be on the road by 10 AM."

Keough was amused by her confusion. "To answer your litany of questions it's 8 AM, no you didn't oversleep, so obviously it's not noon." Meryl slapped him on the shoulder. "And when did you become a smart ass! We both know that's Jameson's job." Her attempt at humor made him smile.

"Did you tell her?"

"Nope, I just told her we had something to tell her but I didn't let her know we're married if that's what you're askin'"

"Yes that's what I was askin', I love you Keough Teal Montana."

He leaned over and kissed her cheek. "And, I love you Mrs. Meryl Montana. Now how about we have our coffee, get packed and hit the road to Casa Montana."

A few rooms down the hall Annabella was just about to brush her teeth when she heard someone at the door. It was the same young man with a pot of coffee and a very large slice of coffee cake. "Good morning Miss Annabella, the kitchen sent this up thinking you might want something for breakfast. The coffee cake was baked this morning. Hope you slept well."

"Yes, yes I did. I haven't slept this long and this well in years. Must be the huge dinner I had last night – and thank you for asking." Annie sat on the edge of the bed thinking how relaxed she was. No patients, no reports, no rounds and best of all, great coffee. *I'd better get going. I want to be in Malta by noon. Only fifty miles to go and I'll finally find the guy my mother slept with, but...suppose he's dead too. The information on the back of the book Sophie was reading had to be at least four years old.*

Annie double checked the room to make sure she had everything. Walking through the lobby the aroma of bacon and fresh biscuits filled the air. *A person could gain five pounds just by inhaling.* The gentleman behind the desk asked if she enjoyed my stay. "Yes, very much so and please tell the young man who carried my overnight bag and delivered my dinner thank you." The gentleman smiled and said he would. She turned around and accidentally bumped into an older man who was waiting to check out, knocking his coffee onto the floor.

"Oh SHIT, I'm so sorry! I didn't see you. Here, let me get you something to dry off." She reached into her pocketbook and pulled out a wad of tissues and proceeded to wipe his shirt.

He laughed and said, "Darlin', if you only knew how many times I've spilled stuff on me you wouldn't be so upset. Heck, once I dropped an entire container of horse stable disinfectant on me. It's the cleanest I'd ever been back in the old days when I was riding the rodeo circuit. I didn't have to bathe for weeks!"

Annie offered to have his shirt cleaned and buy him another cup of coffee.

"No thanks. However, if you want to have a cup with me and my wife before you leave it would be our pleasure. And, how about I treat you to some grub. Those pancakes and bacon smell pretty dang good. So, what do ya' say?"

"I say yes and thank you, sir."

He frowned and said, "Sir? Sir was my dad. My friends call me KT and since we're now coffee mates and all, KT will be fine."

For a moment she thought she lost consciousness. *Did he just say KT? No, he couldn't be.*

KT tapped her on the shoulder. "Hello? You look like you saw a ghost. Are you okay Miss…?"

She collected herself and said, "Annabella, my name is Annabella."

"Okay Miss Annabella how about we head in and find a table – I'm starved." She finally got her legs to move. *He couldn't be, no way! Is this Keough Teal? Should I ask?*

Before she could speak, an attractive older woman walked in and gave him a kiss. He quickly held her hand and walked over to introduce us. "Miss Annabella this is my wife Meryl. We just got married a few weeks ago so I guess we're still on our honeymoon."

She congratulated them and attempted to make small talk. *I can't believe this! I'm having breakfast with my deadbeat dad and his new wife! What the fuck!* She didn't remember much of what they talked about. She vaguely remembered something about Hawaii or was it France? She totally zoned out. She did remember eating the pancakes. *They had a hint of nutmeg in them.* Her mother used to add a pinch of it to her batter too. Strange she had to come all the way to Montana to remember that. Meryl and KT were chatting about how good it would be to see Rose and their granddaughter Charlotte. They asked Annie where she was from and where she was headed. She told them she was from Los Angeles and she wasn't headed anyplace special.

"I'm a doctor at Los Angeles Metro Hospital, Head of Oncology. I have tons of vacation time so I decided to travel for a few weeks. Don't know where I'm going next – maybe Utah. Then again, my mother always wanted to see the Painted Desert. I may head that way."

Keough said he'd been there and it's beautiful especially at sunrise. "So, is your Mama with ya'?"

She hesitated and thought *no she isn't you son of a bitch, she's dead thanks for asking.* She politely told him she'd passed away years ago. His tone of voice quickly changed as did Meryl's. "Oh, I'm sorry darlin' please accept our condolences." Keough added, "And please forgive an old man for his insensitivity."

Meryl leaned over and whispered something to him. He nodded his head. "My bride and I would love it if you came with us and stayed a spell at our Montana ranch in Malta. Come to think of it you remind me of my daughter-in-law, Rose. I know she wouldn't mind another intelligent gal to chat with. We old geezers bore her to death."

Meryl nudged him. "Speak for yourself Keough. Rose and I have wonderful conversations, ya' old coot! Most of which involve you and something boneheaded you've done."

As they continued debating who was the oldest and silliest, Annie realized had Keough known about her he would have been a good father. Keough added that it was almost Thanksgiving and that nothing is more entertaining than a Montana holiday shindig.

"Keough's right," said Meryl "Please come with us. I know Rose wouldn't mind. There are so many rooms she probably wouldn't notice another guest was there for weeks. And, maybe she won't strangle us for not telling her we got married."

Keough chuckled, "Yep, she would never murder us in front of a guest. So, what do ya' say, come with us. You'd be doing us a favor. We'd like to live to see our second anniversary. Consider it payment for my shirt."

Not only is he handsome, he's funny. She understood why her *mom liked him. But she decided to hold her cards close to her vest for now.*

"Okay, I accept upon one condition. You let me pay for breakfast and take you both out to dinner later–deal?"

Keough pretended to spit on his hand. He extended his hand and said, "Deal." He gave Meryl a quick kiss on the cheek. "Okay Darlin', we'd better get goin' before she changes her mind and leaves us with the check. They walked Annie over to her car and then Keough and Meryl got into their truck. Before Annie started the car, she rolled down her window and asked Keough the ranch's address so she could set her GPS. He laughed and pointed toward a huge thicket of trees miles away on the horizon. "You won't need a GPS or whatever that is. Just drive your vehicle in that direction. That darlin' is the Montana Ranch."

She put the window up and thought D*amn, who are these people? Their ranch looks to be the size of Rhode Island! Mom, if you're listening Keough seems to be a good guy. I'm not ready to tell him who I am but I believe he'd be okay if he did know. I know his wife would be. She seems to be good people. Wish me luck!*

Chapter 12

"Amelia, is there anything special you would like me to cook for Thanksgiving dinner?" Cecilia was starting her holiday shopping list. This process generally meant that there will be enough food to feed the entire county.

"Cecilia, whatever you make you know we will devour. Remember that Christmas when Morgan and Raymond fought over the last turkey leg?"

"Yes I do Amelia, and if my memory serves me well it got ugly very quickly. I don't want that to happen again. Maybe I should get two turkeys."

Paul and I love the holidays. It's the only time all of the family can come together. We're so spread out all over the country that Thanksgiving and Christmas is a huge event at the Montana Ranch. I miss Jannine and Morgan so much. And there are times I miss chatting with Jameson. He's starting to look more like Joe every time I see him. Last year he started a journal about twins who'd been separated at birth; later finding each other, as well as writing an essay about his experience as a recovering alcoholic. The New York Times even picked up his article.

Living with Raymond has been a life changing experience for him. I know Joe would be proud to call him his brother. Keough's warmed up to him and has accepted him as his son. However, I believe it was more Meryl's doing than his. They've become very close – Meryl and Keough. I'm glad they're staying through the holidays. I know Kurt will be excited to see him. Speaking of Kurt, lately he seems to be a bit out of sorts. I'd even say reclusive since Keough's been away. Maybe it's my imagination. Strange thing about twins, they seem to know when the other isn't well or unhappy. I wonder if Keough is sensing that something's wrong with Kurt.

I told Cecilia I'd have a list of people for her by the end of the day. She's a stickler for getting things organized. Unlike me she's a planner. I'd procrastinate and we'd end up having salad at the local trucker's hot spot for Christmas dinner.

"Don't worry Amelia I'll take care of everything. You just enjoy your family." Rose stopped her and asked, "What do you mean YOUR family? If you think you're not a part of this family you're crazy. In fact, we wouldn't be a family without you. We'd all be naked and starving!" Cecilia broke into a wide smile.

"I consider you all my family too." She said. When Lash hired me I knew nothing about working for a famous celebrity, nor did I have the experience of managing a huge estate like the Montana Ranch. But he saw something in me I didn't see in myself – confidence. I learned to understand his rather peculiar and but always respectful behavior."

Rose walked over and gave her a hug. "Cecilia, not only are we well fed, you have become more of a mother figure to me and definitely a surrogate grandmother to Charlotte."

Rose looked at the clock. It was already after 10 AM. "I'd better let you go Cecilia or you'll get stuck in Malta's downtown traffic – all five cars."

While Cecilia was out, Rose decided to fix a late breakfast. She remembered Joe making his famous nutmeg pancakes for them when they first met. She had not had them for a while and decided to try her hand at duplicating them. The aroma alone was worth the challenge. She never considered herself a good cook; never needed to. There was always a new restaurant opening in Manhattan or a reliable take-out place that had great Szechuan chicken.

The griddle was packed away in the attic along with Joe's extra large coffee pot. Paul wasn't home so Rose had to go up and retrieve it herself. Paul is so helpful around the house. Not that Joe wasn't willing, it's just that Paul really enjoys doing household chores much more than Joe did.

Rose climbed up to the attic with her flashlight. She made a mental note to ask Paul to fix the finicky light switch. The kitchen ware box was in the back of the attic. She stepped over boxes of Joe's things to get to them. Saddles, rodeo ropes, old boots took up most of the floor. In her mind, she knew she needed to let go of his things but her heart wouldn't let her – not yet. Thank goodness the box marked Joe's Cowboy Cooking Utensils was in front of the other boxes. His old cast iron skillet and griddle were just as he left them. There was an old bandana with his special stash of nutmeg wrapped in it sitting on top of a pile of coffee stained papers that looked like handwritten recipes. "Well I'll be damned, he knew how to cook." *Joe, are there any other secrets about you that I should know?* Rose placed the papers on top of the griddle and carried everything down the attic steps.

"Okay Joe, let's see if you have your infamous pancake recipe in this bunch of stuff." Rose thumbed through them and found what seemed to be a pancake recipe, but she was sure it wasn't for a family of three because it called for two dozen eggs. *It must be the recipe that'll feed 40-cowhands.* Curious, she continued to search the pile until she found his cryptically written recipe. *Well I'll be damned again! His famous pancakes recipe begins with one box of Aunt Jemima's pancake and waffle mix. I swear there is so much I never knew about you.* Mixed in with the recipes was what looked like a half finished manuscript of about thirty-plus typed pages. She put a pot of coffee on and started reading:

Chapter 1

As she stood in front of him, he looked up at her with his weathered face and tired eyes from being out in the elements so much. His long, full, salt and pepper mustache had the slightest little curl on the ends. His hat flattened hair matched the mustache. Bat's dark green eyes could not believe such a lady was standing in front of them. As her beautiful tanned skin and full thick lips started to meet he couldn't believe what was about to happen. They embraced each other as if they had been together for a life time. As the night wore on the passion followed, Bat still in awe over what was happening could not help himself; as he was always the gentleman to a lady's thoughts and beliefs. The flames from fire place seem to grow higher, as the shadows seem to play out a black and white movie on the walls. She took control and at same time he lost his own control of what was going on. Still there was something bothering her that mesmerized him. He took her face in his rough but gentle hands and ask very softly, "You seem so familiar, May I ask your name? She smiled and whispered I'm the one you've been dreaming about your entire life.

Lou's scratching at the kitchen door broke Rose's concentration. She had forgotten she put Lou outside. After scooping some food in his bowl, she sat back down and continued reading. Flipping through a few pages, Rose noticed a date in the upper right hand corner – March 14, 1970. Joe must have written this in high school. When we first met he said he'd always dreamt of a beautiful golden-skinned woman who was the woman of his dreams. He probably started this manuscript in search of her. *No wonder he was so passionate about marrying me. I was the woman he wrote about. I am the woman of his dreams. It took me a moment to regain my composure. What else don't I know about Joe? Who was this incredibly fascinating man I married?*

"Not bad for a horny teenager. Maybe I can turn it into a short story but then again if Joe wanted it finished he would have finished it himself. But why would he? He married his dream. How many men can say that about their wife? I know two who could – my Paul and of course, Joe. I'm a pretty damned lucky woman."

Rose didn't realize she was talking out loud until she heard two voices agree with her. Raymond and Jameson stopped by on their way to town and brought some cheesecake to have with their afternoon coffee.

"Raymond, how are you, hon? And Jameson, where the hell have you been? I haven't seen you for months." They both came over and gave her a hug

Jameson opened the cabinet and got three small plates. "I'm fine Rose. In fact, I'm doing very well. I just returned from the South Pacific, hence the half-ass white boy tan. I swear Montana men don't tan very well do they? But between the beautiful ocean waters and white sands I feel revitalized. And the best news is since my adopted dad died, I've stayed sober–how's that for an accomplishment!"

Raymond and Rose both gave him a high five. "Jameson, I'm so freaking proud of you and I know your mother is too. Have you spoken to her recently?"

He shook his head. "No Rose I haven't. Part of my getting sober is to learn to rely on myself. Plus, I know she's in good hands with Keough.

Raymond started to grumble. "Are we going to eat this cheesecake or talk it to death? I'm starved!"

Rose laughed because Raymond is always starved. He brought over three coffee mugs. He also noticed the manuscript lying on the table. "Is that one of yours?"

"No, it was one of Joe's first attempts to write a novel from high school.

Raymond read a small portion of it, put it down and shook his head, "Even as a kid he was a horny bastard and a lousy writer. He only had three working brain cells. One focused on coffee, one on sex and the other on you Rose. That was the intelligent cell. I'm so glad he found you. You know that you were his only redeeming grace. If it wasn't for you I would have smothered him in his sleep years ago. I'm not joking – in his sleep!" We laughed at Raymond's statement and had a good laugh at Joe's expense.

Raymond and Jameson were about to leave when Cecilia came in loaded down with groceries. Jameson helped her carry them into the kitchen. She thanked him and asked Raymond how he was doing. Then she insisted both he and Jameson come over for Thanksgiving dinner. "Cecilia, when have I ever, and I mean EVER, turned down your cooking. Of course I'll be here and so will my appetite." Jameson also accepted the invitation. He asked if his Mom and Keough would be coming back to Montana for the holidays.

"They called and they will be here for the family festivities," Rose confirmed.

Rose heard the front door open and shut again. Paul was home early. He gave Raymond a hug and shook Jameson's hand. He kissed his wife on both cheeks. "So what are you lot rabbiting about now? I could hear you laughing from the driveway."

Rose explained what Raymond said about Joe and pointed to the manuscript on the table. Paul's demeanor changed from jovial to brooding. Rose could see from his expression that he wasn't amused. After Raymond and Jameson left, she asked about his sudden mood change. "So tell me, what's the matter Paul? You haven't been yourself for a few weeks. Is there something wrong? Is it something I've done?" It took a moment for him to gather his thoughts. Then he spoke.

"Poppet, you know I love you, so please don't take this the wrong way. Ever since we've been married there isn't a minute that goes by when Joe's name hasn't come up. Honestly, I don't know how to live with that or how to compete with his ghost. Lash Jackson Montana was larger than life and his character of Montana Joe was just as popular. It's not your fault Amelia. If I'm to stay married to a legend's widow I guess it's just something I'll just have to accept." Paul kissed me again and walked away.

His painful admission left me speechless. How did I not see this? Was I too involved in my own grieving process to notice my husband's feelings? Rose walked into the living room, Paul wasn't there. She looked out the kitchen window and saw him sitting by the barn cleaning the one of the saddles Kurt brought out to clean. He looked so despondent. Her heart was breaking for him and she felt ashamed. After Joe's inevitable death this wonderful man kept her from losing her mind. And all anybody could say was how much Lash would be missed and what a magnificent man he was.

Rose put the kettle on and made two cups of tea. She thought he could use a break and an apology. The walk over to the barn gave her the chance to think about what I was going to say. *What could I say? The entire time we've been married Joe has been between us. It was like I was married to two men; one tangible, the other always there in spirit. It's not fair to Paul. I have to make a decision.*

"Paul, I thought you could use a nice cup of tea." He took a cup from his wife's hand, sat it on the tack room workbench and continued cleaning. "Paul, can you stop what you're doing for a minute and sit down with me." He took a long sip and sat his cup back on the workbench. Rose put her tea down and sighed. "Paul, I'm sorry. I'm sorry for making you feel the way you're feeling now. I married you because I love you. Along with Charlotte, you're the most important person in my life. Lash will always be a part of our life but he's not MY life anymore – you and Charlotte are. I'm hoping you can forgive me for my insensitivity today. Can you forgive me? Will you forgive me?"

He stood up, took Rose's hands and placed them over his heart. "Poppet . . . Amelia, from the minute we met you had my heart. Even though at the time, your heart belonged to someone else. I love you, I love Charlotte, but more importantly I love our marriage. As long as you still love me I can endure Joe being a constant in our lives. I loved him too. However, I prefer not to be referred as, *Husband Number Two* in your eyes or the eyes of Joe's fans. I want to be the one you WANT to be with all the time, not just when it's convenient."

Rose stood up directly in front of him. "Paul, you are not, nor will ever be second best, or a convenience. I love you and Raymond, Keough and Charlotte love you too."

Paul took the last swallow of his tea then hugged her. They hugged in the barn for a while until they heard Kurt clearing his throat.

"I don't want to interrupt, but I was sent out here to tell you that my niece is wondering what's going on? She said it must be an adult thing so it would be best if I came out and asked."

Paul laughed. "She is quite the clever girl – must get it from her Mum. Also, Sawyer called and asked if it was okay to call Charlotte after dinner. I thought I'd better run the call by you before I tell her he called."

"Thank you Kurt and yes I'm glad you told me first. I'll let her know after we've had a conversation about boy/girl phone privileges."

Kurt winked and continued up to the bunkhouse. Rose and Paul ended their conversation and promised to work on the Joe issue later. *Perhaps it was time to let go of his belongings?* A few weeks ago Hanna suggested auctioning some of them off to raise money for his favorite charities. Rose had considered it a wonderful idea; that they would get together after the holidays to sort his things out. She also told her this is the first time all of the Montana's are coming home for Thanksgiving and Christmas. She insisted that it would be a special event and stress free. And since Rose and the clan view Hanna an honorary Montana they expected her to join them. She said she'd be happy to attend.

The couple walked back to the house. Paul stopped for a moment and kissed Rose.

"What was that for?"

He smiled and said, "Do I need a reason to kiss my lovely wife. I love you Amelia. And, please promise if I ever act like a bleeding jealous pillock again, you'll seriously thrash me about the head with cricket bat."

She returned his kiss and winked, "I promise."

Chapter 13

"Morgan . . . MORGAN! I need you to come over and help me put on my shoes! Oh my God, I can't see my feet!" *Who knew human flesh could stretch this tight in seven months. I'll never tease Rose about her pregnancy flap again.*

"MORGAN MONTANA, where the hell are you? I can't reach the other shoe and I think I have to pee again."

Morgan closed his eyes and rubbed his neck. "I'll be there in a minute. I'm in the bathroom." *Jeez the only time I get to sit down lately is when I need to pee and I can't pee because she keeps yelling for me!* "Let me wash my hands Hon and I'll be in to help you."

When Morgan found out that Jannine was pregnant, he was ecstatic. The thought of another Montana coming into the world had me excited, not only about my future, but the future for this new little human being who will carry on the Montana name. *Its times like this when I wish Dad was still around. I know he'd have his chest puffed out as much as I did when I first heard the news.* Jannine's bellowing snapped Morgan out of his daydream. "I'm coming Jannine. I'll be there is second." He dried my hands and raced down the hallway. She was sitting on the edge of the bed crying. *Oh Lord, this is my cue to not ask why but to agree with whatever she says.*

"Morgan, I'm sorry I yelled at you. I'm sorry I can't find my shoe and I'm even sorrier that I think I just peed myself."

He helped her up and sure enough the side of the bed was damp. He hugged her and helped her into the bathroom. "Honey, there's nothing to be sorry about. You know how much I love you and as this is our first pregnancy we're both learning, so please don't be so hard on yourself."

He held on to her arm as she stepped into the shower. Morgan could tell she was upset. He had never seen her upset. Jannine was the tough one in the marriage. Hell, she's tough in everything she does. That's why he fell in love with her. Rose hired her because she could hold her own in any situation – except now. She's vulnerable and needy, but mostly she's scared. Her husband couldn't blame her because he was just as scared. He was trying not to show just how nervous he was about being a father.

Jannine is a daddy's girl. She was the love of his life. He never knew who his father was. Morgan grew up not knowing Lash. He didn't know about him until he was in his mid-teens. He had no idea what it was like being the son of the famous, Lash Jackson Montana. Morgan's mother did the best she could, but after she died he felt the need to find out more about him. When Morgan showed up on his doorstep he was surprised by his instant acceptance and kindness. He didn't know me. He didn't know I existed. He could have rejected me on the spot as some bastard kid trying to con him out of money. But he didn't. He never did. From then on he accepted him as a Montana. When Rose was pregnant with Charlotte, Morgan told Lash that he would be there for his baby sister. As her big brother, he also promised Lash he would always love and protect her. And the fact that she's twenty years younger than Morgan was never an issue. He knew she was going to be an incredible aunt to her little niece or nephew.

Morgan handed Jannine a towel and helped her out of the shower. She said she felt much better. *At least she isn't crying anymore.* "And, I found your other shoe. It must have fallen behind the bed when you tried to get up." *Why did I say tried?*

That started her crying again. "Morgan, I never had to try to get up in my life. Now something as simple as standing up is like an Olympic event and, I'm fat!" There was nothing he could say that wouldn't be taken the wrong way. So he changed the subject and asked her if she still intended to go to Montana for the holidays.

"Are you joking? Of course I'm still going! There is no way I'm turning down Cecilia's holiday spread. Hell, it'll be the first time I won't have to unbutton my jeans after dinner." *Now that's the Jannine I love.* He happily agreed with her. She'd stop crying and was smiling again –his job was done.

While she was getting dressed, he removed the bed linen and took it down to the laundry room. It gave him a moment to ponder how their lives have changed and how much he missed Lash. "Dad, I know you can hear me so please if you have any fatherly advice I'd be kindly beholding if you would bestow it on me."

A few seconds later his cell phone vibrated. "Hello."

"Hello big brother this is your sister Charlotte. Mama was thinking about giving Jannine a baby shower. Is there anything else you all need or something special she'd like to eat besides pizza?"

Since the moment she found out she was pregnant, Jannine's parents brought every baby item the couple would ever need and the only thing Jannine craved was pizza – pineapple with mushrooms to be exact. The combination made me gag. Nevertheless, if she craved it he'd run out and get it. "Anything Cecilia makes I'm sure will be fine."

"Okay Morgan, I'll let Mama know. I'm so excited that you and Jannine are coming for Thanksgiving and Christmas. We're going to be like a normal family! Not the famous Montanas – just the Montanas. I miss you Mo' Mo', love you." She hung up before Morgan could tell her he loved her too and he loved the fact that she still called him *Mo' Mo'*. She was two-years-old when she gave him that nickname. He was more surprised by how much she'd grown since Lash died. The fact that she'll never know him broke his heart. *I mean it's not like the world will ever let her forget who he was and still is. She will always be the daughter of the famous Lash Jackson Montana. However, knowing my little sister, it won't be her title for long. She's her own person just like her Daddy and Mama.* Rose will insist that she be her own person. *Speaking of Rose I'd better check on Jannine.*

Morgan brought the luggage into the bedroom. Jannine had fallen asleep with her shirt half on. He didn't have the heart to wake her up. He pulled the quilt over her and went downstairs to recheck the flight information.

His cell phone rang again. This time it was Rose. "Howdy, Rose, I was just thinking about you. I just spoke with Charlotte."

"Yes, that's why I'm calling. She said you both are still planning on coming for the holidays!"

"Yep, we are. She really misses you, Rose and in her current condition she needs someone to support her through these bouts of pregnancy blues. She's huge for seven months. At first we thought she was having twins since they run in Lash's side of the family. But the doctor said it's just one BIG baby."

Rose chuckled. "I miss her too Morgan. She's like my baby sister. It'll be good to see her."

The sound of footsteps distracted Morgan. "We also have something else to tell you, but, I've got to go Rose. *Her Royal Highness* is awake and hollering for me to help her into the bathroom again!"

Rose laughed. "Okay, I'll see you soon. Love you both. Rose hung up and thought, Hmm, I wonder what they want to tell me? Guess I'll find out when they come for Thanksgiving.

Jannine shuffled into the bathroom hallway. "Who was on the phone? Was it for me? Was it the office, because if it was I was going to tell them to shove whatever they need up their firm-butt-cheek-implanted asses. I'm on freaking maternity leave and they're still calling me! The minute I get back to work I'm going to ask for a huge raise!"

"No, it wasn't the office; it was Rose. She's just checking to make sure we're still coming to the ranch for the holidays."

Jannine's brow wrinkled, "I hope you told her HELLS YEAH! I'm pregnant – not incapacitated. I'm so excited to see her and Charlotte. I miss them so much. She's like my skinny, older and extremely attractive sister. And I'm her fat, swollen ankles, nothing-fits-me-anymore, younger sister."

Jannine started to cry. Morgan walked over to her and gave her a hug.

"Why are you crying? I thought you were excited about going to Montana."

She wiped her nose on his shirt. "I don't know. It seems I'm always on the verge of tears – hormones I suppose."

Morgan gave her another big hug and said that he loved her swollen ankles and wacky hormones. "After all you are carrying our kid. How cool is that!" He saw a faint smile appear.

"Yes, I am and they'll be lucky to have us as parents. Not to mention my crazy Japanese parents who are already spoiling him or her rotten. Did I tell you the latest of their pre-baby overindulgence? Mom is redecorating my old bedroom into a *Degas* themed nursery, complete with a recreation of his *Ballerina paintings* if it's a girl. And, if it's a boy a *Fredrick Remington* motif." They laughed at the possibility of their kid being an art critic when he or she grows up.

"Well darlin' we better start packing. I've checked in five pieces of luggage; one of which will be my stuff."

Jannine kissed her husband. "And that's why I married you. You know me well Mister Montana and I really need to pee, so can we cut this admiration society short or you'll be doing another load of laundry!"

Chapter 14

"If there was ever a time to ask Keough *are we there yet* it was now." Apparently, the one-hour drive from the hotel to the ranch that Annie calculated took over two hours. She guessed she used to driving in Los Angeles where the speed limit is 70-miles an hour on the freeways. *Geez, Keough, would it kill you to put your foot down? I just saw a turtle pass us chasing down a crippled snail.* A few minutes after her internal rant the group arrived at the ranch entrance. Annie lowered her window to take a much needed breath of fresh air. There was a slight chill in the air. Autumn in Montana felt so refreshing. It was much different than Los Angeles. And completely different than the exhaust-laden fumes that were always present outside the hospital.

Her heart started to race in anticipation of meeting Keough's family. *I wasn't this nervous performing my first solo surgery. There was also an odd feeling of homecoming. It was strange, because I'd never been to Montana before. However, Keough's snail-pace driving allowed me the opportunity to enjoy the Malta scenery. It was breathtakingly beautiful as well as majestic. Mom, you would have loved living here. She could feel herself starting to tear just thinking about her mother. Come on Annie, get it together. Mom didn't raise a wimp.*

Taking another deep breath, she collected herself and continued driving. She was about five-car lengths behind Meryl and Keough's truck. It occurred to her that there was no need to concentrate on driving; it was a private road *This ranch is freaking unbelievable; not to mention overwhelming. Who lives like this?*

Keough pulled over to the side of the road and stepped out of his truck. He walked back towards Annie's. "Well Annabella welcome to the Montana Ranch. I know it's small but we like to call it home."

She put her car in park. He opened the door and extended his hand. "I bet there's nothin' like this in Los Angeles, well maybe in the Sierra Nevada Mountains, but you gotta admit it's pretty impressive, huh?"

She shook her head. "No we do not Keough – I'm speechless. And ALL of this is Montana land?"

He grinned, "Yep, every last bit of it. My son's done a good job with his cowboy writin'. I'm prouder than a polecat of both my sons." *Both of his sons? I thought he had only one son – Lash Montan.*

Meryl walked back to meet us. "Isn't this the most beautiful country you've ever seen Annabella? Its grandeur never ceases to amaze me. I was born not too far from here in a smaller town named, Dodson."

Keough chimed in. "Yes, she's just a small town gal who done good, just like Lash and Jameson. And I now get to call this sweet lil' lady my wife." He leaned over and kissed Meryl on her cheek. She winked at Keough, and then asked, "Okay, so what were you to chatting about? Did I miss something important?" Keough kissed her again, "Nope, darlin' I just wanted to show Annabella the lay of the land."

Meryl laughed and asked Annie her opinion of Malta. "Like Dorothy said, we're not in Kansas anymore – that's for sure."

She smiled at Annabella. "I'm so glad you decided to come with us. You are a darling young lady. The kind of woman I wish our son Jameson would meet. We can only hope darlin'."

Meryl paused for a second, looked at Annie and then followed through with a puzzling statement. "You know Annabella, for some odd reason you seem very familiar to me." *I bet I do, seeing that your husband is my father! But that's a conversation for another time. I need to make sure I want to be a part of this complex family before I break the bastard child news.*

She politely thanked Meryl for her hospitality and kind words. "And please, call me Annie. Now that we've shared a breakfast and traveled together I think formalities can be waived."

Keough started walking back to the truck. Meryl and Annie were still chatting. He stopped for a second, turned around and said, "Well ladies, if we're finished with all of the niceties let's get moving. There's still twelve miles before we get to the front door."

Meryl gave Annie a quick hug. She said, "We'd better get going. It looks like we may get some snow." *Snow, I thought. I haven't seen snow since my ski trip to Lake Tahoe. Maybe I should have packed some winter clothes . . . oh wait – I don't own any winter gear!*

The group just cleared the thicket of Pine trees when Annie saw the house in the distance. *Casa Montana, it looks more like Hotel Montana. I'd never seen a private home as large as this one. This guy Montana Joe or Lash Joe, whatever his name was, must have been worth millions. I bet his wife is an obnoxious diva who married him for his money and fame. But then again that's not how Keough and Meryl described her. I don't think he would be as friendly with her if that were the case. For now I'll hold my judgment. I followed them pass a small pond, over a short bridge and on to a circled driveway. I expected a cowboy valet to come out and take our car keys.* Keough parked his truck beside a small barn and Annie parked beside him.

The three walked down a gravel path and onto a stone walkway. Keough announced, "Ah, home sweet home. There's nothing like being home for the holidays. Heck, they should write a song about it." The two women laughed knowing he surely knew there was already a song with those lyrics.

A lovely older woman opened the door. "Oh my goodness, hello Keough, Meryl . . . and who is this lovely young lady?" *Lovely young lady? I'm feeling about 100-years-old after that long drive. However, I'll take young lady anytime I can get it.*

Keough started the introductions. "Cecilia, this lovely young gal is Annabella Harrison. Or, should I say Doctor Harrison. She was headed to Malta or Billings I'm still not sure, but she's traveling alone and we thought we'd treat her to some good old fashion Montana hospitality and cooking. You are cooking aren't you Cecilia?"

Cecilia nodded and walked over to me. "Welcome to the Montanas. It's a pleasure to meet you. Come in and make yourself comfortable."

"Thank you and please call me Annie."

Cecilia smiled, "Well, Annie, I hope you're hungry. There's plenty to snack on if you are. Make yourself at home."

She turned to Keough, "And to answer your question, of course I'm cooking Keough and I'm making everyone's favorites, so I hope you all brought your appetites with you." She walked over to Meryl and hugged her. "It's so good to see you again Meryl. I hope you and Keough enjoyed your trips."

Meryl smiled, "Yes we did, very much so. In fact we loved traveling together so much . . . we got married." She held out her left hand and showed Cecilia her rings.

"What a surprise! Oh Meryl, I'm so happy for you! Does Rose know?" Meryl shook her head. "No she doesn't. We wanted to tell her in person. So for now, mum's the word. Is she at home?"

"No she's not. She went to pick up Charlotte from school. She should be back in about an hour. I'm sure you all could use something hot to drink. I'll put on a pot of fresh coffee. Or would you prefer tea Annie?"

"Coffee is fine!"

"I made a coffee cake this morning. Help yourselves. Either way, I'm so happy to see you two and it's such a pleasure to meet you Annie."

Keough walked up to Annie and said, "Didn't I tell you Annie? We Montanas are a friendly and hungry bunch. Better get used to it."

Meryl and Keough continued chatting with Cecilia while Annie made her way to the couch. She was still trying to grasp the course of events that occurred and how the universe brought all these people together. Starting with not knowing who her father was to finding out he's actually alive and not dead like her mother had told her to picking up Sophie's Montana Joe novel at the coffee café and seeing his name on the back of the book and finding out his son was Lash Jackson Montana. Not to mention getting lost, then stumbling into him and his new wife at the same hotel. The entire situation was like a bad soap opera! Saying the situation was overwhelming was an understatement. And, the grand finale, the climax to this series of bizarre events; she was sitting here, in the house of his son, as their house guest for the holidays. "THIS IS FREAKING UNBELIEVABLE!" She must have startled Cecilia because she came out the kitchen asking if she were okay. Annie realized she had shouted it aloud.

"I'm okay, thank you Cecilia. So sorry if I startled you." *Jeez, now she must think I'm some kind of lunatic. I swear I'm in the Twilight Zone!*

The roar of a very large truck engine snapped Annie out of her catatonic daydream or nightmare as it were. A few moments later the front door opened. *This is when my already weird day gets even weirder.* It was the British guy she met at the truck stop. *OH MY GOD, I'm in Montana's version of HELL or bizarro version of The Wizard of Oz!* He froze in his tracks and stared at Annie. The two both stopped breathing for a second.

In unison they said, "You're the guy/young lady from the Utah truck stop! What are you doing here?"

Their mutual boisterous recognition brought Meryl, Keough and Cecilia rushing out from the kitchen. Paul was surprised to see Meryl and Keough and even more surprised to see her." Everyone sat down. The situation had to be explained.

Paul told them he'd run into Annie at a Utah truck stop. "She was rabbiting on to herself. I was worried about her…?

"Annie, my name is Annie." She then explained to Keough that after Utah, she got lost. "That's when I bumped into you and Meryl."

Paul scratched his head. "So Luv, how did you end up here? It's not like our ranch is easy to locate. I've lived here for a while and I still require my bloody GPS to guide me to the house."

At this point Keough chimed in. "Meryl and I met her as we were leaving the hotel and invited her to breakfast. We got to talkin' about Malta. One thing led to another and we invited her to join us for the holidays. Ain't that right Annie?"

She nodded.

"And did you know she's a doctor?"

Paul nodded. Keough walked up to Paul and put his arm around his shoulder. "Well, now that everybody knows everybody can I get back to eatin' my coffee cake?"

"Speaking of cake when's Rose getting home? Meryl and I have something important to tell y'all." Cecilia tried not to let on about their surprise.

Paul suggested that they wait for Rose and Charlotte to share their news. They agreed. It also gave Annie the chance to study the Montana family dynamic.

After an hour of chatting and laughing at Paul's exaggerated story about Annie, Rose finally arrived home. Hearing Keough and Meryl's voices, Charlotte came running into the kitchen. She screamed, "Pap-Pap! I'm so happy to see you! Did you bring me a surprise? Oh, and hello Miss Meryl. I missed you too!"

Rose walked into the kitchen with an arm full of Charlotte's library books and a small white bakery box. "OH MY GOD, Keough, Meryl and a beautiful young lady who I don't think I know." She put the books on the table and the box on the counter.

"Hello Darlin'! Lord it's good to see ya'." Rose hugged him and said it was good to see him too. She hugged Meryl. "Meryl, you look gorgeous. Life is good – yes?"

Meryl smiled and said, "Yes, better than good darling." She held up her hand. Rose dropped onto the kitchen chair. "I'll be damned, you two got hitched! This is the best holiday gift ever!"

Charlotte started singing, *Here Comes the Bride* while Paul and Keough exchanged a manly hug. Annie thought, *I feel like I'm an extra in a movie. I don't know these people well enough to get excited or to participate in their excitement.*

Keough noticed Annie's awkwardness and hugged her shoulder. "I know this is a bit overwhelming for ya' darlin', but heck, this is just another day at the Montanas. You never know who or what will turn up. Just go with the flow and you'll be okay." He was so nurturing and kind. *How much I would have loved him being around as my father. Then I became angry because he wasn't around. I need a drink – many drinks!*

Rose came over and properly introduced herself. "So, Keough tells me you are a doctor and you're from Los Angeles. What brings you to Malta of all places if you don't mind my asking?" For a second she panicked. *Do I tell her that I finally found my deadbeat dad and want to rip him a new asshole for abandoning me and my Mom? Okay Mom a little help would be nice right about now.*

Annie explained that she was taking some time off to make a difficult job decision.

Rose perked up. "That's really interesting because I did the same thing. That's how I met Lash. Wow, what a coincidence." I smiled and nodded. "I truly appreciate your hospitality. Keough and Meryl literally kidnapped me; saying that no one should spend the holidays alone – so, here I am. I'd love to be a part of your holiday celebrations. However, I don't want to impose on your kindness, so I'd better be on my way. It's getting late and I have no idea how to get back to the ranch entrance or the hotel."

Rose stood up, "You are not leaving tonight or tomorrow. If Keough and Meryl invited you to come for the holidays you're welcome to stay HERE as long as you like. In fact, it'll be cool to have someone closer to my own age to hang out with. So what do you say?" *I thought how bad could it be? It's not like I have any place to be and it'll give me a chance to get to know Keough* "Okay, I'd love to stay. Again, thank you Rose for your kindness – it's appreciated." Rose hugged her guest and announced to everyone that she'd be staying.

Paul also announced that if anyone heard her talking aloud to herself not to panic. "She has this dreadful habit of shouting out the most absurd things at the most unpredictable times. You've all been forewarned. I'll explain later Rose."

Rose laughed and shrugged her shoulders, then turned and asked Annie if she'd like a glass of wine. I said I'd love a glass. "If you have anything stronger that'll work too." She gave her a huge smile and said, "Okay now we're talkin'."

Reaching in the upper kitchen cabinet she brought down a bottle of whiskey. "Joe used to pour a bit in his coffee after working with the horses – medicinal purposes he'd say."

Rose and Annie chatted until midnight. *She seems more like a sister than a new friend. In fact since Keough is my father and Lash was his son that makes me Lash's sister and Rose's sister-in-law. Crazy shit, indeed!* Everyone else had called it an evening and headed to bed. Charlotte came into the kitchen and gave her Mom a goodnight hug. She gave Annie a hug too. Annie thought the child's gesture odd as most kids don't hug strangers but Charlotte said that Annie was her new friend. She then made a startling comment. "Mama, Annie has the same color eyes as me! How cool is that!"

Rose looked and said, "Yes, she does, the same beautiful eyes sweetie, the same sleepy beautiful eyes as you do. Goodnight Baby Girl."

Charlotte made a face and said, "Okay, I know when I'm not wanted. Goodnight, Mama and Annie. See you in the morning." Rose said, "Goodnight again drama queen, now get goin'."

Rose waited until Charlotte left the room then she made another comment about her eyes. "My husband had those same blue-gray eyes. Come to think of it so do Keough and Kurt."

"Kurt? Annie asked. "Kurt – I don't think I met a Kurt tonight." Rose explained that Keough has an identical twin brother named, Kurt. Rose said she'd introduce him to her tomorrow. "It's getting late Annie, and you've had a long day. You must be exhausted." They ended their conversation with another shot of whiskey, and then said goodnight. Rose had already showed her the room she'd be staying in and told her to make herself at home.

"I'll have Paul bring your luggage in tomorrow morning. She handed her guest a pair of brand new pajamas. "In my single days I used to be a serious shopaholic. My weakness is soft silky pajamas. They seem to help me sleep. Well, at least that's the story I'd tell Joe. We look to be the same size, so these should fit. Sleep well Annie. I'm so glad you decided to stay

"Me too Rose, me too – goodnight." Annie crawled into bed and thought, *no one in LA will believe this, hell I can't believe it myself.*

Chapter 15

Jameson and Raymond had finished closing the last cabin for the season. Not many folks stayed during late autumn or the winter months – too much snow and ice. Jameson's turned out to be a pretty decent fellow. Nothing like the drunken New York putz Raymond first met sleeping by the side of the road. *What a difference a few year make. Joe would be proud of how he turned out. Come to think about it I must admit I miss that exasperating asshole with the shit-eatin' grin. He was my dearest friend and my worst enemy when it came to irritating me.*

Raymond yelled for Jameson. "If you want lunch you'd better come in now or I'll be tempted to eat it all."

"Okay Raymond, let me finish the last bit of work on this broken hinge."

Raymond told him he'd leave his plate on the stove, *nothing worse than cold venison stew.* He poured a cup of coffee and sat outside on the porch. Winter was quickly rolling into the mountains. The air was crisp and chilled his face. He looked at his reflection in his coffee cup and said, "Who is this wrinkled face man staring back at me?" *Damn, I'm getting old, and almost as ugly as Joe.* I chuckled to myself. *What I wouldn't give to hear his gravelly western voice tell me that I'm older and uglier than he is and then me telling him to shut up or I'd scalp what little hair he had left.* It was a bit chilly so Raymond went back inside for a sweater. He took the last photograph of him and Lash together off the mantle. He remembered that day fondly. Rose took it the day she found out she was pregnant with Charlotte. Those were happy times. *Thank goodness I still have a copy on my cell phone. But Rose knows I'm old school. I love the feel of paper photographs in wooden frames. I guess you could say I'm a tactile sort of fellow. I laughed and put it back onto the mantle.* "Joe, I promise to keep Rose, Charlotte and Jameson safe. They are my family just as you are. I love you my brother." Raymond went back outside to collect his thoughts.

Jameson had finished his lunch and noticed his friend sitting on the porch. He went out to sit with him. He also noticed his tearing eyes.

"Thinking about Joe again, huh Raymond? I miss him too Raymond. I never had the chance to meet him or know him. Hell, all my life I thought I was an only child. And then to find out that not only did I have a brother, but a twin brother and an entire family I never knew about…it's crazy Raymond. "If there was ever a time to drink that was it. But don't worry, I've been sober for a while and have no plans on starting again. Plus, you would scalp me for sure."

"Jameson, you need not worry, my scalping days are over. And since Rose gave me this new cell phone I'll just send out mean tweets about you on Twitter and a cruel meme of you on Facebook. Welcome to the age of social media my friend."

Jameson almost spit out his coffee laughing. "Raymond you are truly an awesome dude! And I want to thank you for literally saving my life. I would have eventually died at the bottom of a bottle if it weren't for you and Rose. You believed in me when I didn't believe in myself and for that I'm seriously thankful.

"Speaking of thankful, Rose called. She wants me to remind you about Thanksgiving dinner. She also said we should plan to stay for the holidays. Saying that the roads get icy and she didn't want us getting stranded out here. And, it'll be the first time all of the family will be together since Joe died. She also asked if you'd bake your pumpkin spiced pies."

"Of course I will and I'll call her tomorrow to confirm. It'll be good to see the whole family – especially Nadie. She is growing up so quickly. Where has the time gone and when did I become an old decrepit redskin or to be politically correct, an aging Native American? I can barely get up from this porch chair without huffing and puffing." Jameson offered his arm and Raymond pulled myself up.

"You know Raymond you've been complaining about being out of breath for a few days. Maybe you should have the doc check you out. When was the last time you had a physical?"

Raymond could tell he was being sincere so he told Jameson he would call next week after he and Jameson cleared the dead wood from the cabin side roads. "After that I promise I'll call the doctor and schedule a complete checkup." That seemed to satisfy Jameson who went back inside to clean up the dishes. Raymond looked up at the sky. "Winter is coming and it's going to be a bad one. I can feel it in my bones." He stretched and rubbed the small of his back. "Maybe I should put a Jacuzzi in my cabin – couldn't hurt. Well, I'd better go and help Jameson clear the roads." *Yes, I'll get a Jacuzzi ... must purchase a Jacuzzi! And I think I'll go to bed early tonight. A good night's sleep and I'll be right as rain tomorrow.*

A sharp knock at the bedroom door startled Raymond awake. It was Jameson. He wanted to know if he planned to sleep all day or were they going to go get the tractors and trucks fueled up. Raymond turned over and looked at the clock – it was 9 AM.

"Oh my God Jameson why did you let me sleep so long? The day is half over."

"Raymond, its only 8 AM, put your glasses on." He was right, it was only eight, but still, Raymond usually arose at six o'clock. *Why am I so tired? Maybe the doc will prescribe some super vitamins for me. I'll call him later.* Jameson already had the coffee perking and the gas cans loaded in the trucks – *God bless him!* I told him we could grab something to eat on the way. As we were walking towards the truck he asked Raymond if he was feeling better. Raymond told him he felt great and ordered him to stop worrying.

"I'm old Jameson and old people have old bodies and old problems like getting quickly agitated by young people constantly worrying about us old folks."

Jameson shrugged, "Okay Raymond, if you say you're all right I'll leave it at that – let's get going."

As much as Raymond hated Jameson worrying about him, he knew it was coming from a place of concern and love. He told Raymond that he considered him a second dad. Raymond took that as a compliment as he considered Joe a brother. However, the more he thought about it, Jameson was indeed like a young son – an annoying, over caffeinated son, but nonetheless a son. Both men had honorable souls and good spirits. Jameson's spirit used to come from scotch whiskey, but not anymore. Joe's was coffee – too much coffee! He always smelled of dark roast. *But I learned to love him and his addiction to the wicked bean. What I wouldn't give to sit and have a cup with him. Why can't I let him go? He's been dead for years and still, I miss him. So does Rose, even though she's moved on with Paul I can tell she still misses him. I miss my friend. And if I had to be honest with myself, Joe was my only true friend. I felt my eyes welling up again. I wiped them with my bandana and started up the truck.*

Raymond and Jameson had been on the road for a few minutes. The sky was overcast but the sun would peek through. Jameson was about a half mile ahead of Raymond when he noticed him slowing down and then coming to a complete stop. He rolled his window down and pointed. A beautiful herd of deer appeared from the forest and were about to cross the road. The buck had a huge rack – eight points. All looked healthy and well grazed. *It was a good sign. Mother Earth was rewarding us for our kindness and due diligence in keeping her in high spirits.*

After the herd safely crossed, Raymond pulled up next to Jameson. "You should treasure this experience. It's a sacred sign that we are in fact taking better care of our planet, and not fucking it up for our next generation – truly a good thing. I don't make it a habit of cursing that often, but it was the only word that described my feelings."

Even Jameson was surprised to hear him drop the F-bomb. The two continued their trip to the Fuel and Livery Depot when they saw the first signs of winter–high altitude snow. It was beginning to cover the tips of the Lodgepole pines along the timberline. Jameson stopped again to take a photo with his cell phone. Raymond admitted it was beautiful, but he knew if they didn't get things done before December they'd be in trouble. Raymond was used to the isolation; however, it may be a problem for Jameson.

An hour into the drive, the two stopped to get something to eat. They had arrived at Jimmy's to refuel the trucks and grab a quick coffee. The bell on the door alerted Jimmy that someone had entered the store. He was in the stock room and yelled he'd be out in a minute.

"Hello Jimmy, its only Raymond and Jameson. No need to rush. I'll just help myself to the coffee and sweet rolls if you don't mind."

Jameson heard him chuckle. "Okay, Raymond. Go ahead and help yourself."

Raymond started pouring my coffee when Jimmy came from around the corner. "Howdy Raymond, how's things going out in your neck of the woods?"

"Same stuff, different day Jimmy." He poured himself a cup of coffee and the two men caught up on the local news while Jameson fueled the trucks. Jimmy's store was too small to carry diesel.

"Hey Raymond, did you know that Keough and Meryl got hitched. They're on their way to Rose's to give her the good news."

"No, I didn't Jimmy. I'm happy for Keough and Meryl." "They've both had such terrible losses; Keough losing Joe and Meryl's husband's unexpected death. This is good news indeed. But don't tell Jameson. Let Meryl give him the good news."

"But getting back to old Keough; he's really stepped up for Rose and Meryl. It's a shame Joe isn't around to see all this happiness."

Raymond agreed, "You're right Jimmy, but don't let his death fool you. That mangy son-of-a-prairie-bitch is still haunting me. Like I told Rose, he's worse than bedbugs!"

The two laughed because Jimmy knew exactly what he meant. Jameson walked in while we were laughing and topped off his coffee. "Okay, what did I miss?"

Jimmy and Raymond finally stopped laughing to let him in on the joke. At first he laughed, and then the jovial conversation changed. Jameson leaned against the counter and took a sip of his coffee. "I never knew Joe. I never had the opportunity to know him as a brother or a friend. I wish I could say I love him and miss him as much as you guys do. But I don't. Sadly, I just never knew the guy. Only the articles I've read in the newspapers and the stories Rose and Keough have told me."

Raymond could see that Jameson was genuinely disappointed. And he walked over and put his hand on his shoulder. "Jameson your brother was a fine man, a pain in my ass, but a fine man. I'd be happy to tell you all the stories I know about him." He nodded and continued sipping his coffee.

Raymond looked at his watch. "Well Jimmy, we'd better get going. I don't want to be stranded if an unexpected snowstorm hits."

"I'm gearing up for a snowy winter too." He told Raymond to wait a second and went back into the stock room. He brought out a sack of sugar and two sacks coffee. "This should tide you over until you can make another trip back. Consider it an early Christmas gift.

"Why thank you very much Jimmy. I guess I'll see you later; more than likely in the spring." The men said their goodbyes and hit the road.

Raymond and Jameson arrived at the Fuel and Livery Depot. There was a line for the diesel pumps. Jameson held their place while Raymond went inside. He knew Rose would need spring wormers and grain. *I know she'll be happy at not having to make a special trip out here to pick them up. I remember her mentioning something about replacing hinges for the attic door.* He added them to his growing list of Rose items. He paid for the supplies then went back to the fuel line to help Jameson load the gasoline and kerosene cans. "Let's get going Jameson. I feel snow coming. And, you should call your mother. I know she'd be happy to know how well you're doing."

Jameson stopped in his tracks. "Okay Raymond what's up? Come on tell me. I know something's going on by the way you and Jimmy had your heads together. It's bad news isn't it? I knew it!"

He began pacing in front of the truck. Raymond grabbed hold of his arm. "No it's not bad news you idiot. You're mother and Keough have some good news for you and I think you should hear it from them."

Jameson rolled his eyes and got in the truck. "Okay, Raymond, it's not like you'd tell me anything anyway!" He hopped into his truck and slammed the door. As he climbed into his truck Raymond laughed. *He's more fun to annoy than Joe! Ah, someday I'm going to burn in hell for my wickedness.*

The two arrived home just as the snow began to fall. The flakes were large and starting to stick to the trees and grass. Jameson and Raymond unloaded the cans and filled the gas drum. He stored the empties and the kerosene in the metal sheds. The thin layer of ice forming on the small pond beyond the cabins hinted of the falling temperatures.

"It's getting colder and darker out there. Come in before you turn whiter than you already are. I've put the kettle on if you'd like some tea."

"Okay Raymond I'll be in soon. Give me a few more minutes." He came in covered in snow carrying an arm full of wood. Shaking the snow from his hair, he stacked the logs in the log bin.

"I thought we could get a fire started. It's getting colder by the minute." Raymond thanked him for his thoughtfulness. "I really need to buy a winter hat. I didn't need one in Manhattan."

Raymond tossed him an old Montana State University baseball caps. "Here, you can have this one. It belonged to your brother. I'm sure he won't mind." The fireplace was glowing and the kettle was boiling. Raymond brought Jameson a cup of tea and some of the pastries Jimmy had given them for the trip home.

"You know Raymond, I could get used to living out here. It's so quiet and peaceful – nothing like Manhattan. Even the cold is different. The city is bone-chilling because of the concrete and tall buildings. Here, it's cold, yet it's not – if that makes any sense."

"I know what you mean Jameson and it does make sense. You're beginning to understand how nature works out here. The trees block the wind and snow acts as a canopy."

The fire felt good and quickly warmed the cabin. The two men finished their dinner and called it a night. "Oh and remember to call your mother tomorrow morning. I think you'll be happily surprised. Goodnight Jameson."

"I will and goodnight to you too Raymond." Jameson paused for a few seconds then added, "And, thanks for believing in me. It means a lot."

Raymond smiled and touched him on the shoulder, "My pleasure. Goodnight my friend."

Chapter 16

The alarm on Rose's cell phone started buzzing. *It can't be six o'clock in the morning already? I just went to bed 15-minutes ago? I'd better get up and get Charlotte ready for school. Three more days and she's off for Thanksgiving holiday, thank God!* I grabbed my robe and put on a pair of woolen socks. *Good Lord, it's cold in here! I need to get the thermostat fixed in this bedroom.* Joe said we didn't need to fix it because we were such a hot couple. Paul's always too hot. *Maybe he could be my human bathrobe*

The aroma of freshly brewed coffee greeted Rose at the bedroom door, wafting down hallway, straight to the kitchen. *Ah, Paul's up!* Before she could make it to the kitchen he met her halfway holding a cup of coffee. "Morning Luv, I was bringing you a cup."

She kissed him on his forehead. "You are a Saint, Paul Saxton. Remind me to canonize you as the Patron Saint of the Caffeine Deprived. Why are you up so early? I thought it was my turn to get Charlotte ready for school?"

He took hold of Rose's hand and led her to the living room window. She rubbed her eyes. "Oh my God, when did this happen? There must be at least a foot of snow out there!"

Paul chuckled, "Yes, that's why I let you sleep. The local news station reported that all schools are closed today. I'm surprised the cheering of every school child in the county didn't wake you up. They're getting an unexpected extended holiday. Would you like a sedative chaser with your coffee Poppet?"

"Hah, that's very funny John Cleese." Rose leaned back in Paul's arms and took in the beauty of the falling snow. "Paul, it's so quiet and peaceful when it's snowing in Montana. In New York all you'd hear is the horrible metal against concrete scraping of the snow plows, horns honking at the cars getting stuck in traffic and the people yelling about the lack of parking. I don't miss it. I don't miss it one bit."

The two walked back to the kitchen for another cup of coffee and waited for the rest of the household to emerge from their bedrooms. She heard footsteps coming from the guest room side of the house and an almost audible good morning – it was Annie. Rose poured her a cup and placed it in her hand.

"Morning Annie, I hope you slept well." She yawned. "Yes, thank you for asking Rose. It took me a while to fall asleep because I'm used to all the noises of the city. But once I did, I tell ya', I slept the sleep of angels! One thing's for sure, when I get home I'm going to buy a new mattress!"

Rose smiled and topped off her coffee. "I'm happy you slept well Annie and I hope you're hungry because I was about to make breakfast. We thought we'd let Cecilia sleep in this morning since schools are closed."

Annie took another long sip of coffee. "Yes, again thank you Rose. I'd love breakfast! I'm starving. It seems a good night's rest stimulates my appetite. Since I've been traveling I'm eating more. I swear I didn't know there were so many fast food joints that served breakfast all day."

Meryl and Keough were the next to awaken. Both looked like they were in desperate need of coffee. "Well good morning love birds, hope you slept well."

Meryl hugged her hostess and said, "It's nice to wake up surrounded by friends, family and in the arms of my adoring husband."

Keough shook his head. "I swear you gals are hopeless romantics." He turned to Meryl and said, "Bein' happy to wake up and seein' this ol' face first thing in the morning, lady you've got to be loco."

She turned around and tenderly kissed him on his forehead, cheeks, and then his lips. "I love every inch of this ol' face and the person it belongs to." Rose told Keough she missed his ugly ol' face too. "Whoa there darlin', now I don't recollect her saying anything about UGLY!"

Rose laughed, "I know I just threw that one in so you wouldn't think I've gone soft and started liking you."

While Meryl, Keough and Paul were chatting and enjoying each other's company, Rose noticed Annabella staring at Keough. It was as if she were dissecting every inch of him. *I wonder what that's about.* Rose dismissed it as idle curiosity. Annie seemed to sense Rose's gaze. Their eyes met and Rose tried to play it off as a joke and asked her if Keough's hideous face mesmerized her. At first the two laughed about it, and then she admitted that he looked very familiar. "Rose, has Keough ever been to Los Angeles or ... Fort Worth, Texas?"

Her question caught Rose off guard. It took her a minute to think of an answer. "Not that I'm aware of, perhaps Fort Worth when he was on the rodeo circuit, but that would have been years before you were born."

Rose's answer seemed to satisfy her guest, so Rose changed the subject to her career.

"So, tell me about the fabulous life of a doctor. Keough mentioned something about you being in charge of the entire hospital." Annabella laughed. "I've noticed Keough has a tendency to exaggerate. I'm Head of Oncology at LA Metro. My mother used to tell me that there were two jobs people would always need. One was doctors – the other, undertakers."

"Your mother was right Annie. She sounds like a wise woman. I'd love to meet her."

Annie slowly stirred her coffee and exhaled. "Mom died shortly after I graduated from Medical School. She was so proud. I can still see her smiling and waving at me when I held up that sheepskin. It's a day I'll never forget."

"I'm so sorry Annie. You have my condolences."

"Thank you Rose. Mom was one of a kind. She lived an extremely exciting life. Not many women had her strength and tenacity. I worked my ass off to make her proud. Being a single parent she always laughed when I would give her Mother's Day and Father's Day cards. I still miss her very much."

"I totally understand Annie. When I found out Joe had terminal cancer I was devastated. He made me promise not to jump in the grave with him. Live your life darlin, he'd say and don't look back. That's the Montana way. So when Paul asked me to marry him, I accepted. It also helped that Paul and I were good friends before we married. He and Joe got along well. I know Joe approves of our union."

While Rose was talking, she noticed Annie fidgeting with her necklace. "What a beautiful necklace Annie."

"Thank you. It was a gift from my mom." She gently tucked it back inside of her pajama top. "My father gave it to her before I was born and she passed it on to me when I graduated from High School."

"Your father must be proud of you too. Is he . . . still living?" *Yes, the bastard is in the next room with his new wife.* "I never knew him. He left Mom before I was born. I guess you could call me an oh-by-the-way-I'm-pregnant baby. However, what I do know is that he was already married and never saw or contacted Mom again. We moved to Los Angeles, changed our name from Harris to Harrison and had a great life and I'm now sitting in a kitchen chatting with the most hospitable woman in Montana."

Rose added, "And you are a welcomed house guest Annie. I'm so glad you met up with Keough and Meryl. It's not often I get to chat with a big shot doctor – more coffee?"

"Yes, I'd love a half a cup."

Rose poured until Annie motioned for her to stop. "Rose, now please don't take this the wrong way. As an unexpected guest I appreciate your kindness and hospitality, but I have to ask . . . Lord have mercy girl, why is your coffee so STRONG? I could finish a 25k run in three minutes if I drank one more cup of this stuff."

"We should have warned you about our Montana coffee addiction. Joe was a Coffeeholic, if there is such a word. And, if it's not a word it should be. Writers tend to write at all hours of the day and night. Joe would perk two pots at a time; one pot to help him wake up; the other to get him through his endless proofreading and editing. One of his friends at our local coffee shop said that he probably pissed dark roast!"

The two women laughed so hard they woke Charlotte. "What's so funny Mama? I could hear you two all the way back in my bedroom."

"Well, good morning to you too Missy. How about you saying hello before you reprimand us for waking you up. And by the way, it snowed – no school."

Her sleepy face transformed into a huge smile. "Wow, this is the best news ever! I have to call Corey. He was hoping for a big snow. I think it's because he didn't want to take today's math test. And, can I ride Daisy Deuce in the snow Mama? Please? Maybe Annie would like to ride Daisy. She's really nice Annie and she loves the snow too." Annie looked at Rose as if to say, *it's your call Mama.* "What say we get you some breakfast first and let me think about it – deal?"

"Deal."

Annie walked over to the kitchen window. "It's beautiful. I never get to see snow living in Los Angeles. If it's okay with you I'd love to go out riding with Charlotte. I haven't ridden in a while, but Mom taught me how and I loved it. I guess it was from her years of working in Fort Worth at that cowboy café. She was one tough gal from the stories she told me. Hold on, I have a photo of her in my wallet."

She went to her room and came back with a small faded photo of a women leaning against the bar in what would be considered men's western gear, with her arms folded. "Wow, your mom was beautiful and she has on the necklace she gave to you. What a wonderful memento. I bet it had to be rough being black and working in a cow town like that."

Annie agreed. "There weren't many women working in Fort Worth. Mom was half Cherokee, so believe me she took no shit from the saddlebums and rodeo cowboys."

Rose gasped. "I can't believe this. I'm part Cherokee too! Maybe my family is related to your family. How cool would that be? Speaking of Native Americans, you must stay and meet Raymond Winterbee. He's one of our dearest friends, well, more like family. He's full blooded Blackfoot. He'll be joining us for Thanksgiving, if he can get here. We didn't expect this much snow this early in the year. But that's Montana for you."

Before she put the photo back into her wallet Rose asked her about the ethnicity of her father. "As a writer I'm naturally curious about people's lives and their backgrounds. Would it be safe to assume that your father was not black? Your complexion is as beautiful as Charlotte's. You could be her mother. It's the blue gray eyes. They're stunning. At first glance I would have pegged you as another one of Keough's long lost children. I understand he was quite the ladies man back in the old days. At least that's what Kurt tells me. Both of them swap so many tall tales I never know when they are telling me the truth or a tissue of lies."

The question took Annie off guard and she paused to collect her thoughts carefully.

"Yes, you are very observant Miss Rose. My father is Caucasian. Mom was a live-and-let-live kind of person. Back in those days I'd say she was very much the liberated woman. She taught me love people for who they are not what they are."

"Joe used to say, 'Folks ain't allowed to hate you for what you can't change, in short you never hate people for their race or the color of their skin. It's a code we Montanas live by.'"

Annie said she was raised the same way. "As a doctor I know firsthand when I'm operating that everyone bleeds red. And, as I too am a curious person remind me again . . . who's Kurt?"

"Kurt is the only sane Montana in the bunch. He's Keough's identical twin brother. The only way I can tell them apart is by their clothing. You'll meet him soon. In fact he should be coming over for his morning thermos of coffee. He stayed on after Joe died to help with the ranch. He also hires all the ranch hands. Would you like more coffee Annie?"

"No thank you Rose – I'm good. And again, thank you for your kindness. I feel honored being welcomed by such an amazing and might I add famous family. I have to admit I've never heard of Montana Joe or his hundreds of popular western novels. I'm a trashy-novel-sit-on-the-beach-and-fall-asleep-while-reading sort of girl."

Rose laughed and told her that she'd get along well with her best friend, Jannine. "She and her husband Morgan, who happens to be my stepson, will also be coming for the holidays. However, with the snowstorm I'm afraid their flight might be cancelled."

"Rose, if you're expecting more guests perhaps I should stay at a hotel?" The look on her face caused Rose to laugh aloud. "I'm serious Rose; I don't want to be an imposition for you and your family."

Rose walked over to Annie and held out her hand. "Hello Annie, we're the Montanas. Have you seen the size of this freaking house! It's HUGE! Not to mention we have a three-bedroom fully furnished bunkhouse. I'd have to call your cell phone to make sure you're still here. You are not an imposition you are our house guest. Lash used to say, '*You're only a guest once at Casa Montana. After that you're part of the family. So you'd better get used to making and drinking strong coffee.*'"

Annie was speechless. "Rose, I can't thank . . ."

"Annie, you already have; just nod and say okay."

"Okay Rose. And if it's okay with you I'll get dressed now. It seems I'm going to ride a horse in the snow with an adorable cowgirl."

Rose could see Charlotte and Paul coming down the hallway and heading toward the kitchen. Both were dressed as if they were traveling to Antarctica. Paul pulled the scarf from over his mouth.

"Rose, it seems our daughter thinks it's a good idea to go for a ride in a blizzard. Is this something you approved?"

Rose turned her head so he wouldn't see her snickering, "If it's okay with you darling - yes."

Paul's brow wrinkled. "Hmm, me thinks there is a load of rubbish floating about here. Charlotte told me to ask if it was okay with YOU."

Annie whispered, *I think we've been royally played."*

Rose nodded, "More like suckered."

Annie took a deep breath. "I guess I'd better get dressed Rose. You wouldn't happen to have a heavy coat, boots, gloves and a bottle of whiskey?"

"Yep, I sure do!" Rose pointed her to the hall closet. "Oh, and the whiskey is on the top shelf next to the refrigerator. I'm assuming it's for medicinal use – am I correct?"

Annie laughed. "Yes Rose. Even doctors need a little help especially if I'm expecting to have a few bones reset. Wish me luck!"

"The snow will cushion your falls, so don't worry."

"Rose, being the observant person I am I noticed you pluralized the word *fall*. Is there something I should know about these particular horses?"

Rose shook her head. "Nope, it was just a verbal slip."

Annie squinted. "I don't like the word *slip* either. How about a supportive thumbs up?"

Finally, everyone was dressed and ready to ride. Rose watched as Annie, Paul and Charlotte started their trek to the barns. The snow was beginning to taper off to a light flurry. She watched from the kitchen deck as they happily trudged through the knee deep snow until they were safely inside the barn. *I'd better call Kurt and let him know they were coming. He's going to need to get the tack and saddles out of the tack room.*

"Good morning Kurt. Nice weather we're having, huh?"

"Well, hello, Rose. How are you doing this fine snowy morning."

"I'm wonderful, and I thought I should give you a heads up. You're going to have company in a few minutes. Your grand-niece thought it would be a fun activity to go horseback riding in a blizzard."

Kurt pulled the bunkhouse shutters open. "Yep, I see them. Do you want me to talk them out of it or should I get the horses saddled?"

"It's okay to saddle them because I don't think they'll be riding for very long. One of them is from Los Angeles and I don't think she's much of a snow bird. But you may have your hands full with Charlotte. She'll stay outside until she's blue."

Kurt chuckled. "Okay Rose, I'll take care of them and afterwards I'll be over for coffee and some of Cecilia's coffee cake. There's still some left over, right?"

"Yes, I'll save you a big piece as a thank you for looking after our company and by the way her name is Annabella, but she prefers to be called Annie." Kurt said he appreciated the call and headed downstairs to the tack room.

Charlotte ran ahead of Paul and Annie. "Hello, Uncle Kurt! It's your favorite niece. I'm sure Mama called to tell you we're going horseback riding!"

"Yes she did Charlotte and she also mentioned that we have a guest riding with us." Paul and Annie walked in behind Charlotte brushing the snow off their hats and shoulders. Kurt walked up to Paul and gave him his customary manly handshake and pat on the back.

He then asked Paul if he would start the introductions. "Kurt, this is Miss Annabella Harrison; Annabella this is, if you haven't noticed, Keough's twin brother, Kurt."

Annie extended my hand. "Hello Kurt, it's very nice to meet you. And, I have to admit if I didn't know Keough was in the house I'd swear you're the same person."

Kurt laughed. "Yep, that's my ugly twin brother. And as you can clearly see I'm the handsome one."

Annie smiled, "Funny, that's the same thing he said about you – being the ugly one."

"Well, Annie, since we're now such good friends they'll be no hand shakin'." He walked over and gave me a gentle fatherly hug. "Welcome to the Montanas. You are officially part of our crazy-mixed-up-family. You'll either love us or hate us; but we'll always have your back if'n you ever need us or get into trouble. It's the Montana code."

Kurt walked with us to the stable area. Annie made mental observations of her stable surroundings. *These stables were more elegant than my LA apartment. Now I understand why Rose kept him on. He's got to be a hard worker to take care of all this property.*

Kurt put on his barn coat and cowboy hat and accompanied us to round pen area. "It looks like we're goin' get more snow. Kurt pointed towards the Nimbocumulous clouds looming on the horizon. You two say inside the round pen area. It'll be safer." Paul agreed. Charlotte baulked saying she was a good rider and wanted to show Annie the tricks she taught Daisy Duce. Annie whispered to Charlotte that she wasn't as good a rider as she was and she'd be so embarrassed if she fell off, so she would be grateful to Charlotte if she taught her to ride Daisy inside the pen. Charlotte agreed. Paul and Kurt mouthed thank you to Annie and she winked back in acknowledgement before mounting Daisy. Charlotte already had her horse walking around making a nice path for her new friend to follow. Annie had to admit that she was having fun. Even though she knew how to ride, she hadn't ridden in a while but as Rose said Daisy was such a gentle creature a 2-year-old could ride her.

Charlotte and Annie rode around the pen for thirty minutes or so when Kurt noticed Charlotte's face turning red. He whistled and announced that the rodeo was over then motioned the two to come back to the barn. Of course Charlotte made one more lap around the pen, then loped Daisy Duce into the barn. Annie carefully walked Daisy in behind her.

"Okay Charlotte you are the best riding instructor I've ever had. Next time perhaps I'll be able to get Daisy to lope."

She smiled, "Next time? So, that means you're coming back to visit us!"

Annie glanced over at Paul and Kurt. They turned their heads so she wouldn't notice them laughing. "Yes, I'd love to visit again, if it's okay with you."

"YES! You could be like my big sister. Seeing that I'm an only child sometimes I get sort of lonely with nobody to hang out with I love Mama and Paul, but it'll be fun having someone else to talk to." She put her face next to Annie's "See, we even look alike. The same color eyes and skin."

Kurt nodded, "Yes, you two do resemble each other." Annie noticed Kurt quietly studying her face. He said, "If I didn't know better I'd say you were a long lost Montana."

Paul also nodded, "It's not like it hasn't happened before Kurt. Jameson, Joe's fraternal twin brother never knew he was a Montana. He'd been adopted as an infant by the Wellesley family. It was a surprise to all of us. In fact, he recently changed his name to Jameson Wellesley-Montana. It's a long story Annie; one I'm sure you'll hear during your stay, which may be a while – it's still snowing."

Yes, there's going to be an even bigger surprise story for Keough. One I'm sure he'll never see coming!

Chapter 17

Cecilia announced that dinner would be ready in half an hour. Rose thought *I feel like I gained five pounds from the aroma.* "Thank you Cecilia. Whatever you're cooking it smells amazing!" While dinner was being prepared Rose checked her emails. One was marked URGENT from Charlotte's school—an announcement that classes would resume Thanksgiving break but the week's homework was attached. Charlotte was not happy to hear that although school was put on hold, homework was not.

"I thought I was going to have a real vacation – no homework!"

"No such luck kiddo. We'll start reviewing your assignments after dinner. Thank goodness our Wi-Fi was still working or we'd truly be living in the Ice Age."

Annie came in and asked if she could use my computer to log on to her work emails.

"Sure, let me log out."

"I appreciate it Rose. I'm sure they didn't expect me to be away this long, but if I have to be stranded, I'm happy it's with you folks. I could have been stuck in Utah with Mormons! Nothing against Mormons but I'm just saying it would have been an entirely different experience."

Rose laughed, "Annie, there's no need to ask. As long as you're here please feel free to make yourself at home."

"Thanks! I shouldn't be very long. Most of them I'll delete."

"Take your time Annie but I'd suggest you finish soon. Once Cecilia serves dinner it's everyone for themselves. I've witnessed an entire turkey disappear in five minutes!"

"I'll keep that in mind. I won't be long."

For a brief moment Rose reminisced how Annie checking her emails brought back memories of her flagging down Paul's truck to check and see if she'd received replies from Joe; a memory both she and Paul fondly remember. It seems like only yesterday since he's been gone. *Goodness how time flies.*

"I'd better check on Charlotte to see if she's finished her first page of homework and not chatting with Corey."

"Again, thank you Rose for your kindness."

"No problem Annie. If you need me I'll be in the family room."

Annie took the laptop into her bedroom and logged in. There was a flood of emails – two marked URGENT. She opened them first. One was not so urgent. One of her patients had a non-life threatening problem and needed to return to the hospital. She was discharged the same day. The other was much more urgent. The hospital needed her back by the Monday after Thanksgiving to be interviewed by the panel of doctors for the Chief of Surgery position. She started to panic knowing that there's no way in hell she could get back in two days – not with this snowstorm. *Maybe I can video conference? I'd better call and update them on my whereabouts and the severe weather conditions in Montana. Perhaps they'll postpone the meeting? I can only hope! I'd better call Myers right away!*

"Hello, Los Angeles Metro Hospital Oncology, Myers MacNamara speaking."

"Hey Myers, its Annie, I need a favor."

"Well, hello Annie-I-need-a-favor. Where the heck are you? The reception is terrible!"

"I'm in Montana, Malta Montana to be precise. Listen, I need you to reschedule my COS interview. Malta just got hit with blizzard and I'm stuck here. I can't get back to California."

"No can do Doc, they've been postponing it for days waiting for you to respond to their email. They assumed you didn't want to be a considered a candidate. I tried to call you but I kept getting an out-of-range-message. But more importantly . . . what in the name of Jesus and all of his disciples are you doing in MONTANA! I thought you were going to Tahoe?"

It took a minute for Annie to process what Myers said.

"Myers, you're telling me that they've eliminated me from their applicants. ARE YOU FREAKING KIDDING ME?"

"Wish I was Doc but I just received the word today. I'll forward you a copy of the letter."

Oddly, after the initial shock, Annie felt a sense of relief.

"Don't bother Myers. To be honest, I wasn't sure I even wanted the position, and now I honestly don't know if I want to come back to LA Metro at all. I've turned down more prestigious positions. So finding another won't be a problem."

"Hey wait a minute. What about ME? You're trusty Administrative Medical Assistant and Cappuccino Fetcher! What am I supposed to do? If you're leaving you'd better damn well take me along with you, Doctor Harrison?"

"Myers, don't worry. I wouldn't think of leaving you behind. You know way too much about me. And, I know you well enough to know you'd go on Jerry Springer, put all my business out on the street, and we'd end up in a fist fight."

Myers laughed. "Okay, I'm going to hold you to that or Springer will be getting an anonymous phone call from an angry caffeine deprived Irishman."

"Thank you Myers, you are a sweetheart. I'd better go the reception is getting worse."

"Okay Annie, I'll keep you updated on who they decide on. But before you go I've got to ask . . . eh, why Montana?"

"Myers that is a story we'll have later over a bottle of Kilballys, I promise."

"I'm going to hold you to that Annie, because you know what they say about Kilballys? Of course the good stuff's better, but you gotta ask yourself . . . is it five bucks better? Their official slogan should be *Settle for Kilballys*."

"Hah, hah, so now you're calling me a cheapskate. And here I thought we were pals. Anyway, I've got to go Myers, you're breaking up. I'm only catching half of what you're saying."

A second later the call dropped. Annie noticed her cell phone battery was running low. She started to charge it but a thought of defiance popped into her head. *Why bother. It'll be nice not to be on call for a change.* She turned it off and shoved it into her pocket.

There was a timid knock on the bedroom door. It was Charlotte. "Hello Annie. Mama and Cecilia wanted me to tell you dinner is ready."

"Come on in Charlotte."

"Mama said if you were still on the phone, not to disturb you and they'd keep your dinner warm. Is everything okay? You look sort of sad?"

"Well, yes and no Charlotte. I just found out that I didn't get a position I applied for, but I'm sort of relieved that I didn't get it.

What that also means is I don't have to rush back to California. Would it be okay if I stayed a little longer?"

Charlotte ran over and hugged her so hard Annie felt her back crack. "Yes, yes it's okay! Mama will be excited to know she'll have someone her age to hang out with."

"And how about you? Will it be okay with you? It means you'll have to teach me how to get Daisy to lope like Daisy Duce."

Charlotte laughed and said, "No problem! I can't wait to tell Pap-pap and Meryl. I know they'll be happy too."

"Let's hold off on telling Pap-pap and Meryl until I get the okay from your Mama – okay?"

She nodded and grabbed Annie's hand. "Okay and let's go eat, I'm starving. Mama says it's because I'm growing, but I think it's actually Cecilia's cooking. She's the best!"

We went into the dining room and the table was beautifully set. Annie commented on how lovely everything looked, but Rose said she only goes all out when special guests visit the ranch.

Keough, Meryl and Paul were already seated. Keough quickly stood up and pulled out Annie's chair.

"There you go Annie. Have a seat and loosen you're jeans. Welcome to dinner at the Montanas."

Everyone laughed at his humorous and gentlemanly display of first-class manners.

"Will Kurt be joining us," Annie asked.

Keough said he'd be up later. "He's what I like to call the cleanup guy. If there's anything left over, he inhales it like a vacuum cleaner and never gains a single pound! If he wasn't my brother I'd hate him. Hell, I do hate him – only joking."

Now I understand why Mom liked him so much. He's charming, loving and witty. Great qualities for a father figure and his brother Kurt also has the same qualities. I guess it's a twin thing.

Everyone had finished dinner when Kurt walked in. He asked if there were any leftovers for him.

Keough laughed out loud, "Nope, not a crumb. We didn't realize Annie's appetite was twice her size. Sorry brother, as always you're a day late and a dollar short." Keough looked over at Annie and winked. Meryl rolled her eyes and told Kurt yes and they were in the kitchen and still warm.

Annie started fidgeting with her necklace as she tended to do when she was happy or nervous. This was a happy fidget. Meryl commented on how lovely it was.

"I noticed it earlier today. It's such a beautiful lover's heart necklace Annie. And, if I may be so bold – who has the other half? They must be somebody special."

Her happy fidget turned into a nervous one. She paused and told Rose it was extremely special as it was a gift from my mother before she died. Annie looked directly at Keough.

"My father gave it to her before he abandoned us."

Keough could tell that it was a touchy subject for me. He got up from the table, walked over and hugged jer. For a second she was taken aback. *Do I punch him; tell him who I am or what!*

She was about to explode when he took her aside and explained. "Annie, I totally understand your feelings toward your father. I was a lousy father; a God awful, terrible father to my sons and daughters. *Daughters, he has other daughters? How many kids has this guy spawned!* "I was a drunk, a saddlebum and worse – a coward. It took me years to contact my son Lash and tell him why I couldn't be in his life, until it was too late. He died a few months after we reconciled. If it wasn't for Kurt I may have never confronted him. With all this being said Annie, anger only creates more anger. If you want to know you're father then I say find him, if'n he still alive. Do you know if he is?"

Annie wanted to scream. She could feel her blood pressure rising and pounding in her head. Here is a man who she has HATED all her life and he is now giving her kind and loving fatherly advice. All she could do was thank him for his thoughtfulness and excuse herself.

As she was leaving the dining room, she glanced at Kurt. She noticed he looked as though he'd seen a ghost. *How very odd.* She asked him if he was okay. He uttered something and walked into the kitchen. She followed him and asked again if he was okay.

"Kurt you look pale." Annie reached out to take his pulse. It was rapid. "You'd better sit down, take a few deep breaths. Did you eat today?" He finally stood up and said he felt much better and thanked her for her concern. Rose walked in to check in on Kurt. The cowboy tried to brush it off by saying it was low blood sugar from not eating, but that didn't sound like the truth to her. He was fine until the necklace conversation. He insisted he was alright and thanked Annie again for her in-home doctor's visit and that his check would be in the mail. Annie still thought his reaction to her necklace was rather odd to say the least – oh well.

Cecilia announced that dessert was ready for anyone who wanted some. Annie moved out of the way because everyone came barreling into the kitchen. Charlotte explained to me that no one in their right mind passes on Cecilia's dessert. Annie didn't know what she made but the aroma was intoxicating. Rose revealed to us that it was her famous or as they like to call it her infamous Peach Pecan pie and Apple Crisp with homemade whipped cream. Cecilia also said there was a pot of coffee brewing.

"I will pay you a million dollars a month to leave the Montanas and come be my chef in Los Angeles!" Annie gasped.

Before she could answer Rose threatened, "Them's fighting words Annie. Did I mention that we Montanas all own shotguns and aren't afraid to use them on people who try to steal our Cecilia."

The kitchen erupted in laughter while Cecilia dished out the warm sweet deliciousness. Rose also told Annie that it was no use asking her for the recipes. "She'll go to her grave with them. Trust me I've tried – I failed."

After dessert everyone started filing out of the kitchen to relax. Rose asked Annie to stay behind for a minute.

"I noticed you chatting with Kurt. Is he okay? He would never tell me if he wasn't feeling well. He's stubborn just like the rest of the Montanas."

Annie nodded, "Yes he seems to be fine; nothing organically wrong. BP, pulse, respiration; his pupils didn't look dilated, everything seems to be okay. However, he looked upset or perhaps shocked is a better word."

"Well, I'm glad you were on call *Doctor Annie*. I'm also very happy you are able to extend your stay. Not that you can go anywhere until the snow melts. Paul, Keough and Kurt will start plowing tomorrow. Yes, we have our own snow plows. We have to or we'd never get out of our driveway; especially if there was an emergency – hence my asking about Kurt."

Rose's ability to adapt to this rugged environment impressed Annie. She knew she couldn't do it. She walked over and gave her a hug. "Rose, your tenacity to live in this terrain astonishes me. I must admit you are one of the most amazing women I've ever met. I don't know if I could live like this. If there's not a Szechuan restaurant within walking distance I start to panic. No wonder Lash Montana fell in love with you. Lady, you are one in a million."

Rose shook her head. "Okay, now you're just sucking up. No need, you've already endeared yourself to all of us. It's something that seems to happen time and again at Casa Montana. Annie, you're now stuck with a ready-made, completely over-caffeinated, family of lunatics – lucky you."

Annie had to laugh at her assessment of her gratitude. She had never sucked up to anybody including world renowned surgeons; however, the Montana family had her humbled – beyond humble. Paul poked his head in and asked if everything was okay? Rose said yes and asked if he wanted a cup of tea.

"I would NEVER refuse a cup of tea." Annie offered to make it for him. It was past Charlotte's bedtime and Rose wanted to make sure she wasn't chatting on the phone with friends. She put the kettle on and reminded Paul it would be an early start tomorrow. The driveway and road would need to be plowed. He nodded and said he would come to bed directly after his cuppa. She gave him a quick kiss on the cheek and left.

Paul spun a chair around and straddled it. "So Luv, what's the story with you and Keough? It seemed to me that you were a bit… hmm…brusque with him earlier. I also noticed Kurt's reaction to your necklace was a tad peculiar."

Annie didn't know what to say to Paul. Paul knew she was hiding something. She decided to trust him.

"Paul, of all the people I've met on this trip I believe you know me better than most. You saw me freak out on more than one occasion."

She made him promise to keep her secret between them. "I'm not ready for the rest to know why I'm so familiar with the Montana family, especially Rose. She's been so kind to me and I respect her too much to unload this on her – not yet."

Paul adjusted his chair and leaned forward. "Okay Annie, I'm listening." She told him she'd be back in a second. She came back with a photograph and handed it to him. He took it from her and studied it for a second or two.

"She's beautiful Annie. Quite the impressive cowgirl outfit I must say. Who is she?"

She paused for a second then answered him. "She's my mother Paul, *Sylvia "Sylvie" Harris.*" He commented that it was rare that she married someone named, *Harrison.* "Not much of a stretch to remember. Most people's last names usually change once they wed another person. You only needed to add an O and a N. Brilliant!"

Annie sat beside him and explained. "No Paul, Mom never married my father because she later told me that he was probably married and that's why he left without saying a word. Maybe she didn't want him to find us. So she changed her name to Harrison and we moved to California. I recently discovered who he is during this trip. All my life I've hated this man for him leaving Mom. I swore when she died that I would find him and let him know that he has a daughter. I wanted to hate him . . . but I can't. He turns out to be a pretty decent human being. I know if he'd known about me he would have supported me and Mom."

Paul rubbed his chin. "So tell me Annie, who is this dodgy prat who turns out not to be so dodgy after all?"

"You know him. In fact you know him very well. The dodgy prat you refer to is sitting in the living room. My father is Keough, Keough Teal Montana; Teal being my middle name."

It took Paul a few minutes to process what she had said. He stood up and walked over to the cabinets and retrieved a bottle of bourbon. "I believe I need a drink."

"While you're at it pour me one."

The two sat quietly for a moment to mull over Annie's shocking parental confession. Paul broke the silence. "Right, let me wrap my head around this. You are Keough's daughter, correct?"

She nodded. He continued, "So that makes Lash and Jameson and their sisters your half brothers and sisters." She nodded again. Paul let out a sigh and smiled. And that makes me your brother-in-law! That's bloody brilliant! And Rose would be your sister-in-law!" Paul took another long swig of his drink, empting his glass. "I think I'll have another drink, how about you Luv?"

"Yes, I'd love another Paul." She asked him to keep this conversation confidential until she figured out when to tell Keough, and Paul agreed. "That's pretty heavy news to spring on him seeing that Meryl and he are getting married."

"Paul, I don't think that's going to be a problem – they're already married. That's why they're here. They wanted to tell everyone their good news."

Paul laughed, "What . . . really? I must be the only person who didn't know this! What bloody great news. Be that as it may, I'll keep your secret under me hat, okay." Annie thanked Paul for not discussing our conversation. "You're more than welcome Annie. But I must ask, why me? Why are you telling me?"

"Because you could have called me a lunatic when I was babbling to myself at the gas station, but you didn't. You were worried. That worry translates into caring for me. I appreciated that more than you'll ever know." Annie hugged Paul and thanked him for being a sounding board.

"No need to thank me Annie. I'm happy you trusted me with your secret. I'll keep me gob shut until you're ready to tell Keough."

"Again, I appreciate it Paul." I started to walk away when he asked me to wait. "I understand your attitude toward Keough; however, I'm in a bit of a quandary regarding Kurt's reaction. He was clearly unnerved by your necklace. Might you know why?"

Annie shook her head. "No Paul, I haven't a clue. But I'll sleep on it." Paul finished the last of his drink and said goodnight. He left her in the kitchen to finish her drink.

Annie questioned whether she had made the right choice telling him about Keough. *I guess it's too late now – the deadbeat dad is out of the bag.* She poured another shot, downed it in a single gulp and went to bed. I thought *medicinal purpose Annie, medicinal.*

Chapter 18

The smell of bacon drifted into Raymond's bedroom. *Jameson is cooking? I must have overslept.* He put on his robe and walked into the kitchen. "Good morning Raymond, I thought you'd enjoy sleeping in today. Have you looked out the window?" Raymond pulled the shutters only to be greeted by a huge snow drift. "Holy mercy, we got dumped on!"

Jameson laughed, "Yeah we did; fourteen inches to be exact. That's the bad news. The good news is the weather reports say it's going up to forty-five degrees, so it should melt some of it. After breakfast I'll shovel a path so that we can get to the snowplows."

"I'm impressed Jameson. Who would have thought that you'd turn out to be such an outdoorsman? You're nothing like that caffeine-crazed brother of yours. And what I wouldn't give to hear his response to my insults."

"Yeah, me too Raymond, but I'm sure in some realm of the universe he's pissing someone else off until you rejoin him. Which I hope is a long ways away."

"It's funny you should say that Jameson." Raymond told him that he had a dream about Joe. "He was telling me to stay put. When I asked him what he meant, he said nothing. I don't plan on going anywhere, well at least not in this weather. Oh, that reminds me Raymond, Rose called. She said to stay put until the roads . . . whoa, maybe that's what Joe was telling you?"

Raymond chuckled. "No, that's too easy and obvious. That horse-shit-for-brains brother of yours is much too wily for THAT to be the answer to his message. I'll call Rose to let her know we're still coming for Thanksgiving. Even if we have to dogsled we're not going to miss out on Cecilia's cooking."

"Let's eat breakfast and get going. There's a lot of work to be done if we hope to get out of here anytime soon."

The two finished their breakfast and suited up to plow. *Thank goodness we bought extra fuel and new winter boots.* Jameson was already outside. The snow was deep well past his knees. He threw a large snowball at the window to get Raymond's attention. Raymond flipped him the bird. *I swear he's becoming more and more like Joe every day, but in a good way. He's not as annoying as Joe. I don't think anybody could ever be that annoying! There were times I could have kicked him right up the ass! Speaking of kicking, where did I put those new boots? Yes, now I remember. They're in the hall closet.* He carried the box to the bedroom. It took him a few minutes to undo the laces and put them on. *Whew, I'm already out of breath. I've got to lose some weight. I could blame Cecilia's cooking, but I know it's my late night snacking.* He walked over to the bedroom mirror *Raymond, you're sweating like a Saturday night whore in a police lineup. I hate getting old and fat! And, my shoulder is stiff again. I'd better rub it down tonight or I'll be in a world of hurt tomorrow. This is no time for me to start slowing down. Jameson will never let me hear the end of it. I'm constantly telling him that I can outwork him – even at my age. I'd better take a couple of ibuprofen.*

By late afternoon Raymond and Jameson had finished plowing their road. The main road was clear but the snow drifts beside the road were over six feet high. Thank goodness their area still had cell phone reception. He called Rose and left her a message. He said they were still planning to come over for Thanksgiving, so don't even think about taking their plates off the table. He said he would bring the two bottles of wine that Rose and Joe brought him back from Italy and she didn't have to call back unless she needed him to bring something else.

Jameson and Raymond decided to call it a day. They headed back to the cabin. Most of their road was already melted. Raymond asked Jameson what he'd like for dinner. He said the only thing he wanted was to take a hot shower and snooze for a few hours.

"I think I'll do the same, I'm aching a bit and suddenly, I'm feeling very tired."

Jameson suggested the two have something light to eat and make it an early evening. "You look beat Raymond."

His friend nodded. "I feel beat. But it's nothing a good night's rest won't cure. Thanks for your help today Jameson. I'll make sure to brag about your hard work to your mother and Keough at

Thanksgiving dinner." He chuckled, said thanks then headed off to his room to take his shower.

Sitting on the edge of his bed, Raymond rubbed his arm and shoulder. *It must be the cold or just old age stiffness. Either way I think I'll take a hot bath with Epson salt. It's an old remedy for old folks.* Raymond must have soaked for thirty minutes. The hot water felt good on his tired muscles. He had left his robe by the heater so it would be nice and toasty when he got out of the tub. *Hmm, that feels much better.*

Jameson must have started dinner while he was soaking. His friend knocked on the bedroom door.

"Raymond, I heated up last night's stew. No need to cook when we have leftovers."

"Great idea. I hated wasting food."

What a transformation for Jameson. He told me he never cooked when he lived in Manhattan as there were too many amazing restaurants and gourmet chefs. "Plus, I didn't know how to cook. Neither did the spoiled rich airheads I used to date," he would add. "One actually asked me where milk came from. She said, Do they ship it frozen or in liquid containers? I shit you not Raymond. That's when I knew I had to date a more intelligent class of women."

Raymond had laughed at him for having to suffer that kind of pain. "Jameson, you've come a long way since the day I found you sleeping on the side of the road with empty mini bottles of booze thrown about the seat. I'm pleased to call you a good friend. If you noticed I don't have many friends. Since Joe died I can honestly say you are the only person I can tolerate. That's why I live so far from the city. I love my quiet little piece of Montana paradise."

He agreed. "I never thought I'd enjoy quiet – until now. Thank you Raymond for setting me on the right path. If it weren't for you I think I'd be in some center for the drunken over privileged and still be a drunk."

Raymond nodded, "Jameson I believe it's your Montana blood that keeps you strong. Joe was strong, Charlotte is just as strong. And Rose, well let's just say she's the strongest woman I've ever met. Anybody who can marry Joe and put up with me, Keough and Kurt surely deserves a Medal of Honor."

The two finished their dinner while sitting by the fireplace. Full stomachs and the warmth of the fire caused them both to drift off.

Raymond awoke an hour later and poked Jameson to tell him he was going to bed. Jameson mumbled something and headed off to his room as well. Raymond set his alarm for 6:00 AM. *I promised Rose I'd bring dessert for Thanksgiving. I'll make it tomorrow because it's always better the day after.* Uttering a quick Blackfoot prayer, Raymond thanked his spirit ancestors for watching over him and his friend Jameson and fell asleep.

Raymond had already been up for an hour when Jameson woke up.

"How come you didn't wake me up?" Jameson asked.

"You needed the rest just as much as I did yesterday. I'm still exhausted so I can only imagine how you must be feeling. You did a lot of the shoveling before we drove the plows."

Jameson thanked him for his concern, but reminded Raymond that it's part of his recovery to stay on a schedule.

"I enjoy sitting on the porch in the morning. I love closing my eyes and listening to my surroundings – like you taught me. It's soothing. Something else I never did in Manhattan. Mainly, because it was NEVER quiet. Did you know I'd never seen, let alone heard a hummingbird until Rose pointed out one to me?"

Until that moment, Raymond never realized how much Jameson had changed until now. Montana was good for him. *I only wish Joe was here to see his transformation.* Jameson excused himself saying he would start packing the truck for their trip the next day.

"I know you're going to think I'm crazy but this will be the first family Thanksgiving that I'm excited to attend. I'm beginning to feel like one of the family – a true Montana."

Raymond walked over to him and patted him on his shoulder. "You've always been a Montana Jameson. Never forgot that."

They headed back to the kitchen. "I'd better get Rose's dessert prepared or she'll rip what little hair I have left out of my scalp."

Jameson chuckled. "Hey, I thought no more scalping references!"

Raymond smiled, "You're right Jameson. Maybe I should trim it before we go so she'll have nothing to pull out."

Jameson was about to walk away when he stopped. "Oh, I almost forgot. I'd like to bring Mother to one of your drum circles this spring. I know she and Keough are close but I know for a fact she misses my dad – my adopted dad. Maybe he'll comfort her during one of the ceremonies?"

"Yes, that would be fine with me. I like Meryl. She's is genuinely a wonderful lady. Her only flaw is that she fell in love with that prairie flea Keough."

Both men shared a belly laugh at Keough's expense, and then went about their chores. Raymond was up to his elbows in flour when the phone rang. "Hello, Winterbee Cabins and Lodges, Raymond speaking."

"Oh, aren't we formal. Hey Raymond its Rose. I'm using my cell phone because we're having problems with the landline; must be the snow."

"Hello Rose. I didn't recognize the number. It's so good to hear your voice. How are you folks holding up out there? Is it still snowing?"

"No it stopped and everything is starting to melt. That's why I'm calling to find out if you and Jameson are okay and still coming for Thanksgiving?"

"Absolutely. And at this moment I making the dessert you ordered from Winterbee's Home Bakery."

"Great and thanks Raymond. You know how much Joe and . . . I mean how much Paul and I love your desserts."

There was a moment of silence then she apologized for her slip of the tongue.

"It's okay Rose. I totally understand. Joe was such an important part of both our lives it's to be expected."

She went on to tell me about the altercation she had with Paul feeling overwhelmed by Joe's memory.

"Raymond, why can't we let Joe go? It's not like Paul doesn't understand how much Joe meant to all of us. We love Paul, I love Paul. So why is this still happening? And it seems to happen more around you."

"Rose, Joe was larger than life. His death will never diminish that. Paul loves you very much. He never tries to compare himself to Joe. He loves you and he loves Joe just as I still do. Joe was much more like my brother, than a friend. He will always be in my heart and that's where he will stay; out of respect for you and Paul. Does this make sense to you?"

"Yes, it does Raymond. How'd you get to be so wise, and don't give me any of that Blackfoot bullshit."

"I'm old Rose and I've learned a thing or two along the way. I'm willing to pass it along to you whenever you ask. I love you Rose."

"Thanks Raymond and I'll see you and Jameson Thursday. Love you too."

Raymond went back to the kitchen. *Lord, why am I still achy? I think I'll brew some herbal tea. That might help. I don't want to feel like this on Thanksgiving. I plan on eating my weight in Cecilia's cooking.*

By midafternoon the roads were just about clear. Jameson gave the shaded spots of the road one more plow. The main roads were pretty much dry. Those Montana Department of Transportation or as residents call them *MDOT* fellows do a damn good job keeping the roads safe. By that evening we had everything loaded into the truck. Although the Montana Ranch was a little over 45-miles away, Raymond wanted to get an early start in case the weather took another turn for the worse. Late autumn or early winter in Montana can be extremely unpredictable. So many inexperienced travelers are shocked by how quickly these mountain roads can become treacherous. Raymond remembered to grab a couple of blankets, flashlights and water in case they got stuck or broke down.

Thanksgiving Eve morning came quickly. It was still dark outside. Raymond held the flashlight for Jameson while he locked all of the cabins and they departed at 6 AM. The two had planned for additional travel time in case they encountered detours or slick roads. Jameson said he'd be happy to drive.

"Don't think I haven't noticed that your shoulder and arm are still aching. It'll do you good to take it easy. So sit back and enjoy being chauffeured."

"Hah, isn't this a twist; you chauffeuring me. I bet your New York friends would find this amusing, seeing that it's typically YOU being driven around."

He smiled. "Yep, things have sure changed Raymond. And for the better, wouldn't you agree?"

"Yes, you're not the obnoxious asshole I used to know. Now you're just obnoxious . . . but in a good way."

Jameson laughed out loud. "Okay coming from you Raymond I'll take that as a sincere compliment."

Raymond buckled himself in and pointed at the road. "Alright Jameson or should I call you, Jeeves; we're off to the Montana Ranch – posthaste."

The two were halfway to the ranch when Jameson decided they needed a rest break. Raymond believed the break was more for him than Jameson. Occasionally, Raymond noticed his friend side-glancing at him. Finally, he asked Jameson if HE was okay.

"Yes, I'm fine Raymond. It's just that you look like you need a leg stretch. And, I need to use the restroom. I shouldn't have had that third cup of coffee. My bladder is about to burst and we need more window washer fluid. The road salt and melt is making the windows blurry. I'll fuel up at Jimmy's and we can take a quick break."

Raymond agreed. "That reminds me; perhaps my herb order had arrived. There's nothing like fresh Tarragon in chicken pot pie."

The two spotted Jimmy's place in the distance. About a half mile from his parking lot, Jameson noticed a car with its hood up on the side of the road. Two women were leaning against the car door, one with her thumb out. Jameson slowed down, but didn't acknowledge them.

"Raymond, normally I would give them a lift, but I've really got to pee!"

Raymond glared at him. "At least pull up beside them so I can tell them we'll be back to help." Jameson huffed but honored his request.

Raymond tipped his hat. "Morning ladies, it seems you need help. We'll be back in a minute to assist you, okay?" One of the women thanked him, and asked if they could bring back two bottles of water for them because her friend needed to take her meds."

Raymond looked over at Jameson. "This lady needs medical attention." Raymond clicked the car lock open and told them to get in and they would drive them to Jimmy's place. "It's only a short ways down the road – hop in." Both women climbed in the back seat of the truck and huddled together. Jameson noticed how cold they were and turned the heater up.

Raymond turned around and asked, "So what brings you two ladies to Montana at this time of the year?"

They explained they had come from an event in Billings and got lost; each one blaming the other for the poor directions.

Raymond smiled. "Then it's a lucky thing we came along when we did. There's not much traffic along this part of the highway, especially at this time of the year. The roads can get pretty dicey."

One of them mumbled something about the other one and they started arguing. "Just be glad you are safe, enjoy the warmth of the car. We're almost there."

Jameson pulled the truck up to the store door so they could go directly inside. There was so much slush he didn't want them to get their shoes wet. Jameson told Raymond to go inside while he parked the truck. "Looks like you could use some water too. You look a bit pale." Raymond chucked at the comment thinking *a white man telling me I look pale – that's a first.* A few minutes later Jameson came rushing into the store heading directly to the restroom and so did the two ladies. Raymond wondered how long have they been stranded? All three came out looking relieved. Jimmy came over with two bottles of water and a cup of coffee for Raymond and Jameson.

"I'm surprised to see anyone out this early in this weather. Where are y'all headed?" He asked. Jameson said that they we're headed to the ranch for Thanksgiving. Jimmy smiled. "Now that's the place to be for the holidays. Tell everyone I said Happy Thanksgiving okay." He then turned to the ladies and asked them the same question.

"We might be spending the holiday in the car if we can't get it fixed," the shorter of the two women replied.

Jimmy offered to have his mechanic tow it to his store's parking lot and he'll take a look. "If he can't repair it today, where are you two staying?"

They looked at each other and shook their heads. "At the moment we're staying here unless you know of a hotel close by."

"I'd be happy to ask the mechanic to drop them off at the hotel," Jimmy offered. "It's not too far from here."

Both women thanked him for his generosity. Jameson asked them if they were going to be okay and if so he and Raymond were going to be on their way.

"Yes, we're fine as long as there's coffee and a restroom." We were about to leave Jimmy's when Raymond turned back and extended his hand. "I can't believe I'm so rude today. My name is Raymond and that young fellow making his way through the ankle deep slush to our truck is my friend Jameson – and you are?"

The shorter woman said her name was Mona and the taller was Chinchilla. "Well it's nice to meet you both. Chinchilla, what an unusual and beautiful name? Are you Native American?"

She shook her head. "No, the short story is, when I was born my hair was so soft my father said it felt just like his pet chinchillas. Sadly, the name stuck."

Her story made Raymond chuckle. "Okay, Chinchilla and Mona, perhaps we'll meet again." He started out the door when he thought *if they don't have a place to go for Thanksgiving maybe I'll ask Rose if they can join us.* "Well ladies I know you'll enjoy the hotel in downtown Malta. Nice place with great staff. If you need help again please ask Jimmy to give us a call and we'll be happy to oblige. Have a wonderful day."

As we drove away the tow truck pulled into Jimmy's parking lot. I thought *they'll be okay. Now if only my shoulder would stop aching. I'd be okay too.*

It was about nine o'clock in the morning when Raymond and Jameson reached the ranch entrance. The Good Samaritan delay and the slick roads lengthened their travel time. Jameson asked Raymond if he was feeling better. Raymond lied and said he did.. As much as he appreciated Jameson's concern, he didn't need him hovering over him the entire holiday.

"I'll take a couple of aspirin when I get to Rose's," then he changed the subject. "Although winters are harsh in Montana I never get tired of how beautiful the snow looks on the mountains. It's like a white blanket tucking the valleys and meadows in for the long winter nights. To be honest though, I love looking at it from the comfort of a nice warm house or truck."

Jameson laughed and agreed. The house was quickly coming into view. Jameson exclaimed how excited he was to see his Mother and Keough. "I hope they're happy with the way my new life is going. It's a far cry from the drunken rich guy I was in Manhattan, huh?"

"Yep, you were a piece of work, that's for sure. But you've turned out to be a fine man Jameson. I dare say as fine as you're brother."

He was surprised by Raymond's kind words and so was Raymond. He had never compared anyone to Joe. Joe had been his moral support when he felt defeated.

"Wow Raymond I'm honored. That must have been difficult for you to admit."

Raymond rolled his eyes. "It was . . . so, don't get used to it." He smiled and turned his attention back to the road. A few seconds later Raymond heard Jameson whisper, *I love you too Raymond.*

The two men finally arrived at the house. Raymond saw Kurt standing outside of the barn and waved. Jameson drove up to the barn and parked.

"Well, hello strangers welcome back; awful good to see you both again. It's been too dang quiet around here without ya'. The front door is open, so go on in and get warmed up. Raymond you look at though you could use something medicinal."

He shook his head and said, "No thank you. However, I would like a cup of hot tea. I'm sure Paul has some of his special brew stashed somewhere in the cupboard."

Kurt laughed. "I'm sure he does Raymond." Jameson went in first, hollering if anyone knew of a good place to stay for the holidays. His commotion brought the household running into the living room.

"OH MY GOODNESS is that my son I hear!" Meryl raced down the hall to welcome him. "It's so good to see you sweetheart."

She stood back and looked at him. "I swear you look like an entirely different person! Look at that rosy glow. Have you been working outside? Are you getting enough to eat?"

He hugged his mother. "Yes, to all-of-the-above. And you Mother have a new healthy glow as well. You tend to glow like that when you're happy. So, what's or should I say who has you glowing?"

As if on cue Keough walked into the living room. Meryl lovingly locked eyes with him as he gave her a morning kiss. "Okay, there's my answer. "Morning Keough, it's good to see you. You guys look ten years younger. What have you been doing . . . or should I ask? Never mind, I don't want to know."

Keough paused for a moment and glanced over at Meryl. "Hmm, your mother's got me on some new-fangled Pagan or Paleo diet. But she thinks it's helping my cholesterol so I do what she tells me."

Jameson chuckled. "Sure, it's the new diet. If that's your story …"

Keough laughed and gave Jameson a fatherly hug and also told him how well he was looking. Keough whispered, or it could be that we got hitched." Keough motioned for Meryl to hold out her hand.

"Wow, congratulations! I'm really happy for guys."

Everyone came running into the living room to welcome the two men. It was good to be with the extended family. The only person missing was Joe. *I know you're here in spirit my friend. I can feel it.*

Rose was still in her pajamas and so was Charlotte. They ran over to say hello to Raymond and Jameson. She mentioned that Paul was in the kitchen making his morning cup of tea. Raymond excused himself and walked in to greet him.

"Where can an old guy get a decent cup of tea around here?" Paul swung around in surprise. "OY RAYMOND, hello mate, how're ya' doing! I've missed having our quiet afternoon rabbit over a nice cup of tea."

"Thanks Paul, I've missed you too and is there anyone who can translate what you've just said." Both had a hearty laugh over the language barrier.

Rose and Charlotte came into the kitchen; both giving Raymond another huge hug. Raymond scooped Charlotte up in one arm and hugged Rose with the other. "How are my two favorite Montana girls? My goodness you're getting so big Nadie. I may have start working out if I'm going to continue lifting you up."

Charlotte giggled. "Then I'll stay little forever Raymond." He gave her another hug then put her down. *My arm is still aching.*

"Hey, what about me, do I get a big Raymond bear hug too?" Rose demanded. He wrapped his arms around her.

"Rose, I believe you get more beautiful every time I see you. It does an old man's heart good to have someone like you in his life." Rose gave him a quick kiss on the cheek then headed back into the living room to chat more with Jameson. Raymond said to Paul how lucky he was to have such wonderful women under one roof. Paul agreed telling him that most of the time they're fine until one of them wants the television remote then a declaration of war ensues.

The kettle started to boil. Paul took out two cups and heated them before making tea. "That's the secret to a nice cup of tea Raymond – heated cups." Raymond asked if he had any herbal tea.

"Yes, I think Rose has some Chamomile tea floating about." He found the bag of loose tea in the cabinet.

"Thank you Paul. This will do fine. But I have to tell ya', I've been feeling a bit tired lately. I'm sure it's just all the winter preparation. You know I'm not getting any younger."

Paul nodded, "Who is Raymond? We're all starting to slow down."

Raymond took a sip from my cup. "This tea is really helping – thank you."

Paul motioned for Raymond to sit down. "I have to ask, should I be worried? Is everything okay?"

"Yes Paul, I'm okay. I'm just tired. For some reason this cold weather is making my bones ache. Maybe I should retire to Florida, hah!"

"Not a chance my friend, the state of Montana needs you and so do we."

Raymond laughed. "Oh, so now I'm a state treasure, huh. Perhaps I should proclaim myself one of Montana's Natural Wonders."

The house phone rang. Before Paul could pick it up, Rose had already answered it. Her scream stopped our conversation mid-sentence. She ran into the kitchen and announced that Jannine and Morgan made it to Montana. "Their flight finally arrived and they're renting a car; so, we don't have to pick them up from the airport. I can't wait to see them. It's been way too long. She says they have another surprise for us? I wonder what it could be. We already know they're married and she's pregnant. Knowing Jannine she got a tacky tattoo or probably shaved part of her head and dyed the other part turquoise, but who cares, I really miss that girl."

Raymond agreed with her. Jannine always kept us on our toes. "She's a wild child that's for sure isn't she Rose."

Rose nodded, "That she is Raymond."

All of the excitement was starting to wear on Raymond and he asked Rose if she wouldn't mind him taking a quick nap before dinner. "Jameson and I hit the road pretty early and I'm feeling a bit worn out."

"Of course Raymond you never have to ask. You know where the guest rooms are; pick one and nap as long as you like. Leave your shoes outside of the door so I know where you're napping. This house is so large I could easily forget which room you're in. Or, press kitchen on the intercom when you wake up. Either way, I'll come check on you in about an hour and let you know when everything's ready."

"Thank you Rose. You are my angel of mercy."

Paul walked me to the bedroom. "Raymond, if you need anything, I mean ANYTHING, let me know, okay."

"You are a good man Paul Saxton and thank you for your concern. Now, if you don't mind I think I'll commence to sawing logs."

"Okay Raymond rest up my friend." The last thing Raymond remembered was Paul closing the bedroom door behind him.

Chapter 19

The pilot instructed the passengers to fasten their seatbelts. The flight from New York to Billings' was fine, but the small puddle-jumper to the regional airport was like being bounced around on a carnival ride. Poor Jannine had her eyes closed the entire time. When the plane finally landed she said she would have kissed the ground if she knew she'd be able to stand up again.

"I swear Morgan if you ever mention anything about my New York driving again I'm going to punch you in the throat."

Morgan instinctively knew to keep my mouth shut. If they had rented a car and drove from Billings to Malta it would have taken longer, but the ride would have been much more comfortable. Morgan knew anything he said would only add to his already impending demise.

"And, we still need to rent a car!" She screeched. I thought *I'd better rent a luxury vehicle. It may help to smooth things over.*

The small airport was roughly 30-miles from the ranch. There were large snow banks on both sides of the road. The road itself was wet, but drivable.

"We should be at the ranch by noon Jannine. Will you be okay until then?"

She nodded. "Just get me to a restroom quickly because I've got to pee and puke." The two dashed into the car rental, her going towards the women's restroom and me to the counter. The woman behind the counter smiled as if she knew exactly what was happening. She welcomed us and then said she totally understood.

"I was like that with my third child. She sat on my bladder for five months and wouldn't move."

"I'm sorry." She took hold of my hand and said, "Honey, right now it may seem like a crazy, whirlwind time but once that precious baby is in your arms you won't remember anything except that sweet little face looking back at you."

Her eyes were tearing as though she was reliving her experience. Morgan asked her how old her third child was, because it seemed as though she's just given birth. "Oh, she's 15-years-old, but a mother NEVER forgets." I thought *I hope Jannine doesn't act like this when our kids in high school! He or she would murder us in our sleep!*

By the time Jannine came out of the restroom, Morgan had finished the paperwork and had the keys. There was only one problem. All they had left was a compact car – a Prius. *Well Morgan, beggars can't be choosers. It was new and at least the heating system and sound system worked.*

Jannine didn't look happy. "So, is this Montana's version of a luxury car? Please don't attempt to answer that, it'll just piss me off more than I already am. Not at you Morgan, you've been wonderful the entire trip. It's just I'm so miserable everything is pissing me off. I miss Rose and I know you're going to think this is sappy, but I really miss Raymond. He's such a father figure to all of us. I don't know what I would do if he wasn't around." I glanced over at her and thought *where's this coming from, Raymond's as healthy as a horse – healthier.*

The ride to the ranch was quiet mainly because Jannine slept the whole way. As much as Morgan loved her it gave him a much needed break from her BAPS, Bitching-About-Pregnancy-Stuff. They had just passed the ranch entrance when she woke up. "Morgan, how long have I been sleeping?" She yawned.

"Judging from the puddle of drool on the seatbelt, I'd say about an hour. We're on the ranch road and should be at the house in about 15- minutes. I was going to surprise you but you woke up. Anyway . . . SURPRISE."

"I'm so excited to see everyone. I can't stop squirming in my seat. It's because I have to pee again, but most of all I'm just so happy to be home."

"I've always felt like this was our home and now it will be. Well not this home but once Rose hears we're leaving New York and moving to Montana she'll be so happy."

"Oh Morgan, I'm crying. I never cry because I'm happy. I only cry when I can't find Pradas in my size. Damn these pregnancy mood swings!"

Morgan leaned over and gave her a quick kiss on the cheek. "That's okay sweetie, I couldn't love you any more than I already do." That was his 'down pat' answer to everything she'd say while she was having one of her emotional hormonal breakdown.

Morgan turned into the driveway. "Another minute and we'll be at the front door Jannine. Do you need me to help you put your shoes back on?"

"Nope, I've been putting them on for the last three minutes – I'm good."

Morgan noticed there were more cars parked outside than I expected. That was a good sign. Everyone was able to make it to Casa Montana for the holidays. He was very happy to see Raymond's truck. *I told Jannine he was okay. Maybe now she'll stop worrying about him. I only wish Dad were here.*

Lou ran up the driveway and barked out his welcome Before Morgan could knock, Charlotte flung open the door and screamed. "Morgan! Jannine! I've missed you guys! Mama they're here!"

Rose came running from the kitchen with Paul beside her. I gave her a huge hug and Paul our usual manly half hug. "Mom, you look just as beautiful as the last time I saw you. It's so good to be home."

The two barely made their way into the house when the entire living room came to greet them. It took ten minutes to hug and kiss everybody before they were able to take their coats off.

Jannine dashed directly to the bathroom. Afterwards she said that now she could concentrate and occupied the family with her tales of pregnancy. Rose and Morgan made their way toward the kitchen. Morgan noticed there was a new face he didn't recognize, sitting at the kitchen table drinking coffee. She was about to stand up when Morgan asked, "So Mom, who is this lovely lady?"

"Morgan this is Annabella Harrison, Annie this is my son, Morgan." She extended her hand. "It's so nice to meet you Morgan. Your family is unbelievably hospitable. And please call me Annie."

"Hello, Annie and welcome to the Montana ranch where there's always room for one or in our case dozens more visitors. The more the merrier should be our motto."

Annie laughed and said how honored she was that Keough and Meryl asked her to stay for the holidays.

Rose said it was a long story. "They always are Mom but they're never dull. Anyway, I'm sure Annie, Jannine and I will have the opportunity to hear about it during our stay. By the way, where is my bride and future mother of my child?"

Rose pointed to the crowd of people surrounding her on the couch. "I think she's buried somewhere in the midst of all of them. She seems happy so let's just leave her alone for now."

"I saw Raymond's truck outside. Where is he?"

Rose explained that he wasn't feeling well and is in one of the guestrooms taking a nap. "I checked on him a few minutes before you arrived and he's okay – just a bit achy from the snowstorm."

Morgan said that Jannine had been worried about him. "I'll tell her he's here and okay."

Paul asked if he wanted a cup of tea, seeing that he was going to put the kettle on, he might as well put enough water on for two.

"Yes, thank you Paul and how has my favorite truck driver been. Whenever I see a big rig making its way through Manhattan traffic I always think of you. So, how's driving these days."

"To be honest Morgan, I miss the wife and kid so much, it breaks my heart whenever I leave to go back on the road. It's not like I have to work. I've got enough money of my own to last me a lifetime. So for now I'm semi-retired."

"I'm happy for you Paul. You, Keough and Kurt have done well keeping this ranch running. Dad would be over-the-moon happy. I wish he was around to see his first grandchild."

Paul walked over and put his arm around my shoulder. "He's always around. You know how proud he is of you." Morgan smiled as Paul talked about him in the present tense. "This ranch is his ranch. What you must understand is that he only allows us to live on it. Quite decent of him I must say. "

Rose was able to tear Jannine away for her adoring crowd. They came into the kitchen arm-in-arm chatting and laughing. Before Rose could introduce Jannine to Annie, Jannine walked over and introduced herself. "Hi, I'm Jannine. Who are you?"

Morgan turned to Annie and said how modest and shy his wife was and that he hoped at some point in her life she breaks out of her shell.

Paul almost spit out his tea. "She is rather forward, isn't she?" Morgan whispered to Paul "She has the tact of a bulldozer. " Paul had to turn his back to keep her from seeing him laugh.

Annie said, "From what Rose has told me about you I feel as though I know you already."

Jannine smirked. "Then I guess you know that I'm her biggest pain in her well-toned derrière."

"No, she only told me of your magnificent taste in fashion, hence me wearing my favorite pair of Tory Burch flats in your honor."

Jannine's eyes widened. "Oh My God, I love Tory's line of shoes almost as much as Prada. I like you and your taste in shoe designers – we are officially best friends. Besides Rose, I've have no best friends. Can you imagine?"

Annie didn't know whether to laugh or nod so she quickly changed the subject. "Tell me Jannine how did you and Morgan meet? Rose has already told me her love story. I'd love to hear yours."

Annie turned and winked at Morgan, Rose and Paul. It was her subtle cue for us to make our escape from Jannine's passionate fashion conversation.

Paul and Morgan decided to have tea outside. The cold air felt good after being stuck on a plane and in a car all day. The sun had melted most the snow from the kitchen deck. Paul asked how things were going in New York and if they would buy a house once the baby arrived?"

"It's funny you should mention our buying a house Paul. Jannine and I have decided to sell the condo and move somewhere else. We don't want to raise our kid in New York City. Heck, if it wasn't for Jannine's career I'd be out of that city in a Montana heartbeat. In fact she decided quit her job."

Paul raised his eyebrows. "Oh, now that's interesting. Rose hasn't mentioned anything to me about her leaving her position?"

"That's because she quit two days ago. Jannine misses Rose more than she lets on. Rose was not only her boss but her mentor, sister figure and one of the only friends she's ever had. She resigned because she wanted to spend more time in Montana. If it's okay she's going to ask Mom if we could stay here for a little while because we have an announcement to make."

Paul hesitated to ask but he said, "Go on then. You might as well tell me. It seems I've become the King of Secret Keeping at the Montana Ranch."

Morgan laughed at Paul and how proud he was of his new regal title. "Jannine and I have decided to move back to Montana. We want to start looking for a house after the holidays. I didn't want to mention anything to Mom until I ran our plans by you. After all, you two are married now and we would never want to impose."

Paul asked Morgan to sit down. I cleared the snow off one of the chairs and sat. "Morgan, I'm only going to say this once so listen carefully. You are family."

Confused, he asked, ". . . *and*"

"There's no *and* Morgan. You and Jannine are family, the Montanas are a family. Family takes care of family. It's sort of a forever thing, if you catch my drift." He smiled and continued drinking his tea. Morgan was learning quickly that Paul was a man of few words, but his carefully chosen words spoke volumes. The cold made Morgan shiver so they decided to take their conversation back inside. Paul instinctively put the kettle back on for another cup of tea.

Morgan laughed as he noticed that Paul's addiction to tea was as bad as Dad's addiction to coffee. "Paul how many boxes of tea would you say you consume in a year?"

He rubbed his chin. "Frankly, I couldn't tell you however, I've noticed quite a few tea growers have named their sons Paul."

Chapter 20

Rose looked at the time and realized she'd forgotten to make a hair appointment. She wanted it to look good for the holidays. *Since I'm getting my hair done perhaps I should just have him come to the house and do all of us. I'm sure Jannine and Annie would love to be pampered. Maybe Meryl might like a new do.*

There was so much noise in the living room, Rose took her cell phone into the bedroom to make the call. The phone only rang once.

"Hello, Lots o' Locks Salon, this is Ginger. What can I do to tame your do?"

"Hello Ginger it's Rose. How've you been you red-headed-dreadlocked Diva?"

"Well, Hello Miss Rosalita. It's been at least 4-months since I've seen those lovely locks of yours. Hmm, I thought you didn't love me anymore. How are you dear?"

"I'm doing well Ginger."

LeRoy Cradstaff is the owner and head stylist for Lots o' Locks Salon. His twenty-inch red dreadlocks branded him with the nickname of Ginger. He was the best stylist in Billings and he knew it. Styling awards covered the walls of his work area, as well as photographs of him posing with famous people. Rose was tired of driving to Billings just to get her hair styled, so she offered to relocate him closer to where she lived. She even offered to pay for his travel expenses and new licenses, if he could be her personal stylist. He accepted and now lives closer to Malta. Being a top hair stylist was not his main vocation. After serving 4-years in the military, LeRoy started out his civilian life as a contractor – plumbing and heating being his specialty. When the company he worked for went bankrupt he went to Cosmetology School and the rest is Glam History. He loves being hit on by both sexes. He'd boast, "Sorry, I'm spoken for. My heart and soul belong to Rose Montana-Saxton."

Ginger's girlfriend still laughs at his devotion to Rose admitting, "He'll drop-stop-and-roll for you Rose, and I have to plead with him to fix our drippy bathroom faucets!"

"Ginger, I was wondering if you could come out to the house and make a few women beautiful for the holidays"

"How many is a few Rosie and is Cecilia cooking holiday dinner? If she's not that is a deal breaker, my sweet, and I'll order Chinese."

"Of course she's cooking and you'll never guess who else is coming to dinner?"

"Hm, let me think, Sydney Poitier, The Three Bears. Rose you know I dislike guessing games."

"Well, she's already here and she's your favorite New York Diva . . . it's Jannine!"

"Don't tease me Rosebud. Oh my God, is Jannine really in Montana! I love that child. She's almost as crazy as I am."

"I've just booked you for the entire day. I will have to call two other clients and tell them I have to cancel them. They'll probably be snotty about the last minute cancellation but you come first my dear."

"I will pay you for their cancelled appointments, so no worries."
"I'll see you tomorrow?"

"Yes, I'll be there tomorrow bright and early and there will be Caramel Macchiato coffee waiting for me, correct?"

"Yep it'll be ready and waiting, my Ginger-headed-salon-wizard. Thanks much."

"You're so welcome Miss Rose, Ciao bella."

Rose walked back into the living room and everyone had their hands on Jannine's belly. It was like she was Buddha and they were rubbing her for good luck. She told Rose to come over and feel her future niece or nephew.

"Wow, they are kicking up a storm Jannine! I remember when Charlotte . . . " Jannine cut me off. "Rose this is my turn to be the center of attention. Please let me have my moment."

Rose agreed. This was her turn to be adored. Rose noticed Raymond was missing. *I'd better go in and check on him.* I started to walk towards the guest rooms when she noticed Paul coming out of his room. "Is he okay Paul? He's been asleep for a while."

"Yes, he says he's feeling better but would like to sleep a little longer. I told him we'd bring dinner to him if he wasn't up to eating with us tonight."

"That's a good idea. Thanks hon'." "And, thank you for being so sweet and kind. I'm sure he appreciates being looked after. Paul suggested we head to the dining room.

"I do believe Cecilia is ringing the dinner bell. I laughed because Cecilia's idea of a dinner bell was announcing that the food was on the table and don't let her hard work get cold.

The group made our way to the dining room. Cecilia had outdone herself. The table was set with the dishes and crystal stemware Lash had purchased from Italy.

Cecilia said, "Just because tomorrow is Thanksgiving doesn't mean we have to eat off of paper plates Thanksgiving Eve. We are civilized here in Montana."

They all applauded her thoughtfulness and elegances. She asked if Raymond would be joining us as she had set a place for him. Paul said he'd just checked on him and he was still resting. "I don't want to wake him up again. I think he just needs to rest more than anything." She said she'd keep a plate warm for him just in case.

Once everyone was seated, Keough offered to lead them in a special blessing. He glanced over at Annie and noticed she didn't look very happy. In fact she looked like she was annoyed – mostly at Keough. Rose couldn't figure out why. He'd been nothing but cordial to her since they arrived at the ranch. A knock at the door interrupted him. It was Kurt. He apologized for his lateness stating that Daisy decided to go for a walk outside the barn and didn't want to come back. "I had to lure her back inside with a handful of sweet feed." Charlotte giggled at his statement and explained. "Eww, Uncle Kurt you know sweet feed makes Daisy fart. We'll all be sorry tomorrow!" The table laughed at Charlotte's warning.

Kurt hung up his hat and coat, and sat down in the chair beside Annie. "Thank you for saving me a place darlin'. There's nothin' like sittin' next to a beautiful lady for dinner." Annie smiled. "Why thank you Kurt, what a sweet thing to say."

She looked over at Keough who was sitting next to Meryl. "It amazes me how you all are able to remember who's who. I've never seen twins that look so much alike – it's astonishing."

Keough laughed, and then explained, "Annie, it's easy to tell us apart. I'm the handsome and honest one. He's the sidewinder. Isn't that right Rose?" Both men laughed.

Rose shook her head. "Hey, don't pull me into your bucket of lies. Annie, you can't believe a word these two saddlebums say. Isn't that right Meryl?"

"Rose, I think both men are just fishing for compliments and I shall not be dragged into this pissing match. Plus, I'm hungry. Let them piss about while I steal the rolls off of their plates."

She grabbed Keough's roll and bit into it as if it was a piece of tobacco. "Yeehaw Cecilia, they are delicious. Are there anymore in the kitchen?" Rose almost fell from her chair. Meryl was always so prim and proper. It was good to see this lighter side of her.

Jameson was seated on the other side of Meryl. "Mother, you've become a real country hick since you married this man – I like it!" He leaned over and gave her a kiss on the cheek. "Now, if you'll excuse me I think I'm going to call it an early night and go to bed.

"Are you feeling okay, Jameson?"

"I'm fine, Mother, but for some reason I'm exhausted." He said goodnight to everyone and excused himself from the room. "I'll check on Raymond before I turn in. A few minutes later Jameson came back into the dining room. "Raymond's okay, but he said not to hold dinner for him. He said rest is what he needs and that he'd have a big breakfast tomorrow."

Cecilia agreed. She said she'd save both he and Raymond a plate in case they got hungry later. "Thanks Cecilia I'm sure Raymond will appreciate it, as do I – goodnight all." We said goodnight, and thanked him for looking after Raymond." "You're welcome, goodnight."

After dinner Paul helped Cecilia clear the table. The rest of the group headed to the family room. Jannine and Morgan said they were going to make it an early evening too, and headed off to bed. Charlotte had fallen asleep on the couch. Rose grabbed a quilt, laid it over her and left her to sleep. *She's getting so heavy I can't lift her anymore.* As tired as she was, she needed a little something to help her sleep. Rose asked if anyone else would like a shot of something stronger than coffee. Keough understandably declined. Meryl, Kurt, Annie joined their hostess for a nightcap. Rose brought in the bottle of bourbon and a handful of glasses. They toasted to everyone's happiness and health. Paul came in with a glass and toasted with them. Keough added to the toast, raising his glass of cranberry juice, "Here's to my older and uglier brother Kurt. I wouldn't know what to do without you. You keep me honest brother." Kurt smiled, but looked a bit anxious. Keough continued, "My lovely wife Meryl, my wonderful daughter-in-law, Rose, who brought that sleepy little girl on the couch into our lives. And, last but not least, my incredible children Jameson, Lash and my two daughters Katherine and Trish.

Annie felt as though she was about to explode. Keough noticed it as well. "Annie, are you okay darlin'? You look upset? Have I upset you? I know I'm a longwinded old coot, however, if I've said or done somethin' to upset you – I'm sorry darlin'."

Annie stood up and walked out of the room. Rose started to go after her when Paul stopped me. "Let's leave her alone for moment Poppet." "

Why? What is going on Paul? Rose asked. He said he'd explain later if it was okay with Annie. "It's her place to say what's going on and we'll have to respect that."

A few minutes later she came storming back into the family room with something in her hands. She tossed a photo and her necklace at Keough. Her behavior was unsettling. The only person who wasn't upset was Paul. He walked over to Annie and stood beside her.

"Annie, I think it's time you tell him. He needs to know." Meryl looked at Annie and asked what was going on. "Annie, please tell me what's happening? You're frightening me."

"Meryl, I don't mean to frighten you. You have been nothing but wonderful to me. It has nothing to do with you. It's your husband, Keough Teal. We never knew his last name. We thought it was Teal."

Keough looked at Meryl then at Annie and stared at the photo. "Annie, she's beautiful, very beautiful. You keep sayin' we? Who is she?"

His question enraged her. "What the hell do you mean by who is she? You know who she is! She's my mother, you son-of-a-bitch! I can't believe you don't remember her. Or were you too drunk to remember? Her name is Sylvia. You probably knew her as Sylvie

Harris. And my name is Annabella Teal Harris She gave me, what she thought was, your last name. Only to find out it's your middle name. No wonder we couldn't track you down. She worked at the Eight Second Café in Fort Worth, Texas. She died years ago, not that you'd give a damn."

The room became deathly quiet. Everyone was in a state of shock. Rose looked at Paul and he nodded.

Meryl looked at Keough. "Is this true Keough?" She looked at the photo of Sylvie. "Is she your daughter?"

Keough looked Meryl and Annie directly in the eye and said, "I swear to Jesus and all his disciples, I don't know nor have I ever seen this lovely woman. Even in my worst drunken stupors, I would remember someone as lovely as she. Annie, I'm sorry darlin', but I just don't remember her. If I did, I would have looked high and low for both of ya'."

While everyone was arguing Kurt walked over, looked at the photo and necklace. No one saw him slip out the door, until his return. Then he asked everyone to calm down and let him speak.

"I've got something to say and please let me say it and then I'll leave. I'd like to apologies for all of this misunderstanding, and yes, it's my fault – all of it. Keough, brother, I'm so sorry for what I'm about to confess. Annie, I hope you'll find it in your heart to forgive me too."

Kurt told us the story of how Keough was too drunk to ride in the Fort Worth finals. "The rodeo purse was five thousand dollars and growing. That was a lot of money back then. Keough had kids to feed and a wife to support. I knew if he came home empty handed Charlotte would take the kids and he'd never see them again. So, I let him sleep it off in Dallas and I went to the finals instead. I rode and I won. I told Charlotte the money was from Keough and he asked me to give it to you."

I turned toward Keough, "Charlotte never knew. I had to sit and listen to her praising you for staying sober and how she would stay with you, raise the kids with you and she was none the wiser. After the finals I stayed in Forth Worth for a few days. I saw this café went in and had a drink. That's when I met Sylvie. She was one of the toughest and most beautiful women I'd ever seen. There was this one drunken saddlebum who was giving her a hard time. I kicked him out, she thanked me. When she asked my name I couldn't tell her who I was or the rodeo commission would have disqualified me. I would have to give the prize money back and probably would have been arrested. So I told her my name was Keough, Keough Teal. You're Mama and I talked and laughed like we'd known each other for years." He turned to Annie and admitted, "I fell in love with your Mama. However, I knew I couldn't stay. She was a smart gal and eventually she'd figure out I wasn't Keough. So the next morning, I left."

Kurt turned toward Keough and Annie. "I'm sorry brother and I'm extremely sorry to you Annie. I've carried his secret around for decades and it's been tearing me up inside. I'm sorry for what I done, but in hind sight I ain't. I couldn't fail you brother or your family. I loved those kids like they were my own. Why do you think I pushed ya' so hard to make peace with Lash? Father should be there for their kids; even if it means telling a lie from time to time."

He reached in his pocket and walked over to Annie. I told her to open her hand. "Here's my piece of your heart darlin'. Sylvie gave this half to me before I left and she kept the other half. It fits together with your piece. Annie, I definitely don't regret you being the outcome of that secret. I think about your Mama every day wondering where she was and how she was doing. Just last week I found the necklace she gave me. I never stopped thinking about her." Kurt paused for a moment. He walked over to Annie and held her face in his hands. "You've got my eyes." Annie looked up at Kurt. He had tears in his eyes; so did she.

Rose realized they'd finished the entire bottle of bourbon during Kurt's confession. Paul went out to the kitchen and came back with another bottle. He whispered to Rose, *I think this is going to be a long night.* Everyone left the room to give Kurt, Keough and Annie their privacy. It was a shit load of information to digest in one evening.

After several hours of discussion, the three of them came into the kitchen much calmer and civil. Paul, Meryl and Rose noticed there was no blood or bruises. They must have worked things out. Meryl walked over to Keough and hugged him. She asked if everything was resolved. "Yep, we've worked things out as much as we can tonight Meryl, but there is still a lot of healing to do.

Annie and Kurt agreed to talk more in the morning. "I guess I'd better get going." He was about to head over to the bunkhouse when Annie stopped him. She said she had additional questions that needed answers. Kurt put his hand on her shoulder and said, "So do I Annie, so do I. And I promise I'll try my best to answer yours and I hope you can answer mine. But right now I think we all need sleep, goodnight Annabella."

Rose waited until they'd finished their conversation then hesitantly welcomed Annie into the Montana family. "I'm not sure if you're ready to be a Montana and if you aren't that's okay." She joked about how she came here with no father and now she's inherited two.

"Rose right now my head is spinning, so perhaps you can help me get this straight. Am I really a Montana?"

"Yep, Annie I believe you are. A few years ago we found out that my husband Lash had a fraternal twin brother, Jameson who you've just met and now we've discovered we have yet another long lost sibling – that would be you. If this keeps up I'm going to have an extension built onto this house." Annie laughed. "It's good to see you laugh Annie. Being a Montana can be a hell of challenge, but always a good time – another drink?" Rose poured another shot and everyone raised their glasses. "Here's to the craziest ass shit I've ever experienced – cheers!"

Meryl walked over to Keough. She was finally able to smile and let out a long sigh. "What a night. You are one amazing man Mister Montana. Have I told you how much I love you?"

"Yes, yes you have darlin' and, I love you Meryl Montana. Now if it's okay, I'd like to go to bed with my wife. You're still my wife - right? I did marry you? Are you sure you're not some third generation cousin?"

She shook her head no. Keough took a deep breath. "That's good to know I'd hate to find out I've married some other long lost relative." They wished everyone a goodnight and walked arm-in-arm down the hallway to their room.

Paul and Rose walked over and sat beside Annie and asked her if she was okay.

"I'm confused but happy to finally have things put in perspective. And, thank you Paul for listening."

"You're welcome Annie; always willing to lend an ear." He then explained to Rose that she told Paul about Keough being her father.

"He listened to my story, helped me process it until I was able to confront Keough and for that I'm forever grateful. You have one hell of a good man here Rose."

"Thank you Annie – he's a keeper." Annie hugged Rose and then Paul. "And on that note I think I'll turn in. It's after midnight – Happy Thanksgiving."

Rose wished her the same. However, Paul quickly explained it was an American holiday as most of his team stayed in England. Nevertheless, I do enjoy the meals associated with it.

"So what I'm hearing Paul is if I reach for the last turkey leg you won't fight for it?"

Paul looked her straight in the eye and said, "Poppet, try and you'll lose a hand."

The early morning familiar smell of turkeys roasting and pumpkin pies baking was the Thanksgiving alarm clock. Cecilia always started preparing the dinner at 6 AM saying it was 'her time' to rise and shine. Rose felt like a kid waking up on holidays. Cecilia's breakfast buffet was worth getting up that early. She'd set up the breakfast room like a restaurant with the warming trays, white linen and the good china. The rest of the house was still asleep. Rose put on her robe and followed the aroma.

"Good morning Rose, I hope my cooking woke you up and now I can begin my symphony of *The Clanking of Pots and Pans*. You know how much I love cooking on holidays." She handed her a cup and guided me over to the coffee urn. "I think you need this."

Rose smiled and cupped her hands around the hot mug. "When Mister Lash was alive he couldn't wait for coffee so I would set the timer on the coffeemaker for 4 AM. He'd finish the entire pot before breakfast was served. I know I don't talk much about him since his death, but I do miss him Rose. He took me into his home and treated me as if I was part of his family. I never thought . . ."

Rose stopped Cecilia in midsentence. "Cecilia, you ARE family. In fact, I think he loved you more than all of us. When he realized how sick he was he made very clear provisions for you to stay on the ranch unless you decided you wanted to leave. And even then he has an account set up in your name, so you'd never have to work again for the rest of your life."

She smiled and wiped her eyes. Rose could see the conversation was taking an emotional turn so she changed the subject. "Okay, Cecilia . . . I smell sweet rolls. Are they done yet?"

"Yes, they're already in the breakfast room next to the coffee; go on and help yourself."

She grabbed an extra one for Paul along with his large travel mug filled of coffee. He was already up. She handed him his coffee and the sweet roll. "Thank you Poppet. I really needed coffee especially after last night's fiasco. What a bloody unbelievable series of events!"

Rose totally agreed with him. "Yep, I never saw that coming. When Joe would say there was never a dull moment at Casa Montana I thought he was kidding."

Paul sat on the edge of the bed, shaking his head in disbelief. He had the strangest look on his face.

"What's the matter?" He said, "Let me see if I can follow this bizarre family lineage. Annie thought she was Keough's daughter, which would have made her your sister-in-law. However, as it turns out she's actually Keough's brother Kurt's child. So that would make her your cousin? And the man she thought was her father is actually . . . her uncle."

Rose let out a deep sigh. "Paul it's way too early to figure it out right now. How about we wait until after breakfast – deal?"

He smiled, "Deal. Oh by the way, speaking of breakfast, has anyone checked on Raymond?"

"No I haven't. In fact, I just woke up myself."

Paul said he'd go and check. "He didn't have any dinner last night, however, I'm sure he could use a nice cup of tea." He put on his jeans and tee shirt and headed over to the other end of the house to the guest bedrooms.

To his surprise Raymond was already up and dressed. "Good morning Paul. I don't know what Cecilia is cooking but it woke me out of a sound sleep."

Paul gave him a hug around his shoulder. "Good to see you're feeling better Mate. I have to admit I was a bit worried."

Raymond chuckled, "So was I. I haven't ached like that in years. Old age I suppose."

"Oy, enough about old age! I'm beginning to feel the signs of age myself. My bloody wrinkles are starting to get wrinkles."

Rose heard Paul and Raymond laughing so she knocked on the door and asked if it was okay to come in.

Raymond said, "Of course it's okay. It's your house. I'm just happy it wasn't ten minutes ago or you both would have experienced the shock of your lives. I sleep in the nude."

Rose blushed at the thought of him walking around his cabin in the buff. "Okay, now I know you're feeling better. Cecilia said for you to come and get something to eat since you missed last night's dinner."

"I am hungry, that's also a good sign. I try not to miss meals." He gave a gentle pat to his stomach. "You don't get a physique like this from eating salads."

Rose laughed out loud. "He's fine. I'll let the rest of the family know that you're okay; oh and by the way, breakfast is ready."

Rose was halfway to the breakfast room when the phone rang. It was Ginger. He said he regrets he wouldn't be able to come today explaining that his shop was flooded.

"A pipe cracked and the salon had five inches of water on the floor." "I'm so sorry Rosie girl. You know how much I HATE rescheduling my ladies but unfortunately my pipes thought otherwise."

"Ginger it's okay, I didn't mention it to the Jannine, Annie or Meryl so, no harm, no foul." Rose asked about rescheduling when he stopped me.

"Whoa, now who is this Annie you speak of so casually? Do I know her?"

Rose took a breath, "Ginger, that's a conversation that requires a fifth of Tequila."

"Oh My Lord, then I'll call you after the holidays. Okay, stay beautiful and I'll talk to you later."

"I will Ginger. Happy Thanksgiving! And please tell them to send all of the repair bills to me."

Walking back to the kitchen Rose opened the deck door. It felt somewhat warmer than yesterday. She poured a cup of coffee and sat outside. It prompted her to reminisce of her first Thanksgiving with Joe. *It was unusually warm then.* The fresh air cleared her head of yesterday's drama. Rose heard Paul come into the kitchen. He came outside, stood behind her and wrapped his arms around her shoulders.

"What's on your mind Poppet you look lost in thought?"

"I wish Joe were here to see how well this family has survived his death. He'd be proud." Paul nodded. "And it's all because of you Paul. You kept me from sinking into a state of depression and loved my family as though they were your own. After we married you told me there were no stronger folks than Montana folks. You were right."

"Thank you Poppet and I mean it. You are one of the strongest women I know and I will love you always and forever. Never forget that."

"I won't forget. I love you Paul Saxton."

"I love you too Amelia Montana-Saxton." He kissed me twice on the cheek then asked, "Now, if this love fest is over, shall we go inside?" I'm bloody starving."

"Yes that sounds like a terribly grand idea."

He raised his eyebrows. "Ooh, is that an attempt at sounding posh or are you just being cheeky?"

Rose asked which one would get her get me another kiss. He kissed her twice and said, "Brilliant answer."

One-by-one the rest of the household started to wake up. Keough and Meryl were already sitting in the kitchen having coffee. Raymond was having his tea in the living room. Charlotte was hovering over the sweet rolls trying to sneak one in before she had breakfast. Morgan was already on his second croissant. Rose thought, *I swear that boy's stomach is like the Doctor Who TARDIS. It's larger on the inside than it looks on the outside!*

As if he heard her thoughts, Morgan walked over and kissed Rose on the cheek. "Morning Mom, Happy Thanksgiving."

Rose still got goose bumps when he called her Mom. Rose asked him if Jannine was awake.

"Yesterday's travel wore her out, so I thought I'd let her sleep in this morning. However, being the loving husband that I am, I'll take her in a croissant and a cup of tea. That should make her happy. With the little one on its way I want her to rest as much as she can. And yes, I know she's demanding, brash at times and very opinionated but Lord knows I truly love that gal."

Rose thought *you are definitely your father's son.*

Annie looked in the mirror and splashed a handful of cold water on her face. She ran her fingers over the puffiness that had developed under her eyes. *My God, I feel as though I've been trampled by a herd of Montana bison! This is the reason I don't drink very much. I could pose for the cover of Horse and Hound Magazine – no more whiskey for me.*

She heard someone walking toward the door and then a knock. "Annie, it's Rose. Are you awake?"

"Yes, come in Rose. But I must warn you I look like an extra from a zombie film."

"Ha, like you could ever look bad. Wait until you have to get up at 5 o'clock in the morning to get a sleepy kid ready for school. THEN we can play the Who-Looks-Worse game. Trust me I'd win easily!"

She put on a robe and opened the door. Rose immediately handed her a cup of coffee. "Rose you are an angel. But enough about me, how are you feeling this morning? It was an incredibly bizarre night. Were you able to sleep?"

"Annie did I forget to mention I have a kid, horses and a husband whose snoring can be heard well into the next county. When I'm exhausted I could sleep through a global apocalypse."

Annie laughed, "Rose you're sarcasm is greatly appreciated. It helps me to feel normal again."

"Any time Annie. After all we're related so now you're fair game."

Annie smiled and took a sip of her coffee. "Good grief Rose! I thought you said you liked me. This coffee is so strong NASA could use it as a substitute for rocket fuel. One cup of this would put us decades ahead of Russia's Space Program."

"Get used to it Annie Harrison-*Montana*, and again, welcome to the family."

She thought for a minute and said, "You know Rose if a few more long-lost Montanas shows up you could proclaim Montana Ranch its own country – like the Vatican. Keough could be appointed Pope."

Rose laughed so hard she snorted which made Annie spill coffee all over her pajamas. "Annie you are one *bad ass* woman." She dabbed the coffee from her pajama top with a wash cloth and said that it was Rose who was the *bad ass*. They agreed to agree that we were both incredibly *BAD ASS*.

Chapter 21

The day flew by quickly at the Montana ranch. Before the group realized it, it was already early evening. Cecilia announced that dinner was ready.

"Rose, I put you and Paul at the head of the table if that's okay." Before Rose could answer her, Paul said, "Darling, you can put me anywhere you like as long as we can dine on your deliciously prepared feast."

Rose asked everyone to dress casually as no one felt the need to be formal. Everyone was family or extended family. If there was one thing about the Montanas, there's never a reason to stand on ceremony. Like it or not, they were who they were. In fact, the family reminded Rose of the song *Disorder in the House* by Warren Zevon. Disorder was our order and it made sense in an existential sort of way.

Raymond however didn't get Rose's memo. He was dressed in his formal Blackfoot shirt and black slacks attire. Everyone expressed how handsome he looked. Jameson added a loud wolf whistle.

"Thank you all. Although this holiday means nothing to me or Paul; he being British and me being Native American, it still gives me great pleasure to dine with my enemy. So, thank you for sharing your gifts of small pox and dysentery. And on that note, pass the gravy and let the feasting begin."

Rose leaned over to Annie and explained that Raymond's droll sense of humor never ceased to amaze us. She tapped her knife on her water glass and said, "I'd like thank everyone for coming this year and making this the best Thanksgiving I could have ever hoped for. As most of you know, I'm big on tradition. When I was a little girl, one of my favorite Thanksgiving family traditions was to go around the table and ask everyone what they were most thankful for. I'd like to start by saying, although my life changed in the blink of an eye when Joe died; it became a hundred and ten percent richer because of all of you and for that I'm so very thankful."

Morgan and Jannine were next. Morgan said, "I'm thankful for this amazing woman sitting next to me, who is not only beautiful, she's smart and is giving me the best gift of all – a little Montana. And for that I'm forever thankful to my Jannine."

Jannine added, "And Morgan, I'm thankful for you putting up with me and my unique brand of insanity. However, I'm most thankful that you agreed to move back to Montana so we'll be closer to our baby's Godmother. That would be YOU Rose."

"Really! You're really moving back to Montana?" She jumped out of her chair. "You're not shitting me, are you Jannine?"

Jannine laughed, "We shit you not Rose. Howdy neighbor. We're going to start looking for a house in January. And that's what we're thankful for. SURPRISE!"

Paul had Charlotte's ears covered. Charlotte giggled, "Mama and Aunt Jannine said a bad word so can I have their desserts?" You always say if I ever said bad words I couldn't have dessert."

"Nice try Baby Girl, but not a chance. Too much sugar and you become a mini whirling dervish."

Jannine leaned over and whispered, "Don't worry Charlotte, you can have half of mine plus yours, but you have to eat all your veggies – deal?"

Charlotte shook her hand and whispered, "Deal."

Next were Keough and Meryl. Keough started by saying how fortunate he and Meryl were to have found each other, although the circumstances were definitely not the best, referring to her husband's sudden death. "I'm happy she saw something in this old saddlebum, and gave me a chance to prove I was worth lovin'.I adore you Miss Meryl or should I say Mrs. Montana.I'm honored that she said yes and married me. And that's what I'm thankful for."

Cecilia immediately went to the kitchen and brought out three bottles of champaign and a bottle of sparkling cider for Jameson, Charlotte and Keough.

She said, "We never officially toasted your nuptials." Everyone raised their glass in a toast, congratulating them again and wishing them years of happiness."

Rose gave them both a hug. "I can't tell you how happy I am for you two." Keough smiled and said it meant a lot to him that she approved. "I wouldn't want to get my only daughter-in-law railed up.

Rose whispered, "I love you too Keough."

Jameson leaned over and kissed Meryl on the cheek. He then stood up and said he was thankful for his sobriety and he owed it all to his mother, Raymond, Keough and Lash. "When I found out that I had a twin brother I never knew, I felt betrayed. How could a parent keep that kind of secret from their child? But when Mother and Keough explained the situation to me, I understood why. I was a self-entitled jerk, an arrogant drunk and worst of all, I was proud of it. I didn't care about anyone but myself. However, I'm recovering and I'm so grateful to all of you for helping me own up to my problem and still loving me. And, for that I'm thankful."

Charlotte was next. "I'm thankful for all of you and Cecilia's sweet rolls. I'm just sorry my daddy can't be here. Paul, I think you are the best and I love you, but I never got to see my real daddy.I miss him. She kissed her palm and held it up in the air. Happy Thanksgiving Daddy, I love you so much."

Her admission brought tears to our eyes. Rose walked over to her and hugged her. "Your daddy knows you love him Baby Girl. He loves you so much and so does everyone sitting here. "

Charlotte wiped her eyes with her shirt sleeve then rested her head on Paul's shoulder.

Paul said to her, "Remember, not only does your daddy love you Poppet, he's very proud of you. And so am I."

Annie stood up, walked over to Kurt and motioned for Keough to join them. "I'm not very religious. I'm a person of science. I believe in facts and research. When I use the words fate and faith, they are generally followed by the terms *fate worse than death* or explaining to the family of terminal patients to *hold on to their faith* and their loved ones as their condition might improve. What I've learned during this spur-of-the-moment, serendipitous trip is even lost souls eventually find their way through faith and fate. For years I was in the dark about the identity of my father. I knew only what my Mom told me. So trust me when I say I totally understand how you feel Charlotte. However, your Mama was fortunate to find someone like Paul, who loves you as much as he would love his own child – am I right?" Charlotte nodded. "I spent most of my life cursing my father, hoping to find him miserable, down and out, begging me for forgiveness. Instead, I found a kind, gentle, loving man who, no matter how much I tried, I couldn't hate. He didn't know me from Adam, yet he invited me to join his family for the holidays. And his lovely wife Meryl wouldn't take no for an answer. They treated me like a dear friend, even though I was a complete stranger. Had it not been for these two incredible individuals, I would never have found my true father. What are the odds, how did this happen, how could I have been so damn lucky? I've never ever played the lottery. Because I know the odds are against the gambler. Well, I played the odds, and I won. I've won the love of a family I never knew I had; a loving father and a father figure. I'd say that's a true miracle – pure fate. So, to wrap this up before Christmas, I think my odds are pretty good, and that Mom is finally at peace knowing my dad and I finally found each other. And for that I'm very thankful." Kurt and Keough hugged her so tight she disappeared between them. In unison both men said, "Amen."

Annie turned the floor back over to Raymond. He stood up, cleared his throat and raised his glass. "Thank you Annie, your story touched me to the point of being speechless, and those who know me know I'm never at a loss for words. Sorry folks we may need Cecilia to reheat the dinner. I have a lot to be thankful for." There was a flurry of laugher then he started to speak.

"I'm full-blooded Blackfoot. I believe death comes to us in various ways. Some die young, some are taken by accident, most hope to leave from extreme old age – I prefer the latter. I've lived a very satisfying life. I've known many good people, all of them have taught me life lessons I will forever cherish. He paused and rubbed his arm then continued. "Some feel as though the world owes them something and." He paused. "Others, other, oth . . ." We could clearly see something was wrong. He began to sweat, grabbed his arm, then his chest and said, "Oh Shit! I think I'm having . . . having a heart attack. Way to go Raymond, you just ruined dinner!" He dropped his glass and fell to the floor. Everyone froze; everyone except Annie. She immediately went into emergency room mode. She dashed to her bedroom, got her purse and gave Raymond an aspirin. Before he passed out he was able to chew it. Then he stopped breathing. Paul knew CPR and amazingly so did Charlotte. The panic was tangible. Annie kept her focus and continued talking to him. Raymond could feel himself losing consciousness. I thought *this is it Raymond there's no coming back from this trip.*

He felt myself slowly losing sensation of sight, smell, touch, all of them flooding from his physical body. He could barely hear Annie shouting, "Come on Raymond stay with me!" But the pain was becoming unbearable. Drifting into a transitional stage felt so much better. There was no pain and the feeling of weightless was comforting. There was no glowing bright light or a tunnel or heavenly chorus of angels. All he heard was someone calling his name and it wasn't Annie. The voice was familiar, but not yet audible enough for him to recognize. His body was growing lighter; the voice, louder. Finally, it became clear as a bell.

"Well, if it ain't my favorite ol' friend. Howdy Raymond! I hope you brought me some decent coffee because the crap they serve here tastes like that shit you used to make when I was alive. Maybe that's what killed me, hah. Are you still counting the beans before you grind them?"

"I can't believe my eyes! Oh my dear Lord, oh Father of everything that's Holy! Joe! Is that YOU Joe?" He laughed that annoying condescending laugh. The same annoying chuckle that irritated him so much that he threatened to shove his head up a buffalo's ass.

"Now who else did you expect to greet you when you finally decided to pay me a visit?"

"What do you mean *a visit* Joe? I just had a massive heart attack. I'm dead. You said you'd see me later remember. Nadie gave me your message."

"When did you learn to speak Blackfoot and why are you calling my death a visit? What the hell is wrong with you Joe? I swear you are still as fucking loopy as you were in life."

"Hey there's no cussin' in heaven. You don't want the Big Guy kicking you into his fiery hoosegow, do ya'? Trust me you don't want to spend the rest of your eternal life in that place. The coffees burnt and dadgum weaker than cattle piss! I bet they use store brand instant! Hah only joking, you can drink whatever kind you like and it's free all day long. And that's heaven to me. To answer your question *what the hell is wrong with me, eh, I'm dead – ain't that enough?* Anyway, it's good to see you my friend, even if it's only for a short while. I've missed you Raymond."

Raymond asked Joe if he had other friends here.

"Sure, I've got lots of friends here like my mother Charlotte, Wyatt Earp, John Lennon and Randolph Scott, who I idolize. I even went riding with John Wayne; he's a lot taller than I thought. With that being said let's get back to you Raymond. There are two things you need to know: number one, you're not gonna die, well at least not yet. You're goin' to live a long life if you quit stuffin' that bacon in your mouth and exercise. I know you love to eat but watch those saturated fats. You can eat as much as you want when you're here for good, but until then cross bacon off of your shopping list and number two: your wife wants to know why you never remarried."

"Laurie Anne is here? Please tell her that I never forgave myself for her death. If I hadn't gone out that night, if my car hadn't got stuck in that snow bank, she wouldn't have come out looking for me. She wouldn't have skidded on that black ice and crashed into the guard rail. The truck never saw her and she was killed instantly. Tell her I'm so sorry, so very sorry."

"Raymond she's right beside you. You can tell her yourself."

"Hello Raymond." "Oh my God, Laurie Anne, I've missed you so. You're more beautiful than I remember. I'm so sorry."

"Raymond it wasn't your fault. Stop torturing yourself, and please, find someone, love them, be with them and be happy. Please promise you'll do this for me."

Raymond tearfully promised her he would. "Now I must leave, we'll meet again and perhaps you'll introduce me to your new wife when your time comes; which won't be for a very long time. "Maybe we can double date."

"Did you say double date?" Are you with another man Laurie Anne?"

"No I'm not, but we play tennis together three times a week. I've always wanted to learn and this nice young fellow is teaching me. She whispered, *plane crash coming home from Wimbledon.* Well, my dear and sweet Raymond, it's time for me to say goodbye. Keep your promise to me okay? Find a nice woman and remarry or live together, it's your choice. But don't end your life alone. Promise me this Raymond."

"I promise Laurie Anne, I promise."

Joe and Raymond talked for what seemed like hours. He said he had a new ranch and horses and he still writes. "I've written a book about a young gal who meets the love of her life in one of those internet cowboy chat rooms. How wild a story is that? Can you imagine meeting you're future spouse online and then marrying them? Hah, now that the makings of a Hallmark movie. Crazy stuff, huh?"

Raymond didn't want to tell Joe that online dating sites were the current trend and very common. He thought, *why ruin his day. I've already ruined mine by having this freakin' heart attack.*

Raymond nonchalantly changed the subject. "Speaking of dating you know Rose remarried?"

He tilted his cowboy hat back on his head. "Yep, I sure do Raymond. She married that British fella Paul. I'm happy she ain't denying herself of happiness. And I like Paul. He's a good guy."

Raymond also told Joe as much as she loves Paul she still misses him very much.

"Yes, I know she does Raymond."

"Nadie has missed you the most. "She asked me how someone can miss a person they've never met. She's such an amazing child."

Joe nodded in agreement. "Why do you think I try to visit her in her dreams? She's a sensitive little girl. They don't let us do that too often. Not good for the kids, they say. So I pick certain holidays just to let her know that I love her and sometimes I give her annoying messages for my friends – like you Raymond."

"Thanks a lot Joe. I can always count on you to be an ethereal asshole. How's it working for you up here?

Joe laughed, "Now that's the Raymond I've missed."

We continued talking when something caught Joe's attention. It was a flashing light. "Okay partner, it's time for you to head back and join the party. You're about to feel one heck of a huge jolt, as if you've been kicked by a mule. And, I need you to do me a big favor. Please give Rose this message from me."

"What do you want me to tell her Joe?" He whispered his message and told Raymond to swear that he would tell her.

"Well, adios my good friend and remember no more bacon. I don't want to see your face again until you've punched your ticket for good. I love you Raymond. Give Charlotte a hug from her daddy and tell Rose exactly what I told ya'."

"I will Joe, but before I leave I'd like to share the blessing I said at your funeral."

Joe laughed, "Okay, but you'd better make it quick because your stagecoach is coming to take you back to Montana."

He walked over and placed his hand on Joe's shoulder. "May your spirit soar bravely, your heart love eternally and your soul be welcomed with open arms."

Joe smiled. "Thank you Raymond, that was beautiful. Stay well partner and don't forget to ask. . ."

His voice was fading fast. "Don't forget to ask what Joe?"

He turned around and said, "I'll tell ya' later . . . adios mi amigo."

Raymond felt a violent jolt. All I could hear were people yelling. "He's okay. Thank God, he's okay! Raymond, it's Rose. You're okay." Rose turned to Annie, "You did it, you brought him back!"

Annie wiped her forehead. "Thanks Rose, I wasn't about to let this fine man slip away without a good fight. Rose knelt over Raymond and asked him if he could hear her? If you can, just nod your head."

He did as Rose asked, and mumbled that he was okay. He whispered *I'm sorry I was away so long, did I miss dessert?* Rose tried to laugh through her tears. "No sweetie, you didn't miss dessert. You had a heart attack Raymond. And if it weren't for Annie's quick thinking you'd be pushing up daisies and daffodils. Your heart stopped beating for over two minutes."

Two minutes? It had to be longer than that. Joe and I talked for what seemed like hours? Rose continued to tell him that Annie and Paul performed CPR until the medics arrived and thank God they did. They got your heart beating again. The Med-e-Vac team is on its way. They're flying you to Billings and keeping you for observation.

Raymond could hear the helicopter getting closer. He struggled to speak and told me, "Rose, before I go, Joe wants me to tell you something." I thought *Joe? He has a message from Joe? Did he forget Joe's dead?* Raymond tried to give her the message but the medics put an oxygen mask over my face.

"Raymond you can tell me later but now you need to get to the hospital."

"Okay Rose but please, PLEASE Rose do not let me forget to give you Joe's message. I don't want him annoying me though whatever lifetime I've got left." Rose promised Raymond she wouldn't forget and that he could tell her when he came home. The team scrambled past Rose with Raymond strapped to the gurney and quickly shuttled him out the door to the waiting chopper. As they were leaving, Rose noticed Raymond whispered something to one of the medics. It must have been important because Raymond insisted he write it down. Rose made a mental note of it just in case.

Annie gave one of the medics his stats and told him that she was a doctor, a surgeon to be precise, and if they needed her to come with them she'd be happy to do so. He said it wasn't necessary and that his friend, Jameson is riding with him.

"It's a good think you were here or he might not have made it."

Annie agreed. "I know the symptoms of what we call *The Widow Maker* and knew I had to act fast. Oh, one more thing, I gave him an aspirin before he lost consciousness if you'd like to add that to your report. He jotted it down on his chart.

"That's good to know. It most definitely helped in saving his life – again, good job." Annie gave him her card in case the hospital had further questions.

"Okay, will do. Again, I have to say he's lucky you were here. This fellow owes you big time." He started to walk away then turned around. "You should come and work at Billings Metropolitan Hospital. They're always looking for well-train surgeons. He gave Annie his card.

"Thank you Dr. Clearwater." "Please, call me Russell or Russ or Rusty, take your pick. I answer to all three. Perhaps I'll check into it later. Clearwater, that's an interesting name?" Russell said, "It's Blackfoot, and I'd love to explain the rationale behind it. Maybe I can call you later?" Annie brushed her hair away from her face and smiled. He winked and ran out of the door to catch up with the medics.

Rose said, "Is it me or was he just flirting with you?

"I refuse to answer that question Rose on the grounds that I don't want to start blushing in front of company. But between you and me . . . he's hot!"

Rose leaned out the door to get a better look. "Amen to that Sister."

Our admiration of Russ's physique and good looks allowed us a brief moment of levity.

Annie explained to Rose that Raymond had a very close call. "I don't want to scare you Rose, but had I not been here I think he might have . . ." I stopped her midsentence.

"Annie, I'm going to quote Lash's question to me when we first met. I was trying to decipher why I decided to drive west instead of south, how I ended up in Currysville, how I got lost AGAIN and ended up in Meeteetse, Wyoming at the exact same time Joe did. In fact I still can't tell you where Meeteetse it is on the map. But Joe knew. Somehow he knew I'd be there and you know what he said?"

Annie shook her head.

He said, "Rose have you ever heard of fate? Maybe it was just fate that threw us together – plain and simple." "Ain't this the kind of adventure you said you were lookin' for? Well, you put it out there darlin', and now you've got it. It's just our destiny."

"Maybe all of this is YOUR destiny Annie."

Perhaps getting lost brought Annie exactly where she was supposed to be? It certainly led her me to her father. Despite the fact that the man she thought was her father turned out to be her father's twin brother who in fact IS her father. The entire situation was mind-boggling. Was Rose right? Did I put this crazy situation out to the universe and it came to fruition. As a woman of science she was not sure she believed in all this cosmic fate stuff. However, she was willing to consider it as a possibility.

Rose came into the living room and announced that Cecilia was heating up dinner for whoever wanted it. No one seemed hungry. Everyone was still in a state of shock over Raymond. Nonetheless, Cecilia insisted everyone try to eat something. The table was quiet. The group held hands, bowed their heads and each said a silent prayer for Raymond's speedy recovery. Rose thought a little music would sooth frayed nerves. She plugged her cell phone into the home sound system. She thought she selected Andrea Bocelli; instead she must have pressed Brooks and Dunn by mistake. *Boot Scootin' Boogie* blared from the surround sound speakers. It jarred everyone at the table. Rose tried to switch the music but Morgan and Charlotte had already jumped out of their chairs and started line dancing. They pulled me onto the living room floor along with Annie, Jannine. Keough extended his hand to Meryl and asked her if she'd like to have this dance and they surprised us with a perfectly choreographed Texas line dance. Kurt sang along while he joined

Annie and said, "How about cuttin' the rug with your ol' man Annie." Annie smiled and said, "I'd be honored . . . Dad."

Paul came over to Rose and wrapped his arms around her waist and kissed her. "Would you like to do a slow Texas two-step with a gentleman that just happens to have two left feet, Mrs. Saxton?"

"Yes I would Mister Saxton. Should I expect to also have my toes stepped on?"

Paul grinned, "Absolutely, you know you're taking your life into your hands dancing with an uncoordinated Brit – you've been warned." As they danced, Paul told Rose he wouldn't know what to do if anything ever happened to her. "You are my one and only true love, always and forever Rose Montana-Saxon. And, seeing that there's never a good time to bring this type of conversation to light, I thought you should be aware that I've changed my will. It now reflects that everything I have is to go to you, Charlotte and said future children. Tonight's dreadful events were quite sobering and I wanted you to know that I've taken care of you and our family's well- being. But let's talk about this in the morning, as all I want to do right now is to dance with my wife."

They continued to dance long after the music stopped and everyone else had gone to bed. Paul could see she was still shaken by Raymond's heart attack. He assured her that Raymond was otherwise healthy and should be okay due to Annie's quick actions.

"She told me they'd probably keep him for a few days to be sure no damage was done." Paul said, "That sounds correct." "They'll also send him home with a lengthy list of things not to eat, to his dismay."

"Yes I'm sure you're right and I think we should call it a night and go to bed."

Paul pulled her close. "Perhaps you haven't noticed I'm not sleepy well at lease a certain part of me isn't."

Rose smiled, "Are you referring to that extreme hard on you have?"

He nodded, "What can I say, I find you terribly arousing."

"Then we'd better take care of that."

Paul winked, "Yes, I believe we should. In fact I believe this could lead to the *said future children* clause."

Chapter 22

The next morning everyone was still in a daze from yesterday's chaos. All were up, except Charlotte. What a traumatic event to witness at such a young age. Watching someone having a heart attack is devastating enough for adults to take in. She considers Raymond a second grandfather. Rose knew she was stressed, so she let her sleep. She woke up on her own about noon still tired, but hungry. That's a good sign. Cecilia took her into the kitchen and made her a late breakfast. As for the rest of the group, Cecilia instinctively knew to make two pots of coffee. Food would come later.

Rose asked Morgan to step outside on the deck with her. It was chilly; however, in the sun it was comfortably warm. Warm enough to be outside without our coats. Odd weather for winter in Montana. She thanked him for taking Charlotte to the family room when the medics arrived.

"No need to thank me Mom. I love my little sister and protecting her from things like that is just another part of my being her big brother." *He looks so much like his father when he smiles.*

"You'll be a good father went your little one arrives. I can't tell you how happy I am that you and Jannine are moving back home to Montana. It's the best news I've heard in months!"

He said, "Truth be told, we really miss this place. There are times I honestly think I can hear Dad hacking away on his computer and printing out his rough draft manuscripts. I miss him."

"I miss him too Morgan."

Rose saw Charlotte peeping at she and Morgan from the kitchen door. "Come over here Baby Girl. Are you okay?"

She shrugged her shoulders and came over to join us. "How are you feeling this morning?" She hugged her mother and then Morgan. "Mama I'm feeling scared. I had fun dancing last night, but then I started thinking about how Raymond almost died. It made me think about Daddy."

Rose's first thought was to comfort her; however, she thought it best to let her continue. "I dreamt about him. And, Raymond went to visit him in heaven. He told Raymond how good it was to see him but, it wasn't his time and to go back. So he did. I guess he knew how much we'd miss him."

Morgan and Rose looked at each other and then Rose asked her how her Daddy was doing?

"He looks just like his hottie photo." Rose whispered to Morgan that she took that photo when they first met.

To bring a bit of levity to the conversation Morgan said, "So he's still a hottie in heaven?"

That brought a faint smile to her face. "Yes, he sort of looked like you Moe, except with gray hair."

Rose asked her if she knew what Raymond had to tell me." She shrugged. "Nope, he just told me not to worry about him or Raymond and we'd see him when he gets out of the hospital. Oh and one more thing he said he and I must have some kind of connection . . . psychic, I think he said. That's why he calls me, *Nadie*."

Now that I can believe. She's always had this connection with Raymond, so it would make sense that he communicated with her during his heart attack.

Morgan was a bit more cynical about it, asking her if he met Elvis. Charlotte rolled her eyes at him and asked if she could go back inside. Rose nodded and both Morgan and Rose gave her another hug.

Morgan asked, "Mom, do you believe she really communicated with Raymond or was it just a dream?"

"Morgan, I've heard of stranger things happening to people who can converse with people on the other side. Perhaps she does have some kind of connection with spirits – I don't know. However, Raymond seems to believe in it. I've had a similar experience at one of his drum circle events – it was mind-blowing. I swore I heard Joe's voice. If there is an afterlife I hope it has sweet rolls."

Morgan laughed and said that he didn't understand how she could eat so much and not gain an ounce.

"The trick Morgan is to eat so fast you don't have time to absorb calories and, if you believe that one, I've got some ocean side property for sale in Monument Valley."

After a good laugh Morgan and Rose finished their conversation and went back inside the house. They were about to start lunch when the house phone interrupted us. I rushed back inside and saw it was Jameson's cell phone number.

"Hello, Jameson. How's Raymond?"

"Hey Rose. I wanted to call and let you know we arrived safely and Raymond is in the ICU – just a precaution. I would have called last night but by the time they finished working on him it was 3 o'clock in the morning. He's stable and for now they're keeping him in the Intensive Care Unit. How is everyone holding up at home?"

"We're okay but obviously we're worried. That man is the leader of this quirky tribe of misfits and I don't know what we'd do if he drifted off to the happy hunting grounds."

"For now you can stop worrying Rose. He's not going anywhere except to a private room. He's already flirting with the nurses and told one of them he was going to marry her when he gets better. I think his medication is doing most of the talking."

She laughed. "Now I know he's going to be okay. And, with all that being said, how are you holding up?"

"I'm okay, and I have to tell you this entire incident has tested my sobriety. I could have really used a drink last night but I thought if I started drinking and Raymond dies . . . he'd haunt me forever!"

"Yes he would, and so would your brother Lash. Trust me you wouldn't want these two men giving you a wrath of eternal shit!"

"Hah, I agree. Okay Rose, I wanted to give you an update. His doctor just went into his room, so I'm going to cut this conversation short and find out what's going on. I'll call again later today if there's any change. Give my love to everyone. Oh, and tell Annie her ears should be burning. Doctor Clearwater has been gushing about her since he arrived at the hospital. He's been calling her the Angelina Jolie of Florence Nightingales. I have no idea what that means but tell her to be prepared, he's definitely hot for her."

"I'll let her know that she's become a celebrity at Billings Metro."

"Okay Rose, I've got to go. The reception isn't that great here and I'm breaking up. And, I need to charge my phone. Talk with you later. Love ya'. "

"Love ya' too Jameson, and again, thanks for taking such good care of Raymond."

Rose called everyone into the living room and gave them Jameson's update on Raymond's condition. Two people were missing.

"Where are Kurt and Annie?" Paul said he saw them walking over towards the bunkhouse. "I think they were having a Dad-Daughter natter."

"Okay Paul, explain *Natter* to us poor confused Americans."

He huffed, "Natter, as in rabbiting or as you lot call it chatting."

Charlotte smirked, "Then why didn't you just say chatting, you're in Montana for goodness sake not England!"

Paul squinted at Charlotte. "Oh aren't we the cheeky monkey or should I say smart aleck, because I'm in Montana, not England." Their mock argument was a much needed comic relief. He put his arm around her neck and gave her a gentle head noogie. She laughed and tried to wiggle away from his grasp.

Seconds later Charlotte ran back and asked, "Mama, may I call Sawyer? Last time we talked he said he can't wait until we go to see his daddy ride in Las Vegas." For a moment Paul and Rose looked confused, and then we remembered that Bailey's new owner, JT McCabe invited us as his special guests to Cowboy Christmas Rodeo in Las Vegas. Rose told her yes she could call Sawyer; however, they had to make sure Raymond was okay before they say yes to his dad's invitation. The look on her face went from extreme joy to disappointment.

"Mama we PROMISED him we were going! You said we could go. We have tickets!" Rose tried to reason with her. However, being the stubborn Montana that she is, she felt an argument brewing. She looked over at Paul and he whispered *I'll talk to her and help her understand that sometimes family comes first and Raymond is family.* Rose thanked him for his willingness to smooth things over but explained she needed to hear this from me.

"Charlotte, to answer your first question, yes you may call Sawyer, however, hold off on the Las Vegas conversation until later. I'll call Mister McCabe and we adults will decide – is that clear?"

She mumbled something and walked back towards her room in a tween huff.

Rose sat down again and held her head. "Paul when did that sweet little baby girl turn into a stubborn young Montana?" Paul didn't say a word.

He knew it was a rhetorical question. "Poppet there's nothing wrong with her behavior. She's a typical tween. I'd worry if she didn't have a few tantrums. Charlotte is head strong just like another Montana woman I know. Her name is Rose – perhaps you know her?" I thanked Paul for keeping my blood pressure stable.

Rose and Paul went to join the others in the family room and Paul said he would head over to the barn to hay the horses. "I haven't seen Kurt come down from the bunkhouse and, if he and Annie are still chatting I don't want to disturb them. I might as well give the horses their wormers too. It's a horrid job but somebody's got to do it."

Rose walked over and kissed him. "Have I told you what a wonderful man you are Paul Saxton." He winked and continued over to the barn.

Rose went to check on Charlotte when she noticed a missed call on her cell phone. It was Jameson. She called him immediately. *Lord, I hope it's not bad news about Raymond?*

"Hello Jameson, sorry I missed your call. Is Raymond okay? Has he taken a turn for the worse has he?"

"No, Rose. In fact he's doing well. They think he may be released in a few days. That's if he behaves himself and does what he's told. But I'm calling for a totally different reason. To make a long story short, when Raymond and I were on our way to your place for Thanksgiving, we assisted two women whose car broke down near Jimmy's place. They called to thank me and Raymond for our help and to tell us that everything was repaired. When I explained that Raymond had a heart attack they were shocked. One of the gals mentioned that she is a Certified Nurse's Assistant and would be happy to look after him when he returns home, repaying him for his kindness so to speak. Her friend worked at a hotel. She's willing to take on the housekeeping chores until he's back on his feet. And to be honest Rose, I could use the help. I wanted to run this by you before I agreed."

"I'm glad you did Jameson and I trust your judgment. If Raymond feels comfortable with them helping then I say go ahead."

"Great, I'll tell them okay. Their names are Mona Moon Rae and her friend who goes by the name of Chinchilla. Both are a little bit quirky, and I'll need all the help I can get once Raymond's released from the hospital. Oh and they are huge Montana Joe fans – what are the odds!"

I think I stopped breathing for a second. *Mona Moon Ray and Chinchilla . . . oh shit!*

"Hello, Rose, are you still there?

"Yes, yes I am Jameson. You're not going to believe this. . . I know them! And quirky is an understatement. However, they are harmless and they LOVE Lash's books. I'm glad they're able to help you and Raymond. I still have Raymond's house and master keys. Would you like me to drive over and get them settled?

"I was hoping you would Rose, and if I haven't told you lately, you are my favorite sister-in-law."

"I'm your ONLY sister-in-law living in Montana, but thanks for the acknowledgement."

"Again, thanks Rose and I'll tell Raymond you're okay with this."

"You're welcome Jameson. Hey, before we hang up do you know what Raymond wanted to tell me?"

There was no reply. He'd already hung up. "Damn! What does Raymond want to tell me? Oh well, I guess I'll have to wait until he gets out of the hospital – if he remembers."

The household was understandably quiet. No one at the Montana ranch felt blissfully stuffed like they usually felt the Friday after Thanksgiving. Even though the roads were clear, the traditional Black Friday Sale shopping didn't excite them. They were more worried about Raymond's condition than hunting for those pre-holiday bargains. Rose told everyone that Jameson had called and said if his results look good Raymond might be released in a few days. He also mentioned that he'd arranged for home care assistance to help out during Raymond's recovery. His updates seemed to lift their spirits a bit. However, Rose didn't feel the need to mention who would be helping, as she was still trying to wrap her head around Mona and Chinchilla's being sane enough to do anything without supervision.

Kurt and Annie walked in while she was giving everyone the update. Annie was relieved to hear Raymond was doing well.

"Oh, and by the way Annie, Jameson wanted you to know that you are being called a Cardiac Hero and local celebrity by a certain Dr. Clearwater."

She rolled her eyes and blushed. "Maybe I should call him and check on Raymond's stats."

Rose mimicked. "Maybe you should." She looked around to see if anyone was looking, then she flipped her the bird.

"Hey sweetie, I'm just the messenger . . . don't shoot me."

Cecilia came in from the kitchen and asked if they wanted her to make a light dinner. "Rose, if you would like I can whip something up before I go."

"No, Cecilia we're fine. We'll nibble on the leftovers. Leave some of those holiday sales items for me okay. However with the situation being what it is I'll probably shop online this year. I'm just not in the mood with Raymond being in the hospital."

"Oh, I'm not going shopping Rose. I'm driving to Billings to visit Raymond." "We're almost the same age and I know what it feels like to be in the hospital, especially during the holidays. When I was in my twenties, I broke my leg in two places. I was in the hospital for three weeks. It was depressing. I've made Raymond some soup. I know he could use something other than hospital food."

Rose wasn't surprised by Cecilia's thoughtfulness. When she was pregnant she pampered her so much that after Charlotte was born she really missed her doting over her. She was like a Fairy Godmother.

Cecilia put on her coat and hat then promised she'd call as soon as she arrived. "I'll be home later this evening, but if the roads become icy I'll stay overnight at a hotel."

Wishing everyone a Happy Holiday she went on her way. I thought *how sweet of Cecilia to go so far out of her way for Raymond. And . . . why didn't Rose think of doing that! Perhaps it's better for someone his own age to visit. She'll understand what a close call he had. I know Raymond thinks the world of her. I also know how much he'll appreciate her kind and thoughtful gesture. I wonder why they never hooked up.* I laughed to myself and thought *Rose, get your mind out of the gutter.*

"Oh Jeez, I promised Jameson I'd meet Mona and Chinchilla at his cabins. I'd better get going."

Chapter 23

Chinchilla and Mona thanked Jimmy for all of his help in resolving the car situation. "We truly appreciate everything you've done for us Jimmy."

"I'm happy to help you Miss Mona. Getting stuck out here can be bad, especially when you don't know the roads. They can be tricky to maneuver on the best of days. The weather can turn in minutes so being prepared is the key."

"We completely understand that now. In fact, we'd better get a couple of bottles of water, a few power bars and a flashlight – just in case." Chinchilla added two blankets to our order. She said, "If we get stranded again I want to be warm."

Jimmy bagged their items. Chinchilla wrapped one of the blankets around Mona's shoulders. *I should have brought a coat.* Jimmy threw in a couple of sweet rolls for the ride.

"Again, thank you so much. I could get used to this Montana hospitality." He asked where they were headed.

"Back to Raymond's place. You heard about him didn't you?"

Jimmy shook his head. "No what's going on with Raymond?"

"He had a heart attack during Thanksgiving dinner and was flown to Billings."

"Oh my God, I'm so sorry to hear that! Why didn't somebody tell me earlier?"

Mona shrugged. "I guess they didn't want to ruin your holiday dinner." Mona then told him Rose was on her way over to the cabins to let us in. "Chinchilla will be taking care of him until he's feeling better. She's a CNA-Certified Nutty Adult." Chinchilla pinched my arm. "Ouch, I was only joking Chin' she's a Certified Nurse's Assistant."

Jimmy laughed, "Well, ladies again let me know when you arrive and I'll probably let you know when Rose is on her way. She always makes it a point to stop in and pick up her *secret* stash of my cinnamon-raisin rolls, but you didn't hear it from me, okay?"

The two women nodded. "Okay Jimmy we're off. You take care."

Mona put the bags on the backseat and tossed her blankets beside them. Chinchilla was still wrapped in her blanket. Mona shook her head, "If you'd gained a pound or two or ten, maybe you wouldn't stay so cold all the time? You are too thin!"

Chinchilla gave me a rolled-eye glare. "I prefer the term slender."

"Yeah, slender like the crack in my ass! Hell, if you turned sideways you'd be invisible. You know I'm only kidding Chin', in fact I'm really enjoying this road trip. We should take one every year!"

She ignored her friend and mumbled *Never-Again-In-Life!* "Oh for God's sake Mona, just drive already!"

It was midmorning when Rose arrived at Jimmy's store. She checked her pocket again to make sure she had Raymond's keys. *I'd hate to drive all the way back to the ranch. With everything going on I've been a bit forgetful. I dug my hand in my coat pocket and of course they were there. I think sometimes I'm losing my mind. Get it together Rose!* She parked beside the store as she always did when sneaking her pastry stash into the truck. Jimmy's homemade cinnamon raisin rolls were her weakness. He saw her come in and reached for the bag behind the counter.

"Morning Rose, you just missed those two gals. And for the life of me I can never remember their names – odd ones aren't they?"

"Yes, they are very odd, but quite harmless. They're going to stay and help Raymond when he's released from the hospital. The thin gal is a Certified Nurse's Assistant. The other is just an eccentric rich weirdo with a heart of gold. She's the woman I told you about who was obsessed with Joe. She actually believed Lash was the persona and that Montana Joe was real! She still refers to him as the man she hoped to marry, with all due respect to me of course."

Jimmy laughed. "You've really got your hands full with those two gals. I tell ya' I kept my shotgun handy while they were in the store. Just in case they had a loony attack and started throwing stuff."

"Jimmy, they're not violent. They're just East Coast Weird and after working and living in New York City for years, trust me, I know weird. But like I said they're harmless. After all, they've got to have some modicum of sense. Chinchilla's job requires precise skills and judgment and Mona, well—Mona can drive a car."

Jimmy laughed again. "Rose when you put it that way I guess Raymond is in good hands.

"I think he'll be okay Jimmy, besides Jameson will be there too. With that being said I'd better get going. I wouldn't want those two to get lost. The BOLO would sound like something from a George Carlin skit, 'Be on the lookout for two wackaloons. They aren't armed or dangerous. They're just bat shit crazy!'"

Jimmy almost choked on his coffee. "Alright Rose, it's time for you to leave before I require CPR.

"Okay Jimmy, you take it easy and again, thanks for keeping my Cinnamon Raisin Roll Obsession or as we call it, my CRRO our little secret." He gave her the okay sign then waved goodbye.

Rose made it to the cabins in good time. She was amazed how clear the roads were. Not one patch of ice but the snow drifts were still over three feet tall. She parked and walked around Raymond's place. There was no sign of Mona's vehicle.

"Lord, I hope they didn't get lost or even worse, drove over an embankment. Hell, we wouldn't find them until spring thaw." The very thought of them arguing for months while trapped in Mona's car made Rose laugh out loud. *Rose, that's just evil. Perhaps I should go look for them – nah!*

Rose reached in the bag and started nibbling on another roll when I heard a car speeding toward the cabins. Mona and Chinchilla eventually arrived. Both looked extremely pissed off so I chose not to ask them what had happened. Although, I'm sure they'll tell me in great detail whose fault it was. I thought I'd get the conversation started by saying good morning and offering them one of my rolls.

"Morning ladies, it's good to see yo . . ." Before Rose could finish her welcome they were already at each other's throat; each one blaming the other for the wrong turns.

Rose walked between them and shouted. "Whoa, time out ladies! Stop yelling or I'll drive you both into the forest and leave you for the mountain lions! Remember, you're here to help Raymond, not to argue or fight about stupid shit! Do I make myself clear?"

They stopped and uttered a shameful okay.

They parked their vehicles in the gravel lot behind the guest cabins, walked over to Raymond's cabin, and Rose let the two women in. His place was incredibly tidy. Rose never expected two guys to be so organized, but if you're running a business you have to have some sense of order. Once Mona and Chinchilla familiarized themselves with the house they became a well-oiled machine. Rose was impressed by their professional transformation from arguing friends to focused workers.

After a thorough assessment of Raymond's condition, the two sat down and discussed his exercise program. Chinchilla said she would put him on a walking schedule and low-cholesterol diet.

"I've already removed the bacon from the refrigerator and freezer. I'll shop later for turkey and fish. It'll be rough for him the first few days, but he's a smart guy and knows what's best if he wants to stay alive."

If he thought his heart attack was bad he hasn't seen me with my patients. They refer to me as the MDS, Miniature Drill Sergeant."

Rose laughed at her taking complete control of her dear friend's health.

Chinchilla continued, "I like to tell them that it's for their own good and it hurts me more than it hurts them. But we all know that's a crock of shit. I know it really hurts; however, in the long run they understand the importance of my work."

Rose totally agreed with her. She thought of Joe's physical therapy and how painstakingly brutal it was.

Once everything was settled, the three women sat at the table and chatted a little bit about their lives.

"I was an executive at a major law firm when my mother died," Mona began. "Being the youngest of three children it devastated me. They say it's easier when you're an adult, but I don't think I ever recovered from it. My father divorced her when I was 5-years-old and remarried. I didn't want to reconnect with him. My oldest sister however was a hippie and moved to Pago-Pago, so I went to stay with her and her son, Tucker Chapman-Bernard who has his PhD in Paranormal Psychology; or as he like to describe it, *I study and investigate spooky, inexplicable shit.* A few years ago I came back to the states and swore I'd change my life. It was at that moment my belief in divine intervention came about. Someone left a copy of Lash's novel, *Gunslinger's Fortune* on a seat at the airport. I started reading it. I fell in love with the characters *Montana Joe* created, hence my adoration of Montana Joe westerns. It was nothing short of a miracle finding that book. The inscription on the first page read, *To Darlene.* I was shocked because my real name is *Darlene*, Darlene Whittlemire. I changed it to Mona Moon-Rae because Darlene didn't portray my true bohemian inner self. I know people think I'm crazy and overly exuberant but that's because they don't know me. I'm really a loveable person once people get to know me."

That's when Chinchilla chimed in. "Mona is one of the most loyal and kind people I know. She's got such a big heart. It's just that when she loves something or someone she REALLY loves it or them a lot. Her enthusiasm catches most people off-guard."

Rose asked Chinchilla about herself. "Chinchilla, that's a very unique name." She laughed. "The short story, as a baby I was born with a full head of hair. It was so soft my dad said it was as soft as his pet Chinchillas – the nickname stuck. My real name is Claudia Kuilan and I'm from Mount Laurel, New Jersey. The surname is Spanish. My dad is half-Spaniard. Mom's hot-tempered Irish. So Rose as you can see Mona and I were destined to be friends – two oddballs."

"I'll admit you both are the most interesting ladies I've ever met and I lived in New York City. You can't swing a barista without knocking over an oddball. However, I married someone who definitely would have been a kindred spirit to you both. Most people knew Lash as this handsome, squared away, focused writer. That couldn't be further from the truth. He was an impulsive, over-caffeinated, eccentric man who had weird and wonderful ways of showing his love." Rose told them about the chocolate candy kisses and hundreds of rose petal in our shower surprise. I recited his note. *If I kissed the ground you walk on and showed you with roses will you love me forever?*

Mona and Chinchilla started dabbing their eyes with their sleeves. Mona exclaimed, "Rose how could you NOT fall head over heels in love with him?" "My entire life I prayed for someone like Joe to sweep me off of my feet and ride into the sunset with him beside me. I guess it's just not in my cards – but that's okay. I've got great friends and enjoy living vicariously through Montana Joe novels. I secretly thought his Jenna Lee character was based on me – crazy huh?"

Rose went over and hugged Mona. "No it's not crazy, not crazy at all. You are an awesome woman Mona and I'm sorry I misjudged you when we first met. Like Joe always said, never judge a . . ."

Mona interrupted me. ". . . A book by its cover?"

Rose laughed. "No, that would be way too normal for Joe to express. He'd say never judge a person by their outsides, because their insides might be one hell of a great story."

Rose continued to tell them a bit more about her and Joe. She felt they've earned the right to know more about their idol. She told them that he was also highly intelligent man who would sometimes act the naive cowboy. "At first it annoyed me but as I got to know him it was his playful way of letting me know that I was just as smart as or even smarter than him. Did you know he had his Ph.D. in Communications from Columbia?"

Chinchilla's mouth hung open. "Wow Rose, I had no idea! So what you're bragging about is that Lash Montana was not only unbelievably handsome, he was smart, romantic and worth saying again – unbelievably handsome?" Mona and Rose laughed at her candid expression.

"Yep he was all that Chin' and I never took it for granted. I knew exactly how lucky I was. I'm just happy that I trusted my best friends Daniel and Patrick. They told me to take some time off of my 60-hour-a-week career, saying to hell with caution, and take the trip that led me to Joe. If I'd listened to my inner-self I'd still be in New York working myself to death and living in my overpriced condo with my cat."

Chinchilla glanced over at Mona. "Mona convinced me to come on this trip. I was hesitant because as you are well aware Mona can be rather erratic with her decisions. But had I listened to my inner-self I would never have met you, Jameson or Raymond. I can cross meeting a famous person, taking wild western road trip and finding an exciting new friend off of my Bucket List. I was hoping that exciting new friend would be male but hey, the trip ain't over yet!"

Rose learned that Mona and Chinchilla were both kindhearted individuals who just look at the world differently." She felt that she could continue to open up to them. "Now I've never mentioned this to anyone except Raymond. But when Lash found out that his throat cancer was terminal, he began writing a series of emails to send to me after his death. I had no knowledge of this. He advised his lawyer to send them over periods of time to remind me how much he loved me and Charlotte. Did you know he died minutes after Charlotte was born?"

Mona nodded, however my statement left Chinchilla speechless. She said how devastating it must have been. "At least he got to see her Rose."

Rose continued telling them about his emails. "They're starting to taper off, however knowing Lash, I have no idea if they'll ever stop. In fact, I received one email that was entitled part 1 or 2, but I never received part 2 or 2. His entire persona was based on him being unpredictably predictable."

Rose glanced over at the clock and realized we'd been chatting for over two hours. "Well ladies, I believe it's time I got going."

Mona smiled and said, "Thank you Rose Montana for believing in me. I know it was a rough start but I'm happy things turned out the way they did."

Chinchilla said, "Ditto what she said, even though this is our official first meeting, I'm glad to have met you Rose. You're a very cool lady."

Rose told her she was happy to meet her too. And even happier that she was able to help cross three things off of her bucket list.

Chinchilla asked, "So, can you help me cross off number eleven?" Mona squinted at her. "Okay, spit it out Chin' what's number eleven?"

"There is no eleven Mona, but if there were, it would be to meet a good looking cowboy, have a wild romance and marry him like Rose did." Mona said if anybody was going to marry a cowboy it would be her, and not Chinchilla. Of course this admission led to a hypothetical argument; one that would never be settled anytime soon. Rose used it as her chance to exit. *I'll be miles away before they even realize I'm gone.*

It was early evening when Rose arrived home to find dinner ready and waiting. Paul met her at the door.

"Ooh, something smells amazing. Is Cecilia back already?"

He gave her a welcome home kiss. "No, Cecilia hasn't come home yet. I decided it was time for my wife to experience a culinary taste of Paul Saxton's delicacies. I made you dinner. Roasted chicken stuffed with chestnut mushroom dressing and gravy with braised parsnips, and, homemade Yorkshire pudding, or as we call them *Yorkies*."

Rose followed the aroma and low and behold he'd prepared dinner.

"Paul I didn't know you could cook."

He chuckled. "Poppet, when you're on the road as much as I am and you don't want to get a horrid case of dysentery from those off-road diners you learn to make your own foods. You'd be surprised by the gourmet meals one can whip up on a hot plate. Would you like a glass of wine?"

She held up her glass. "Absolutely, thank you! Why don't you pour yourself a glass as well? We'll both need a drink after I tell you the stories I heard chatting with Mona Moon Rae and Chinchilla."

Rose told him about their backgrounds and how they weren't as crazy as they thought. In fact, they were quite normal and talented. "I know Raymond will be well taken care of. They really have their act together more than I could have imagined."

He nodded. "I'm happy to hear that Poppet. I wouldn't want Raymond's health to fail because someone wasn't giving him a hundred and ten percent of their attention."

Rose agreed with him. "Paul, I don't think we need to worry about that. They might seem wacky; however, when it comes to their professions they are squared-away individuals."

"Speaking of individuals, where is everybody? The house is… quiet." Paul smiled and moved his chair beside Rose's chair. "We have the entire house to ourselves my dear. It took a lot of convincing and two hundred pound, eh, I mean dollars to get them to disappear for the evening."

Rose laughed and asked if she wanted to know where they all disappeared to? Paul said if he told her he'd have to kill her and that would ruin their perfect evening. "However, I will tell you that Kurt, Annie and Charlotte went to the theatre or as you lot call it – the movies. So she's in good company. Meryl and Keough went out to dinner. I told them to take their time, as I had a surprise waiting for you when you returned home."

And, what a surprise it was. The table was beautifully set with the good china and crystal. The candlelight enhanced the gorgeous Calla Lily centerpiece.

"Paul this is breathtaking. Have I told you recently how much I love and adore you?"

"Yes, numerous times. Every morning when I wake up next to you and see that magnificently beautiful face of yours, I have to remind myself that I am indeed awake and I'm not dreaming this perfect life."

For a moment Rose was speechless. She knew how hard it was for Paul to be the new husband of the legendary Lash Montana's widow and father to her young child. Paul was a stoic man who showed patience and self-endurance during adversity. Who else would let a crazy stranger into the cab of their truck and commandeer his internet. Rose reminded him of that insane moment which brought a smile to his face, and in turn, Rose was reminded how beautiful a smile Paul had. The corners of his mouth turned upward like he knows something no one else knows. Unlike Joe's lop-sided grin that always looked as though he were up to something.

After dinner, the two retired to the living room for an evening night cap. Paul brought out a decanter of Brandy.

"I thought this would be better than an evening coffee." *I never knew he drank Brandy?*

"Yes Paul that would be lovely and it would warm me up. Rose shivered as a chill ran up her spine. Paul walked over to the fireplace and started a fire.

"This, along with the Brandy should remedy your evening chills." He paused for a moment. "Rose I've got a confession to make."

Oh shit, why does this always happen to me? Why is there always another shoe just waiting for the most inappropriate time to drop? Rose tried to appear nonchalant then asked,

"Oh, a confession? And what would you have to confess?"

He rubbed his chin the way he does when he's trying to find the right words to say. Then he spoke. "Rose, no. . . Amelia, I have loved you since the moment I saw you flailing your arms in the middle of the truck stop lane attempting to flag me down. Then, when you married Lash I thought, what a bloody lucky bloke he is.

She is one brilliant woman and I'd give anything to have someone like her in my life. I kept this admission to myself because I respected Lash and you. The last time I spoke with Lash, he made me promise something that totally threw me. He waited until you and the doctors left his hospital room and said, 'Paul, I know I'm dying, I know I may never see my daughter's birth or her first birthday. Please promise me you'll be there for them; that you'll take care of them after I'm gone. I'll be able to die a peaceful man if I know they're in good hands. And you my British friend have those hands. Love them like I would. And if it's in the stars – marry her. She'll say she's okay being alone and that she can take care of herself; and she's right. But I don't want her mourning her young life away because of me. Because I didn't have the courage to tell her I was dying when I first met her. I know that was a selfish thing for me to do, but I wanted to love and be with her even if it was only for a short period of time. Can you do this for me Paul? Do you know why I'm asking you? Because you are one heck of a fine man Paul. And don't think for one second that I don't know how you feel about my Rose. I know you love her. Like me, you've loved her from the moment YOU met her. What man in their right mind wouldn't love her? Promise me you'll do as I ask. And some day after you've married her. Yes, I'm being presumptuous, and finally settle down with her it's up to you if you want to mention our conversation. She'll hate you for a moment, then, she'll cry. Just tell her I threatened you.'"

Paul said he laughed at the thought of Lash threatening anyone. "I told him I would honor his wishes but I did ask what if she says no to my proposal, what do I do next? And he said 'well pard' put a huge slice of strawberry cheesecake in front of her. Ask her if she'd like some. And when she says YES slip the ring on her finger and tell her you love her as much as she loves that damn cheesecake. And make sure you have a lot of napkins. She tends to drool over it and she'll shed a few happy tears when she says yes.'"

Paul sat beside Rose and took hold of her hands. "A month later he died. I knew I had to carry out his wishes so I did and never regretted a single moment Amelia. I love you beyond words." He paused for a moment and then added, "That's my confession Poppet. I've wanted to tell you for years but couldn't seem to find the right time. I'll totally understand if you hate me or want to thrash me about the head. I won't flinch."

Rose walked over to him and kissed him. "Paul in my heart I've known this all along. It's not like Joe to leave and not have a contingency plan."

Paul playfully wiped his brow. "I thought you'd at least start throwing things at me." I smiled at him. "No Paul I'm happy you told me. And now let's put this behind us and live our lives to the fullest. Joe would want that for you, me and Charlotte."

The two hugged and toasted his being able to breathe after such an emotional confession. Paul stopped for a moment as if he remembered something else. "Oh and one more thing he mentioned, that we give Charlotte a sibling. She'll need a little brother or sister to boss around and protect."

"Are you sure it was Joe who said this or is this wishful thinking on your part." Paul kissed her again. "Poppet you can't blame me for trying."

She kissed him back and said, "Then why don't we start trying tonight. Shall we give it a go, ey?" Paul pulled away and stared at her. "Since when have you become so terribly British? Next you'll be singing, *God Save the Queen* before we make love." Rose blew out the table candles and carried the glasses, while Paul tucked the bottle of Brandy under his arm, and headed off to the bedroom.

Rose didn't know when they fell asleep, but the piecing rays of the winter sun woke her up. It was 8'oclock in the morning. That's late at the Montana house. Rose jumped out of bed in a panic and ran down the hall to wake Charlotte up for school. She was about shake her then realized it was Sunday. Everyone else was still sleeping. Since she was already up, Rose decided to make the coffee. Cecilia was still in Billings, so Rose felt obligated to carry on the morning coffee making brigade. She knew the smell would bring the rest of the household into the kitchen. She poured a cup before the pot finished brewing. *How much did Paul and I drink?* She walked back to their bedroom and noticed the empty bottle of Brandy on the floor. *Okay, that answers my question. He's going to need coffee too.* She went back and got him a cup. "Paul, wake up I brought you coffee." He opened one eye then the other and reached for the mug.

Rose asked if he slept well. "Yes, I haven't slept that well in months. You think it has something to do with our marathon lovemaking session last night. Bloody hell, I ache!"

Rose didn't want to tell him she was feeling the same way. "I'm feeling a bit out of shape too, hon. Maybe we should start jogging."

"Oh my Giddy Aunt . . . jogging; are you completely deranged?" He sat up and looked at Rose and they broke into a fit of laughter.

"Poppet, instead of me and Keough hiring ranch hands, we could rent this place out as a fitness center calling it a *Ranch-to-work* program. Our slogan could be, *The Work is Tough but the Food is Worth the Pain.*"

Their laughter was interrupted by a car pulling into the driveway – it was Cecilia. Paul quickly put on his jeans and tee shirt. They both wanted to welcome her back and find out how Raymond was doing. Paul opened the door before she took out her key.

"Welcome back Your Highness we missed you Luv."

"Hello Paul, I've missed you too," she smiled, "and to quote Dorothy, *there's no place like home* or should I say the Ranch."

Once she was settled, he made her a cup of tea and Rose asked her about Raymond.

She explained that his condition was still fair but he looked better than when he left.

"I told him that he gave us all quite a fright! I also reminded him not to worry and that I'd be preparing his meals once he gets home. This won't happen again on my watch." Rose glanced over at Paul and he whispered *I think you should mention Mona and Chinchilla.*

"Eh, that may not be necessary Cecilia. There are two women who we met recently who will be helping with his care when Raymond was able to return home."

Rose went on to explain about Mona and Chinchilla and their qualifications.

Cecilia paused for a second. "Oh, I didn't realize he had other *women* coming in to help – okay, never mind. So, what would you like for dinner? I hope all the leftovers are gone. If not I'll toss them out. I wouldn't want my family eating three-day old food."

Rose looked over at Paul and shrugged.

Cecilia headed to her room to unpack. When Rose was certain she was out of listening range she asked Paul if she seemed annoyed by Mona and Chin' helping Raymond.

"Personally Poppet, I'd say she seems more jealous than annoyed."

"Yes, you're exactly right Paul." That's when it dawned on me that Cecilia might have feelings for Raymond other than friendship. "Well that would explain her toddling off to Billings."

"Methinks there's a budding romance brewing."

" Methinks you're right Paul."

Chapter 24

"Raymond, if you don't get into this wheelchair right now they won't let you leave the hospital!" Jameson had to fight to keep his friend in his seat until they reached the hospital lobby.

"I'm FINE Jameson! For the love of Dr. Phil, please stop coddling me. I can walk by myself! Just get the truck."

Jameson gave the valet parking attendant a twenty-dollar bribe to bring his truck next. "Raymond, I never noticed until now how much of a pain in the ass you are!"

Raymond shook his head and chuckled. "Yes I am and I can't tell you how many times I've wanted to lock you outside the cabin for the wolves to snack on. I just want to get home. Can you blame me? I've been living on broth and watered down juice for six days— not to mention this thing they've implanted in me!"

Jameson sighed, "It's called a stint. And, I wish they could have rammed one down your throat. Maybe it would keep you quiet for a while and give me a break from your incessant bitching!"

Raymond had to laugh at Jameson's frustration. He recognized that Jameson was a good guy and that he had acted like a real prick to his friend, but he hated being sick and feeling helpless.

The attendant put the truck in park and walked over to help Raymond.

"I'm good, so please don't help me anymore okay." Raymond attempted to stand up and but he felt his legs buckle. "Alright, perhaps I do need someone's arm just for a second until I get my sea legs back." Jameson snickered and said he'd be happy to offer his arm. "Thank you Jameson." He whispered *jerk* under his breath.

"Hey, I heard that!"

"Oh for the love of lard Jameson you're so annoyingly sensitive. "

Jameson opened the door and held out his arm again. "No let me try. I've got to gain my strength back." Raymond reached inside the door and grabbed what some folks call the Jesus handle, and swung himself into the passenger's seat. "Whoever created this extra handle was a genius, I must write the company and sing their praises."

Jameson stared at Raymond and then the parking attendant, who whispered *anesthesia residue; it'll wear off by the time he gets home.* The two buckled themselves in and headed to the interstate.

An hour into their drive, Raymond asked Jameson about his truck being at the hospital. "How did it get here?"

Jameson thought for a moment then answered. "I guess I could give you some of your ancient Blackfoot mumbo-jumbo about the Great Spirit magically transported it to Billings, but the truth is, I flew back to Malta and drove it back to the hospital!"

"Hah, that was a good one Jameson! I guess I deserved that smart ass answer. Perhaps, you haven't noticed, I'm not a very good patient."

Jameson smirked, "Yeah, ya' think?"

Raymond had fallen asleep during the drive but a loud announcement from Jameson that they were home startled him out of his deep slumber.

"Wow that was quick," Raymond remarked unaware that he had napped for almost the entire ride. "Normally, I can't sleep in a moving vehicle. Must be a control thing, huh?" Jameson just shook his head and helped him out of the truck. "It sure feels good to be home Jameson, and who the hell is car is parked in our driveway?" Before his friend could answer, Raymond noticed the two women with the car trouble that they had helped on Thanksgiving standing on his front porch.

"Welcome home Raymond. It's great to see you again and looking so healthy."

Raymond smiled. "I'm happy your car's repaired too. However, I must ask. Why are you two at my house?" He turned to Jameson, "Did you know about this?"

"Yes, yes I did. You'll need more care than I can give you Raymond, especially with the cooking. I can't boil water." He turned his back to Raymond, winked at Mona and Chinchilla and whispered, "I cook very well but he likes to do everything himself."

Jameson spun around and joked with his friend, "Raymond, I'm sure you remember the last time I tried to make you tea."

He laughed, "Yes, I still have the burnt tea kettle sitting on the back porch. Maybe I'll turn it into a planter." Jameson didn't have the heart to tell his friend that it was Raymond who fell asleep and burnt the kettle. "But getting back to these two young ladies, I really appreciate your concern but I'm quite capable of taking care of myself," he insisted. Mona and Chinchilla looked at each other and laughed.

"Yep, that's exactly what Rose said you'd say," Chinchilla chimed in. "Now Raymond, are you going to cooperate or do I need to put on my Nurse Bad-Ass Uniform?"

He shrugged his shoulders and decided not to argue.

Once Raymond was comfortably settled in his room, Jameson closed the door and joined Mona and Chinchilla in the front room.

"Thank you both for your help. He can be a total knob when he's not feeling well, but when I think about the hard times I gave him when I started my sobriety, it's worth every minute of the lighthearted abuse he gives me." Jameson told the two women how Raymond stood by his side during his road to sobriety. "He made me face my demons and I've been sober for three years and seven months. I owe him my life."

Jameson asked Mona and Chinchilla about their lives and how they wound up in Montana. Both Mona and Chinchilla shared how they ended up on the road trip of a lifetime.

"I guess you could say we were in the right place at the right time." Chinchilla boasted. "What's the probability of a nurse and a hospitality worker being rescued by the Montanas, then helping an ailing friend of their family? I mean come on, seriously—what are the odds!"

"Pretty damn good odds I'd say! And speaking of odds, what's the chance you two made dinner? I'm starving."

"I just put dinner on and we're having vegetarian lasagna and strawberry sherbet for dessert. Raymond's got to watch his cholesterol which means no more bacon or those inch-thick grilled cheese sandwiches he's been eating."

Jameson asked her how she knew they were an inch thick. "It's simple. I call it the cheese-to-bread ratio. If there's six slices of bread gone from a loaf and one slice of cheese left in the package then mathematically, you'd have to use at least three to four slices of cheese per sandwich."

"Mona you are by far one of the most, eh, unique people I've ever met."

She arrogantly added, "Hello, I also work in the food and beverage industry!" The three laughed at Mona's somewhat scientific analysis of Raymond's eating habits.

Jameson, Mona and Chinchilla finished dinner while Raymond slept. Soon afterwards, Jameson retired for the night. "Again, Mona, Chinchilla, thanks being here, You've been a tremendous help. If you even need a favor, please don't hesitate to ask."

Mona smiled and said, "It's my pleasure Jameson. Now go to bed, you look like a ghost! You are the whitest white guy I've ever seen! I can tell you're from New York City. You have that florescent light paleness."

"Mona, I have to agree with you. I've never been the outdoorsy type until I came to Montana."

"You know, Jameson, my nephew, Tucker Chapman Bernard or as we call him *"Tuc"* lives in Pago-Pago near the beach. When Raymond's feeling better maybe you both could come and visit us sometime."

Jameson's eyes widened. "Are you shitting me Mona? Your nephew is Tucker C. Bernard; the same Dr. Bernard who wrote the book, *Paranormal Pilgrimages – A Restless Soul's Journey.* I LOVE that book!"

"Yep, one and the same; he's my sister's kid."

"Mona, I have to ask . . . so, what's up with the white streak in his hair? Did he bleach it or is it natural?"

Mona shook her head. "Of all the scientific and logical questions you can ask me, you ask about his HAIR? Raymond was right . . . you are an asshole. I'll admit you're a loveable asshole but an asshole nonetheless!"

Their laughter woke Raymond. "What the heck is going on? Can't an old man get some much needed rest?"

The three apologized and told him they'd try to keep it down so that he could go back to bed.

"Nope, I'm hungry and something smells very good. That food they serve at the hospital, I wouldn't feed to my worst enemy. What's cooking?"

"Vegetable lagasgna, Raymond."

Raymond's face drooped in disappointment. "So, there's no meat in it – correct?"

"Correct. There's no meat in it," Mona confirmed.

"Well, that sucks. I guess I'll have to fry up some bacon to put over it."

"There's no bacon either. You, my fine recovering-from-a-heart-attack friend, are on a no-fat, low-cholesterol diet. There'll be no more clogged arteries on my watch."

He glanced over at Jameson. "Jameson, what foolishness is this – no meat?"

"They are the cooks and I just eat what they prepare, Raymond. Deal with it and besides it's pretty tasty!"

Chinchilla fixed him a plate. "Okay Raymond, dig in."

He took a fork full and sniffed it before tasting it. "Not bad, not bad at all. You all are safe. I won't have to scalp you in your sleep."

Jameson walked over and gave him a hug. "Raymond you must be feeling better because you haven't threatened to scalp anyone in months."

"Jameson," Raymond chided, "I think of scalping you all the time. I just don't tell you. The element of surprise is much more dramatic."

Mona offered Raymond some sherbet, but he passed on it saying he'd have it tomorrow with his lunch. He then said goodnight to everyone and went back to bed. They all thought it was a good idea to call it a night. "Again ladies thank you. It's been a real pleasure chatting with you both."

Jameson started to leave then turned back around. "And Mona, we may take you up on that Pago-Pago trip once Raymond is better." Mona gave him the thumbs up and said goodnight.

Chinchilla asked Mona about Tucker. "Okay Mona, so why am I just now hearing about your famous nephew? Is he cute, and more importantly, is he married?"

Mona pretended not to hear her. "Well Chin' I think I'll go saw some logs – goodnight." Chinchilla tailed behind her asking a litany of Tucker questions until Mona had to close the bedroom door in her face. "GOODNIGHT CHIN'!"

Everyone was exhausted from yesterday's activities. The vibration of Jameson's cell phone on the nightstand woke him up. It was 8:00 AM. Jameson grabbed his glasses and saw that it was

Rose. "Good morning Rose. Sorry I didn't call you last night. We were pooped."

She said she understood and was checking to see if they had made it home safely and if Raymond had adjusted to being home and having Chinchilla and Mona under his roof. Jameson told her how the first night went and how the two women had dinner prepared upon their return from the hospital.

Rose mentioned that she and Cecilia would be coming over to visit. "Okay Rose, I'll let Raymond know."

Jameson was about to go back to sleep when she aroma of coffee coaxed him awake. He peeped into the kitchen to find Raymond up and eating his sherbet.

"Good morning Jameson I thought since I can't have eggs or bacon I'll have dessert for breakfast."

Jameson beamed in amusement. "Good morning and good idea."

"Who called?" Raymond asked.

"Rose. She wanted to know how you were doing. I told her you slept well because I could hear you snoring through the wall. "I thought it was a rock slide. And while that was bad, it was your obnoxiously loud farting that woke me."

Raymond's chuckle resulted in a soft snort which made the two men laugh aloud.

"Anyway, I made coffee in case you were interested."

Jameson went to get a cup when he noticed a dirty plate in the sink. The quizzical look on his friend's face forced a confession from Raymond. "I had a piece of the cold lasagna as an appetizer before my breakfast sherbet.

"As long as you eat healthy and have a hardy appetite you can have anything you want. Just no more heart attacks, okay?"

Raymond put his hand over the left side of his chest and promised to keep his ticker going. "I've known for years that my bad eating habits would catch up with me. I just didn't think it would be so soon."

Jameson heard the bathroom door close and the sound of running water. A few minutes later, Chinchilla came stumbling into the kitchen wearing her sunglasses and mumbling what sounded like *coffee please*. Jameson grabbed a large mug from the cabinet and poured her a medicinal cup of morning brew. She removed her glasses and took a long sip. "Thank you Jameson. You are the best. Why is the sun so damn bright in Montana?"

Jameson suggested, "Well you did mention that you're from New Jersey correct? She gave a sleepy nod. He added, "I think it's because the air pollution is so bad it filters the sunrays.

"Or maybe it's because you're full of shit Jameson – ya' think?"

Jameson laughed so hard his sides started aching. "Ah Chinchilla, I really miss that east coast attitude. You know I lived in New York City all my life until I moved to Montana."

She scratched her head. "Why on earth did you move?"

Jameson reminded her of his drinking problem, and the fact that there is a bar on every corner in New York City and so on. She totally understood.

"I must say it's beautiful here. But it's way too quiet for me. If it weren't for Raymond and Mona's snoring I wouldn't have been able to sleep. I need the noise."

"I get it Chinchilla. It took me a year living in Montana before I could sleep without leaving the radio on. But I wouldn't trade all the clubs in Manhattan for this view."

They stood up and opened the curtains. The tall pine trees covering the looming mountain took their breath away.

"I could get used to this Jameson. Montana is truly a beautiful state." They heard Mona coming down the hallway. "Hey Mona, what do you think about me moving to Montana? I could become a cowgirl and work on a cattle ranch."

Mona rubbed her eyes and squinted. "I swear Chin' it's way too early in the morning for me to process your bullshit. At least let me have some coffee before I have to cuss you out."

Jameson's cell phone buzzed again. It was Rose saying she and Cecilia were about five minutes away. She mentioned that Cecilia had made her special morning breakfast casserole and she purposely made it healthy enough for Raymond to eat replacing the sausage with grounded turkey breast.

Raymond returned to the kitchen fully dressed. "Was that Rose calling again? Is she here?"

"Not yet, but she should be here any minute. And by the way Cecilia's with her."

He smoothed his hair. "Then it's a good thing I got dressed. I wouldn't want to welcome them in my underwear."

Mona was helping Chinchilla set the table for breakfast when Jameson heard Rose's truck pull into the driveway. Raymond beat him to the door but not before he took one last look in the mirror.

"You look fine."

"My hair too?"

"Yes your hair looks fine too. Rose will see that we're taking good care of you."

Raymond agreed. However, Jameson knew his friend was not primping for Rose. Cecilia carried the casserole and Rose carried two small bags. Raymond rushed to open the door.

"Hello ladies, I'm so happy to see you."

Rose handed Jameson the bags and Raymond took the casserole from Cecilia. Chinchilla took the food from Raymond and placed it on the table. Raymond hugged Rose, then Cecilia. Cecilia smiled at Raymond and told him how well he looked.

"Thank you Cecilia as do you. I believe this is the first time you've been to my house. And the first time I've seen you in slacks and a casual sweater. I'm so used to seeing you in your formal blouse and skirt. The look suits you"

Rose could tell that Cecilia was starting to blush so she changed the subject and asked how things were going.

"It doesn't look as though you're starving Raymond. I see Chin' and Mona run a tight ship, huh."

"Yes they do Rose, too tight for my liking. Did you know they threw out ALL of my bacon?"

Rose laughed. "Yes, I was the one who ordered it thrown away. Turkey bacon is your new best friend."

"You are evil Rose. And here I thought we were allies."

Raymond as soon as you're better I'll go back to being my kind and gentile self, but until then I'm your food Nazi."

The table was set and Chinchilla announced that breakfast was being served. Raymond took hold of Cecilia's hand.

"Cecilia I'd like to introduce you to Chinchilla and Mona. These are the two ladies who had the car trouble."

"Cecilia, I was surprised you didn't float in on a heavenly cloud the way these two guys talk about you – especially Raymond." Mona joked.

"Hah, don't listen to them Cecilia." Raymond quipped. "They're just jealous because they fly in on a dark thunder cloud."

I've never met such mean women in my life—torturing an old man the way they do. Yesterday they forced me to drink a green slime drink – a smoothie they called it. I think it had pond scum in it," Raymond continued with his whine. "I had to drink it all or they wouldn't let me have my sherbet. Mean spirited harpies they are."

Mona interjected, "It was KALE Raymond, healthy green kale! And there's more in the refrigerator to drink with this afternoon's lunch." He shook his head.

Rose looked over at Jameson and said, "Jameson, I'm starting to feel sorry for him."

"Rose, if I wasn't a recovering alcoholic I'd have Mimosas with breakfast just to drown out the bickering!"

After breakfast, Jameson let Rose know that he was going into town to pick up their mail. "During all of the commotion I'd forgotten about it. Most of it is bills and advertising, however, on occasion there's a hand written letter from my mother. In the world of emails and texting, there's nothing like a handwritten letter of encouragement. Alcoholism is a day-by-day battle Rose, one I'm committed to win."

Rose acknowledged his success and told Jameson that Joe would have been proud as is Keough and his mother.

"Thanks Rose," Jameson said. "Addiction affects the entire family. I've learned from Raymond to accept help from others without taking it as judgment and replace it with constructive love. I'm proud of me."

Rose gave him a tight hug. "Jameson you are a remarkable man. I can't believe that just a few years ago you were a drunken, conceited, jerk blasting Frank Zappa music in the bunkhouse."

"Aw Rose, don't hold back, please tell me what you really thought of me. But seriously, I'm so grateful to all of you for accepting me as a true Montana and happy to have such an awesome and beautiful sister-in-law."

"No truer words were spoken especially the beautiful sister-in-law part," joked Rose. The two hugged and Jameson put on his coat and started his truck so he could go pick up he and Raymond's mail.

About a mile down the road, Jameson noticed something wedged between the front seats. It was one of his old Mothers of Invention CDs. He popped it into the player. *How it was that these funny these songs sounded much cooler when I was drunk. I guess it was just music to drown out my miserable reality.* He popped the CD out and enjoyed the sounds of the mountains. He had never really appreciated the wind whistling through the hillside or the honking of the snow geese. Jameson pulled off the road and parked by the partially iced-covered river. It was so peaceful.

How much time I wasted hopping from noisy bar-to-bar, buying rounds of drinks for other drunken assholes. Wasting even more time dating dozens of gold-diggers who were only interested in my family's millions. I can't believe what a fucking schmuck I was. I had to come to Montana find the true Jameson. Who would have thought I'd ever change? I couldn't see myself changing my New York lifestyle. But Raymond and Rose could. They believed in me. Mother always did, but I was too drunk to appreciate it. She couldn't have any children and how did I repay her. I blew hundreds of thousands of dollars being a jerk. What a shameful thing for an adopted child to do to their parents. It took my birth father Keough a little longer to stop comparing me to my fair-haired twin brother, Lash. But over time Keough understood that he and I were more alike than he was willing to admit. Our drinking didn't hurt us, but it most definitely hurt the ones we loved the most. "I swear I'll never take another drink ever again!" he said aloud. He wiped his eyes, put the truck in drive and continued on to pick up the mail.

The Post Office parking lot was empty. He noticed the sign on the door which read, *Closed Due to Family Emergency – pick up mail at Jimmy's.* He continued driving hoping Jimmy had made fresh coffee.

His parking lot was full of trucks. *Everyone's picking up their mail I suppose.* Jimmy saw Jameson heading towards the door and handed him the mail. "I'd let you in but as you can see there's no room, but hold on a minute." He went back inside and came back with a very large container of coffee and a box of sweet rolls. "Here you go. Please tell Raymond I'll get up there to see him as soon as I can. I've put in an order for vegetarian baked beans and turkey bacon just for him. Thanks Jimmy, I'll let him know and thanks for the coffee and rolls."

Turning the truck around, Jimmy started to head back to the cabin but decided to pay his mother and Keough a visit. It'd been a few days since Raymond's heart attack and he thought he'd bring them up-to-speed on his condition. Figuring Rose and Cecilia would be there for a while chatting, Jameson knew Raymond would be in good hands. The joy of driving in this part of the country always helped him relax. It was nothing like the bumper-to-bumper Manhattan gridlock traffic. The road was clear and for a moment he could zone out. It was as if he were floating. Jameson was conscious of everything around him and the sounds seemed far away. *Maybe this is one of those spiritual moments Raymond's always talking about.* It was similar to the experience he had at one of his drum circle. However, he felt serene with no sense of panic. Jameson stayed with the feeling as long as he could. He came back to "consciousness" when he heard someone say, *don't look back, keep moving forward.* He stayed calm and asked aloud, "Who is this?" He heard the voice again. *Keep moving forward . . . Lucas.* "Lucas? Who the heck is Lucas? Jameson jotted down what he'd heard and tucked the paper into his shirt pocket.

"Maybe Raymond can explain this episode of weirdness to me. "Or, I'll ask Keough and Mother. Maybe they'll know who this Lucas person is? He poured some of Jimmy's coffee into his travel mug and continued on to the ranch.

It was late morning when he arrived. Paul's rig was still parked by the barn as was Keough's and Kurt's trucks. Jameson noticed Paul's work truck parked in the house driveway, and he pulled into the driveway behind him. His legs and back were a bit stiff. He stretched them out before he knocked on the door.

Paul answered the door with a dish towel draped over his shoulder. "Hello Paul, looks like I caught you in the middle of doing the washing up."

He laughed at Jameson's British use of his term for washing the dishes. "What are you doing all the way over here? Not that I mind you visiting but this is quite a surprise. Would you like a coffee? I just put a pot on."

"No thanks Paul I've still got half a container in the truck. But thanks for asking. Is my mother here or has she whisked Keough off on another bizarre adventure."

Paul laughed, "No, they're both here. They're over at the bunkhouse having a natter with Annie and Kurt. They've all become quite friendly."

Jameson asked about Morgan and Jannine. Paul said they were looking at houses. "Their little one is due in a couple of months so they'll need a home with at least three bedrooms. It'll be wonderful having them so close. Charlotte has already appointed herself as their official babysitter."

Paul and Jameson chatted for a few minutes. "I think I'll take a walk over to the bunkhouse and say hello. Say hi to Charlotte for me."

"I will Jameson and as always, it's a pleasure to see you. I'd better get back to the washing up before Rose gets home. With both ladies away, I get to make me own meals, which usually consists of a cheese omelet and toast. That's about all I can cook except for an occasional bowl of porridge. At least that's what I want them to think. Or I'd have the cooking and washing up duty."

Jameson winked, "Your secret is safe with me Paul."
"Raymond does all the cooking mostly because I've let him believe that I can't cook. Truth is I'm becoming a very good cook. But it's more fun keeping him in the dark or he'd have me cooking every night."

Paul gave Jameson a chuck on the arm, and then went back to the kitchen to finish his cleaning.

Jameson headed over to the bunkhouse. Keough and Kurt were coming out as he was about to knock on the door. "Well, lookie here brother, it's my nephew, howdy Jameson!"

Keough gave him a fatherly hug. "How are ya' son. Your mama's inside jawin' with Annie. I swear them two gals can talk a blue streak. I think their comparing designer shoe stories. So, what brings you to the ranch? Is Raymond okay?"

Jameson reassured Keough about Raymond's recovery and explained he was out picking up the mail when he thought he'd take a quick drive. "I needed to get out and clear my head. So much has happened in the past few weeks. It's a lot to process."

Keough agreed. "Yep, I'm still tryin' to accept Raymond almost dying."

"And let's not forget who saved his life – my daughter, the doctor." Kurt boasted. "In all my years, I never thought that sort of statement would come out of my mouth. I'm so grateful we found each other. I only wish I'd had the good sense and courage to search for her mother."

Kurt showed Jameson the photograph of Sylvie. "She's beautiful Kurt. And so is Annie. I'm surprised she's not engaged or married. A woman as smart and beautiful as Annie would have her pick of millionaires in Manhattan. If she wasn't my cousin, hell, I'd date her."

Kurt bristled. "You keep your eyes off my daughter, ya' heathen."

All three men laughed at his declaration of paternal protection.

"And on that note," Jameson interrupted, "I think I'll head inside to say hello to Mother."

Meryl must have heard Jameson's voice because she came out to welcome her son before he opened the door. "Hello my sweet son how are you doing?"

"I'm well, Mother. We haven't chatted much since you announced your marriage. I miss our mother-son lunches."

Jameson saw Annie and waved. "Hello cousin or should I call you Super Annie, you've become our local hero."

She laughed and flipped him the bird. "For goodness sake, will you all please stop this hero crap! I did my job. After all I am a doctor."

"Yes you are Annie; a very skilled doctor, who was in the right place as the right time," Jameson replied. "I don't know what we would have done if you weren't there."

Annie laughed, "You say that now, but wait until you all get my bill. And on that note Jameson, I'm going to head outside and pester my Dad. In my entire life that's a phrase I've never had the pleasure of uttering." She gave Jameson a pat on the back. "I'll leave you and Meryl alone to talk."

Mother asked her son to sit down. "Ever since you were a baby Jamie, I've learned to recognize that worried look on your face. What's wrong sweetheart?"

Jameson relayed to her what he experienced while driving to the ranch. "I heard a voice, a woman's voice to be precise."

Meryl slid forward in her chair. "What did you hear Jamie?"

I swallowed hard then told her. "It said *Keep moving forward Lucas.* I don't know anyone named *Lucas* Mother – do you?"

She paused for a moment, but then said, "Lucas was the name your birth mother, Charlotte, gave you when you were born. Lash and Lucas—her twin boys. When we adopted you, I changed your name to Jameson after my grandfather. He was a strong man, a vibrant man. He had the values that I instilled in you. And then you began drinking, and became quite arrogant and over privileged. Not knowing Keough's drinking history, I blaming that on your adopted father's side of the family. Pub creatures they were."

Jameson snickered at his mother's term *Pub Creatures*.

'I'm forever grateful to Raymond for putting you on the right path."

Her son nodded. "I'm grateful too Mother; he's been my Spiritual Advisor throughout my recovery. Raymond has me on this holistic healing health kick and surprisingly it seems to be working. I'm feeling better physically and mentally."

Meryl agreed. "So with that being said Jamie, tell me more about these voices you're hearing."

"Mother, I'm not hearing voices. I was enjoying my drive to the ranch when I heard the message. I guess you could say it was an ethereal message. Do you think the message was actually from my birth mother?"

Meryl sighed. "I don't know Jameson. Since I've known Raymond, he has me convinced that spirits visit us when we need guidance. Perhaps that's what happened to you."

"I never believed in his mumbo-jumbo until I went to one of his drum circles," Jameson noted. "I think there's something to his spirit philosophy, or I'm having hallucinations. Either way as long as they don't blame me for Jimmy Hoffa's disappearance, I'm good."

"Why Jameson, you are becoming quite the comedian. Jay Leno beware, Jamie Wellesley-Montana is now doing stand-up!"

As mother and son finished their conversation, Jameson remembered he didn't let Rose and Raymond know where he was. He excused myself and walked outside to get better cell phone reception. Rose's phone rang once.

"Jameson, where are you? We were worried. Did you get into an accident or even worse did you get lost again and end up in the Bitterroots of Idaho?"

"Gee Rose I'm touched that you and Raymond are worried about me. I'm really feeling the family love. But seriously, I'm at the ranch. I decided to take a ride and see Mother and Keough. I'm leaving in a few minutes."

"Okay, I'll let Raymond know. Be careful and we'll see you later. Oh, and can you bring some of Jimmy's . . ."

"I've already picked up a dozen for you Rose. I stopped at Jimmy's before I headed to the ranch."

"Did I ever tell you that you're my favorite brother-in-law?"

"As far as I know I'm your only Montana brother-in-law, and you're welcome. See you soon sweetie, bye."

Meryl walked Jameson to his truck and the two said their goodbyes. Keough, Kurt and Annie also walked over. Keough and Jameson hugged and told him to drive safely.

"Bye Jameson, I'll see you later," Annie said as she gave him a hug. "I'm flying back to California to formally resign from my position at LA Metro."

Her statement took Jameson aback "Wow, Annie that's a surprise. May I ask why?"

She told him about a position opening at Billings Metropolitan. "I think I'm going to apply. Montana is starting to grow on me and I'm quickly becoming a daddy's girl. Isn't that right Dad?"

Kurt walked over to Annie and kissed her cheek. "Yep, Jameson, we finally found each other and I'm never letting her out of my sight – ever." Annie rested her head on Kurt's shoulder and smiled in agreement.

Jameson hugged her again and said how happy he was for her and it'll be good to have her hanging around if for no other reason to keep Kurt and Keough in line.

"Someone has to make them toe the line Jameson. I'll be leaving tonight and back in plenty of time to pick out a Christmas tree with Charlotte. She made me pinky swear so I can't go back on that promise."

He started his truck and waved goodbye. *How lucky am I to be a part of this crazy, mixed up and wonderful ever-growing family. And, I wouldn't change a damn thing!* He cued Frank Zappa in the CD player and headed home. *Home, I really like the sound of that!*

Chapter 25

"Paul, would you help me hang the holly and garland around the front door?" Paul emerged from the kitchen with a step ladder.

"What's the matter Poppet, are you shrinking?" He joked.

"Ha, ha, very funny, no, I just wanted you to come out and help me." Rose raised her arm and touched the top of the door frame with her hand to prove she was more than capable. "I'm able to do it myself, but I love decorating with my husband – so sue me."

Paul held the ladder while she stepped up. *I could feel him staring at my butt.* "Thanks for your help dearest and you can stop looking at my butt."

Paul scratched his head. "Now why on earth would I want to stop looking at such a lovely derriere?" "

Okay, I'll accept your compliment. I guess it's true. Pilates do work." The two exchanged a quick tender kiss.

As promised, Annie returned back home to Montana well in time for Christmas. She was excited about starting her new position at Billings Metro in January. "I've found an apartment close to the hospital, and just a stone's throw away from you all. Well, maybe a little over a stone's throw. At least I'm in the same state. Of course, Dad insisted on checking the place out before I moved in."

Rose laughed at Kurt's transition into fatherhood and becoming a hover parent to his grown daughter.

In charge of decorating the interior of the house, Cecilia seemed to go overboard this holiday season. "Raymond missed Thanksgiving and I want to make certain he enjoys the upcoming holidays."

Paul and Keough decided to cut a tree from the ranch thickets. The area needed to be thinned out so that the younger trees could grow faster and healthier. The ranch's 15-foot ceilings could easily house a 10-foot evergreen tree. As promised, Charlotte and Annie accompanied them on their hunt for the perfect tree. Annie never had a fresh tree so she welcomed this new tradition. Charlotte announced she was going along to supervise.

"Last year's tree wasn't fat enough!"

"Okay, then you can go and help to pick a *fat tree,*" Rose told her daughter. "Please put on some old clothes so you don't get pine sap all over you." She gave Rose a big smile and dashed back to her room to change.

As much as Rose enjoyed the holidays, they tended to bring on a wave of melancholy. She and Joe never got to spend many holidays together. On the other hand, Paul loves the feeling of waking up on Christmas morning and watching Charlotte open her gifts. More than Christmas, Rose loved New Year's Eve. It was always exciting to realize that at 11:59 PM, an entire year would be at her door—an entire new beginning. She remembered telling Paul that to her, New Year's felt like time travel. It was the one and only time, she could leap into a new beginning and new adventure. Rose was also grateful that Raymond was with them to see another year and hopefully many more to come. She couldn't imagine how she could live without him in their lives. And she knew Joe wasn't ready to see him yet. Heaven isn't large enough to house both of them. Rose did miss their banter which on the surface seemed contentious was actually a loud demonstration of their love for each other.

The phone ringing interrupted her musing. I didn't recognize the number; however, I did recognize the area code. It was Silicone Valley, California. *It's probably one of those telemarketing companies.*

"Hello, Montana Ranch, Amelia Montana-Saxton speaking." There was a brief pause, then a vaguely familiar voice answered me back.

"Hello is this Amelia Matthews?"

I thought, *I haven't used my maiden name Matthews in years?*

"Yes, this is she. May I ask whose calling?"

"It's Donovan . . . your brother."

For a second Rose was stunned. She had not heard from any of her family since she married Joe. She paused, caught her breath and then continued talking.

"Hello Donovan, it's been quite a while–years to be exact. What do you want?"

"Yes, it has been. So I guess you're wondering why – correct?"

"YES it has. And, again I ask, what do you want and why are you calling?"

I was not in the mood for twenty questions. More than likely it was a call for money. He was a Trust Fund Baby and the only boy in the family. Father always treated him like the Grand Prince of California.

"Okay, I suppose I deserved your pointed questioning, so I'll cut to the chase. I'm calling to inform you that Father passed away three weeks ago. I thought you'd like to know. His death was big news in California. His obituary was featured in Fortune 500."

Such news should have upset me, but I'd been estranged from him for so long it didn't faze me.

"Well Donovan, I'm sorry to hear about *your* loss. I assume you'll be taking over the company so I know this call isn't about money. Are you still gambling?"

"Amelia, I don't want to get into a pissing match on the phone. Perhaps I can come see you and we can finalize the estate paperwork. I'm taking off the rest of December. I can be on a plane tomorrow. I don't like this anymore than you do, but it's time we resolved this childish feud and handle Father's affairs."

Rose thought the term *Father's affairs* was appropriate knowing that he'd cheated on her mother so many times she'd lost count by the time I was 12-years-old.

"Childish? I'm being childish! Then how about we *children* call our lawyers and let the adults handle it!"

There was a pause and then a long sigh.

"Okay Amelia, I apologize. I didn't want this to turn into an argument. I just wanted to inform you of Father's death and hopefully see my big sister in the process. You are the only family member that answered my call. Our sisters told me they didn't care about Father or his money after he married that gold digger, who by the way you'll be happy to know, received nothing from him."

For a moment she felt some relief that Father had the good sense not to leave her a dime. But she wasn't ready to forgive her brother for not supporting her when she told him she was marrying Lash. It was to be expected from her sisters, but not her baby brother. They had always been close as kids.

Donovon continued. "Oh, and please accept my condolences on the death of your husband. He was a huge public figure in

California. His generous funding supported our New Laptop Program for intercity schools. Our Information Technology Division thought very highly of him. And, I also heard you remarried? Congratulations."

"Thank you on both accounts Donovan. However, about you coming to Montana, let me think about it and I'll get back to you."

"That'll be fine. It was good reconnecting with you Sis. Take care. I hope to hear from you, however, if I don't . . . Merry Christmas."

He hung up before she could respond.

Rose called for Paul to come into the family room. He immediately saw that she was upset. "What's wrong Poppet? Was it the phone call? Who was it?"

"You're not going to believe this, but it was my brother Donovan. He wanted to let me know that our father died."

Paul hugged me. "Oh Poppet I'm so sorry. Are you going to California?"

"No Paul he died weeks ago." Rose explained their running feud and how both he and her father had been estranged from her for years. "He wants to come to Montana so that we can sort out Father's estate."

"Are you up for this?" Paul asked.

"Not really Paul, I haven't seen him in decades. But I consider this an emergency so I told him I'd call him later and let him know."

"Whatever you decide I'll support." Rose thanked him and kissed his cheek. "All in a day's work Poppet. How about I make you a nice cup of tea to sooth your nerves, would you like that?"

"Yes, that would be wonderful, and if you threw in a back massage you'll definitely get laid tonight."

A broad grin spread across his face. "That my dear is a deal."

While the tea was brewing Rose mentioned to Paul that she'd been feeling extremely tired. "I think I need to start taking vitamins or something. I'm not getting any younger you know and between the ranch and Charlotte I'm feeling run down."

Paul reminded her of Raymond's episode. "That wore me out more than you can imagine; almost as much as Lash's death. But I'd do it again in a heartbeat. I honestly don't know what this family would do without Raymond."

Rose nodded in agreement. "Neither would I Paul. He's the first person I met when I came to Montana. I had no idea that he and Joe were friends. Even then he was more like a father to me than my birth father; always ready to expound fatherly advice and wisdom." Rose's thoughts made a wide pivot. "Speaking of which, before they rushed him to the hospital he said he had something to tell me? I'll have to remind myself to ask him about it later."

Rose was about to call Raymond when the phone rang again. It was Joe's former doctor, Theodore Jacobs.

"Hello Theo. My goodness it's been quite a while since we've heard from you."

"Yes, it's been a while Rose, how are you and the family doing?"

Rose told him they were doing well however Raymond gave them a scare.

"I know that's why I'm calling. I wasn't his doctor but the word spread that he'd had a heart attack on Thanksgiving. I just wanted to call and hear how he's doing. I remembered that he and Joe were very close friends."

"I can assure you Theo he's doing well. In fact, he's being pampered by three lovely ladies so he's definitely in heaven so to speak."

"Hah, well it sounds like he's in good hands. I also wanted you to know that I'm retiring next month. Sorry for the short notice, however my replacement is a fine doctor. I believe you know her, Doctor Annabella Harrison."

"YES, I know her extremely well, Theo. She's Kurt's daughter and my new-found niece! You've got nothing to worry about with Annie – she's top notch."

"Indeed she is Rose. I'm very happy she decided to stay in Montana and take the position. She even insisted we hire her personal administrative assistant, some young fellow named, Myers MacNamara. He's smart . . . and via the hospital grapevine, a very handsome young man. The female nurses' assistants are already talking about him and they haven't even met him yet. Annie said he's going to wait a while before she tells them he's gay."

The two chatted for a few more minutes about how life has a way of working out for the best.

"Even in our darkest times, there's always a beacon of light that helps us through it." I said.

"Dr. Harrison is definitely my beacon. I wanted to retire five years ago. After Joe died, I just didn't have it in me to work in the field of Oncology anymore. I was hoping that science would have a cure for this ugly disease by now. Hopefully in our lifetime, but for me . . ." he hesitated, "I can't watch another person wither away. After decades of private practice it gets to a person. But losing friends to this disease, Rose it gets harder and harder. So when I heard Raymond had a heart attack I decided to hang up my white coat and move to Hawaii. I'm leaving the end of January."

"Theo, I totally understand and I'm happy for you. You've earned your retirement twice over. Hell, I thought you would have quit after dealing with Joe. He was screwy enough to send Sigmund Freud running to a psychiatrist."

The two enjoyed the laugh at Joe's expense.

"Well, Rose, I'd better get going. I still have to box up both my home and hospital offices. You and Paul take care; give my love to Raymond and a very Merry Christmas to you all."

"Merry Christmas to you too Theo and please keep in touch now that you'll be a professional beach bum."

"Hah, I promise I will Rose. I'll expect a visit from you all once I'm settled in okay. Take care Rose, Bye."

Rose had just ended the call when Paul walked in. She told him about Theo Jacobs and his new plans. "He's retiring and moving to Hawaii of all places."

Paul clapped his hands, "Good on him! He's earned it. We can add him to our places to vacation."

Rose also shared how Annie was appointed to replace him and is taking over his practice.

"Now that's bloody brilliant! I bet Kurt is prouder than a peacock of that girl."

"Yes, imagine finding out you have a child you never knew about. Must be mind-blowing, especially when you realize they're a big shot doctor." Rose walked over to the refrigerator to get some juice when she started to feel dizzy. Paul came over and held her arm.

"Poppet you look a bit pale. Perhaps you should lie down for a bit."

She agreed with Paul. "Yes, I think I'll take a nap. I haven't felt well since yesterday. All of the excitement I suppose."

He walked her to the bedroom. "I'll make you a cup of tea later, but for now you get some rest." He tucked her in and kissed her forehead. "I love you Amelia."

"I love you too Paul."

Rose didn't remember falling asleep, but she did remember dreaming about Italy and the villa where Joe and she spent their honeymoon. She remembered how warm the sand felt and how the ocean breeze blew through her hair. She woke up smiling and wondering if it was still available for rent. How relaxing it would be for she and Paul to take a much needed getaway. Paul and Rose hadn't really taken a vacation since they had married.

She put on her robe on and walked into the living room. The house was unusually quiet. *What's going on? Where is everybody?* She looked at the clock. It was 6:00 PM and she realized she had slept the entire day away. The family room was completely dark. She made her way to the light switch and before she could flip the lights, the entire area lit up and a roaring SURPRISE echoed throughout the room.

Paul, Charlotte and Annie had decorated the tree. She had never seen anything so beautiful in her entire adult life. Charlotte ran over and grabbed her hands. "Mama isn't it awesome! We wanted to surprise you. Paul said you didn't feel good. I thought this would make you feel better. Do you feel better Mama?"

Rose could feel her eyes well up with tears. "Oh Baby Girl it's lovely." Paul asked if she was feeling better.

"I am. I just needed a nap. I'm feeling much better now especially waking up to this wonderful surprise."

Charlotte gave her mother a huge hug. "This is going to be the best Christmas ever!" She squealed.

"Why's that Baby Girl?"

"Because Sawyer's daddy's rodeo is this weekend and we're all going – right? Sawyer is so excited to see me . . . eh, I mean us. I can't wait!"

Rose panicked knowing she had completely forgotten about the rodeo. "Yes, it'll be wonderful."

Paul looked at her knowing she had forgotten about it. He whispered *"I'll remind you of the details later, okay?"* He then turned his attention back to Charlotte. "YES, it's going to be brilliant, Charlotte. Maybe they'll even let me ride a bull. What do you think?"

His stepdaughter rolled her eyes at him and muttered something to the effect that he'd be bucked off in less than three seconds and hit the ground like a sack of potatoes.

After the lighting of the tree, Rose mentioned to Annie that Dr. Jacobs called, singing her praises. "Yes, he said he was going to call you personally to tell you about his retiring. He also told me about much you and Lash or Joe as he called him, loved each other. He said that your love was a once-in-a-lifetime sort of love; the kind that lasts even after death. Is that true Rose? Do you still love Joe?"

Rose asked her to sit down with her. "Annie, Joe and I had a whirlwind love—an insanely, magical love. It was so romantic people thought it was sickening, saying that no one could ever love anyone that much. Well, Joe did. He did from the moment we met. Our love was short-lived but it felt like a thousand lifetimes. However, my love for Paul is just as extraordinary—in a different way – if that makes sense?"

Annie shook her head. "Rose, I wish I could tell you that I know what that feels like, but I can't. I'm married to my job and never have time for long term romance. Dinner and maybe a movie is my limit."

Rose put her arm around Annie's shoulder. "You are a beautiful woman Annie. I know you'll find someone special when you're ready. And even if you're not ready, it will find you. Trust me I know. When I asked Joe why me? Why do you think we were meant to be together, he simply said one word – fate. And he was right." Sometimes things are just left up to fate. The right place at the right time."

"Rather serendipitous if you ask me," Annie added.

"Yep, that's the exact same word Raymond used when Joe and I first met," Rose countered. "He and Joe were friends long before I came into the picture. In fact, when I first came to Montana I got horribly lost and ended up at Raymond's place. And I stayed in the same cabin Joe used to stay in when he did his research work. How's that for serendipity?"

"Rose that sounds so unbelievably made up that it has to be true. Or like they say, sometimes in life *is* stranger than fiction. I mean, come on. Look at my course of events that led me here. What are the odds?"

Annie went to the cabinet and brought out the bottle of bourbon. "How about a drink to our crazy mixed up and totally insane reality." "I think I'll pass on the bourbon. I'm feeling really dehydrated. I think it's all of the holiday foods. I'll stick to water on the rocks."

We toasted to our bizarre lives and to the upcoming New Year. Annie was about to take a sip when she told me Mona and Chinchilla called and asked if Rose would call them. "Thanks Annie. I'd better call now before it gets too late."

The phone rang once when Cecilia answered. "Hello Rose I'm glad you called…"

"Is everything okay, Cecilia?"

Cecilia heard the worry in her voice. "Yes, he's fine; however, Chinchilla's father was in a car accident. He's bruised from the airbag, but okay. Understandably, she and Mona left this afternoon to be with him. I was wondering, if it's okay with you, that I stay here for the night. Just to keep an eye on Raymond. Jameson is quite capable, however, I'd feel better staying here."

"I totally understand Cecilia and of course it's fine. If you haven't noticed I'm becoming sort of a decent cook. I only burnt two pots this month." Rose heard a muffled giggle on the other end.

"Okay then. I'll be home tomorrow afternoon. Raymond is getting better and better every day. And to be honest I think he's getting a bit annoyed with everyone hovering over him. Again, thank you Rose for your understanding. He also wants me to tell you that you should be prepared for his healthy appetite. He said he intends to eat twice as much to make up for his missing Thanksgiving – healthy foods of course."

"That's fine by me Cecilia. Oh and remind him that he had something to tell me. Do you know what it was?"

"No I can't say that I do Rose but I'll have him call you in the morning."

"Of course Cecilia, have a good night and I'll see you tomorrow."

"Everything okay?" Paul asked when he came into the room.

"Yes, it was Cecilia; she's staying at Raymond's place tonight. Chinchilla's father was in a car accident and she's heading home to New Jersey with Mona."

Paul was about to walk away when he said, "Oh and before I forget Poppet, I promised I'd remind you about the Las Vegas Rodeo this weekend. Charlotte's been pestering me about it and I told her I'd let her know tomorrow."

"Paul, to be honest, there's been so much going on, I really don't want to go. But we promised her."

"I'll tell her yes, but I may stay here, if you guys don't mind."

Paul sat next to Rose and said, "I must admit Poppet, I really don't fancy going either. You've been looking a bit *poolie* lately and I think it's best you take it easy."

Rose squinted at Paul and asked him to refresh her memory of what *poolie* meant. "You know poolie, sick, not feeling well . . . poolie!"

You could have just said SICK! Rose almost said it aloud, but Paul was being so sympathetic that she let it go. "I think you're just run down Poppet. Why don't you stay in bed for a few days and let me take care of everything."

"That would be wonderful Paul. And that's why I love you so much." She kissed him on the cheek so as not to give him whatever 24-hour bug she might have. "With the extra company and all of the drama it's no wonder I'm exhausted."

Maybe my dream about Italy was a good premonition. Conceivably after the holidays Paul and she could take a well-deserved vacation to that charming Villa on Elba Island. She curled underneath their large quilt and drifted off to sleep.

The next morning, she awoke to Paul's gentle shaking. "Poppet, wake up Poppet." The scent of toast, coffee and strawberry jam filled the bedroom.

"Paul, you made me breakfast in bed. You are too sweet! What time is it?"

He sat on the edge of the bed and nibbled on a piece of her toast. "It's 11:00 AM. Why do you ask? Do you have somewhere to go? The answer is no, you don't. So enjoy being pampered for a change and a gracious thank you would be polite."

Rose leaned over and kissed him. "Thank you, kind sir; you are a prince, and why is the house so quiet?"

He hopped onto bed with her. "Well darling if you must know, we have the entire house to ourselves. Annie, Kurt, Charlotte, Keough and Meryl all flew to Las Vegas to see JT McCabe and

Keough took Lou with them so he's taken care of as well. Speaking of Lou, did you know he's 14-years-old? He doesn't look a day over ten. That's seventy or eighty years old in dog life. I should look so good at his age."

Rose asked him about Jannine and Morgan. "Jannine called last night. They wouldn't be going to Vegas because they found a house! She explained that they have to fill out all sorts of paperwork and banking information which needs to be completed before they make settlement. They're so excited about it. Morgan sent photos to your cell phone. However, they did say, they would be back in time for Christmas Eve, which by the way is in seven days."

"That's amazing news Paul! I understand Jannine and Morgan not going to Vegas, but I have to ask, how did you get everyone else to go without me?

Paul rolled his eyes then cleared his throat. "My dearest, as much as you think you are the center of the Montana universe, I am quite capable of taking care of such minuscule tasks on my own."

"Ah but truth be told, it was Meryl who made it all happen." She called for the Wellesley Corporate jet and they all departed two hours ago. Charlotte called from the plane and asked if we saw her waving as they flew over the ranch. Of course I said yes and thanked her for letting us know that she was having so much fun without us."

Rose leaned into him and kissed him again. "Paul you are a natural with children. Now don't take this the wrong way but I'm surprised you never had any of your own. We've never discussed the subject but I have to ask, do you want children?"

He shrugged his shoulders. "I guess. To be honest Poppet I've never thought about having a wee one of my own. Being on the road as much as I was, it seemed like a cruel thing to do to a child and a wife. However, I'd be willing to rethink the subject if you're interested."

"I admire your honesty Paul and to be completely honest with you I think I'm too old to have another baby. I'm almost . . . well let's just say I'm not getting any younger, so if we want to have a child of our own we'd better get started. But the way I'm feeling right now I think I'd rather wear a barbed wire bikini than run around with a toddler again."

For a moment the smile drifted from Paul's face and transformed into a forced grin. "I understand Poppet. And as always you're amazingly correct. Imagine us attempting to run after a 2-year-old; our wrinkled hands grasping our Zimmer frames with the tennis balls on the bottom." They both laughed at his aging vision.

"Paul I'm not saying no. I'm just saying let's think about it, okay?" He nodded and asked if Rose needed anything else before he went to feed the horses.

"I'm good Paul – are you?" He gave her a quick smile that told her he was fine. "You rest and I'll be back in time to fix you lunch."

Rose wondered if she had hurt Paul's feelings. *Does he really want children? Maybe when I'm feeling better we'll approach the subject again. At the moment I feel like I've been run down by a semi-truck. Amelia you need vitamins and a vacation! But for now a hot shower will do.*

The long shower rejuvenated her and eased her aching back. Moving all of Raymond's furniture to accommodate two extra guests took a toll on her muscles. That reminded her she needed to make an appointment for her New Year's checkup. It's something she did every January. She looked forward to starting the New Year off knowing she was healthy and raring to go. It was also a promise she made to Joe after he was diagnosed with cancer. *I'll email my doctor and schedule it.*

Rose realized she hadn't checked her email in nearly a week. She assumed there would be hundreds of junk emails to delete. She slipped on one of Paul's shirts, pinned her hair back into a ponytail and logged in. *I remember doing the same thing before I read Joe's emails. Oh well, that was long ago and now my emails are mostly Charlotte's classroom assignments and freelance offers.*

Rose was, as Paul would say, *spot on* about the amount of emails. There were no less than 100 in her inbox. She scrolled through them, deleting them in bulk, when low and behold one subject title jumped out at her: *Vincent Van Gogh Lends an Ear 2 of 2.* For a second she froze. She stared at it, *Joe's part two of two.* She was debating whether or not to open it or just delete it along with the rest of them. *Oh, what-the-hell Amelia, go ahead and open it. She* took a deep breath and clicked on the email.

To: Rose
Fr: Montana Joe
*Subject: **Vincent Van Gogh Lends an Ear – Part 2 of 2***
My Dearest Rose Darlin',

I guess by now you were wonderin' when you'd ever get part two of two of this email. Well darlin' I wanted to wait a while before having this one sent to you. By now Paul has told ya' about the conversation we had. I'm sorry I couldn't tell ya' personally but you know cowboys ain't supposed to cry and I wouldn't have been able to hold back the tears. I want you to live a good life. I want you and my child to live the life I won't be able to give ya'. Paul is a good man, a fine man, a man I'd trust to raise our child and be with you. Now, I know what you're thinkin'. How in the name of Wyatt Earp I will ever know if you chose Paul. I won't. But I know my Rose Darlin'. I know she's able to take care of herself and she knows a good man when she sees one; besides ME, that being Paul, of course. I don't want you to mourn the rest of your life away. I want you to laugh, love, travel, and sing . . . well maybe not sing, 'cause I've heard you sing. In fact, I distinctly remember your singin' and it ain't pretty baby. But if singin' makes you happy, then sing your heart out darlin' and please understand that's all I ever wanted was your love which you gave me so willingly.

Now, I have another surprise (more like a confession) to tell you. I told you I was a man of many surprises and you know I don't lie darlin' at least not on purpose, but that's another story. This one I hope you and your husband (again, hopefully Paul) will enjoy. Remember the Italian villa we stayed at on our honeymoon. You enjoyed it so much – well, I bought it. It's yours Rose. Take the family there for vacations or make it your personal retreat. Maybe you'll start writing again. Hey, you could write our love story. About how we met, how we fell in love, how this crazy cowboy wouldn't give up on ya'. You're an excellent writer darlin'. But our story is so over-the-top romantic nobody would believe it's true, so I reckon you'll have to list it as fiction, hah, but we know better don't we darlin'. Romance like ours does exist. It's just most folks are too dadgum afraid to take that leap of faith. Just look at what they're missin'. The love of their life could be standin' right beside 'em in the supermarket, but they ain't got the dang courage to say howdy or strike up a conversation with 'em. Being afraid is an awful thing Rose – a terrible thing. Never be afraid to face your fears and be willin' to cross that bridge when you get to it. Don't hesitate! No one knows how much time they have left, so never take time for granted. This cowboy spent so much of his life searchin' for you.

Knowin' you were out there somewhere and wantin' me to find you. Sadly, once we found each other . . . cancer found me. Without a doubt I'd say that's lousy timing. But such is life.

My beautiful Rose Darlin', this is the last of my emails I've asked my lawyer to send. They'll be one more message I've asked Raymond to deliver to you. I hope he remembers.

Until then, give our child a hug and kiss, tell 'em I'll love 'em and remind him or her they're everythin' I've ever wanted and hoped for, even though I haven't met him or her yet or maybe I did. I guess I'll never know.

Well darlin', my eyes are becomin' as weak as this ol' cowboy writer's body. I still have those two daffodils ya' gave me. They're still sittin' over by my chaps where ya' left them. Sorry to say they're fadin' fast, just like me. Be strong for me my Amelia Rose, stay sweet and love me as long as you're able. You'll be in my heart forever.

Tu eres mi amor de verdad, Love, Joe
P.s. If you haven't figured out yet, my valediction is written in Spanish. Ask Morgan to translate for you.

Rose took off her reading glasses and dabbed her eyes with the end of her shirt sleeve. She couldn't hold back the flood of tears. She cried. she cried harder than she'd ever cried. She needed to cry. Because it finally hit her, she never truly mourned Joe's death. She was too busy keeping the Montana Empire together. He's still a huge part of their lives, her life. She chained everyone to him and her memories of him

I thought, *how did he know Paul would ask me to marry him or I had a dream about Italy. It's like his psyche is linked to mine.*

She stood and looked up at the skylight and said aloud, "It's time Joe. It's time for me to let you go. I've kept you in my heart long enough and now it's time to make more room for Paul. I need that room for him Joe, I love him. I'll never forget you, but it's time for me to let go and live outside of the larger-than-life Montana Joe shadow. You've got to help me. Please help me Joe; because I don't know how, I don't know how to let you go? It's not like we had a lifetime of memories together. Our marriage was unexpectedly short lived. But the impact you made was extraordinary. Everything I do or see reminds me of you. "Maybe I should sell this place and build a new home. Would that be fair to Charlotte? I don't know. This is the only home she's ever known. It's our Montana legacy. You built this legacy for us Joe but I don't want it to become your shrine."

Rose sat back on the bed and continued to cry. She cried so hard her throat and face ached. As she was wiping the tears from her face Paul walked in. He walked over to her and held her. He never said a word. He instinctively knew what was going on. He let her cry. After about fifteen minutes he asked if she felt better.

"Honestly, I don't know. I thought that I had accepted Joe's death but obviously I haven't. And I've dragged everyone into my misery. Who does that to their family?"

Paul sat down with her on the bed. "Amelia, you are a brilliant, beautiful and extraordinary woman. Joe saw it, I see it, and the entire Montana family sees it. You are the glue that holds us all together. If it weren't for Joe meeting you, there wouldn't be a unified Montana family. Who brought Keough and Joe together? Who figured out that Jameson was Joe's twin? Who introduced Meryl to Keough and if it weren't for Keough, Kurt would never have found his daughter Annabella. Jannine would never have met Morgan. And most importantly Charlotte, that incredibly beautiful Bah-Bee wouldn't be here. When you connect the dots together, they draw a very lovely outline of Amelia Matthews Montana Saxton. You, my darling, are the key person. Again, I say if it were not for you we'd all be scattered to the winds never knowing we are part of this fantastic family. In fact, you're the Mitochondrial Eve of Montana! It all began with YOU!"

Rose had to smile at his comparison. Paul's observation helped her more than he realized. She was too busy living in her grief to let it go. Rose told him about the email she had received. He clicked on the link and read it.

"Well, Poppet I think it's pretty clear what he wants you to do. He closed the email and started to log out of her email page. She reached over and grabbed his hand.

"Wait Paul, don't log out yet. There's something I must do." She clicked on the folder where she had stored every single email that Joe had sent her. She checked the select all box. Paul placed his hand on her hand.

"Are you sure you're ready to do this Amelia?" She took a huge breath and said, "Yes, Paul, I'm sure. It's time."

"Then carry on Amelia."

Rose clicked delete. In the blink of an eye, hours of correspondence were gone. Paul asked if she was going to delete the deleted files. She wiped her eyes and whispered, "Baby steps, Paul, baby steps."

The two decided to forego dinner. She wasn't very hungry and Paul was too worried about her to reheat Cecilia's lasagna. Paul's other culinary specialty was omelets. He made two while Rose put together a tossed salad. She ached from the crying but felt relieved by her decision to release Joe. She had to stop living in the past or as Joe would tell her *you'll miss the perfect now and have no chance of enjoying the future.* She wanted to have a full life with Paul. She wanted him to have all of her, not just the parts left over from Joe. He deserves that and more.

"Are you happy? Are you happy you married me?" Rose asked.

Before she could ask another question he stopped her. "Amelia, my dear sweet Poppet; YES, I'm happy I married you. I knew what I was getting into and I accept you for who you are. I completely understood that I'd be sharing a part of you with Lash until you were ready to let him go. Lash will always be a part of your life because of Charlotte, who by the way, I love like my own child. She's bright, funny, and fearless just like her Mum. And I wouldn't change one thing – not one! I love you Amelia. Always have, always will."

After eating, the two decided to watch a movie. The deafening silence was broken by one of Paul's favorite films, *Monty Python and the Holy Grail.* Rose hadn't seen it in a while and forgot how hilarious it was. Paul said how he could watch it over-and-over and still laugh at the iconic scenes that have grown so popular through the years.

Paul shouted out the famous lines and then he shouted, "Oh my giddy Aunt, it's bloody brilliant!" Rose laughed at his British expressions. "Paul we've been married for a while and I still don't understand half of what you say."

He leaned over and kissed her on the forehead. "As it should be dearest, as is should be. If you knew what most of my expressions meant, you'd thrash me about the head with a brick."

A few days later, their quiet couple time was over. The house was back to normal, with laughter, stories about the Vegas rodeo, and Jannine and Morgan excited about moving into their new home in Billings. Keough and Meryl decided to stay in Vegas for a few more days to take in the nightlife. Kurt and Annie flew from Vegas to Los Angeles to retrieve her apartment belongings and clean out her hospital office. She told Meryl that she wanted to show off her handsome Montana cowboy father to her friends. They all promised they'd be back before Christmas. Raymond and Jameson stopped by to thank Cecilia and Rose for all their help during his recovery.

"Cecilia told me how often you dropped by to check on me. How lucky a man am I to have two lovely ladies doting over such an old geezer?"

Rose told Raymond how happy they were to see him out and about.

"If only you knew Rose. Jameson never lets me sit around and vegetate; not on his watch? He has me walking a mile every day. I tell you Rose, the man is an evil demon!"

She laughed and said, "It's for your own good, dear. I never ever want to see anything like that happen to you again – understood?"

He nodded yes and took a large bite of carrot stick. "Rabbit food, that's what Cecilia has me eating Rose . . . RABBIT FOOD!" He walked over to Rose and whispered *I'll give you a thousand dollars if you fry me two pieces of bacon.* He dug into his pockets as if the money had magically appeared.

"Ha, no can do Raymond. Keep your money. You do remember between my own money, Paul's funds and the Montana Legacy – we're billionaires?"

"See what I mean Rose that loony prairie flea of a former husband of yours still takes the Mickey out of me. Did I use the term correctly Paul?"

Paul chuckled. "Yes, yes you did Raymond Ol' Chap!" Paul turned toward everyone saying next he'll be singing *God Save the Queen* and eating crumpets instead of toast.

While everyone was being entertained by Paul's repertoire of British slang, she pulled Raymond aside and asked him about the message from Joe that he wanted to tell her before he was rushed to the hospital.

"Rose, the entire episode is a blur. I know I told the doctor to write it down and I don't know what he did with it. In fact there's not much I do remember from that night. I remember feeling light headed and then an elephant sat on my chest or at least that's what it felt like."

As much as she wanted to know what Joe had to say, she didn't want to put any undue pressure on Raymond. Rose told him it was okay and not to worry about it. She also confided in him about deleting all of his emails.

"It's for the best Raymond. I'll never move on if I'm constantly being haunted by his memory. However, I did save the final email I received last week from him. I didn't tell Paul but I saved it in a desk top folder I use for my freelance writing. If you feel up to it would you read it and see if there's anything that helps you remember the message he said to you? I need closure and letting go of Joe and his messages will bring it about for me."

Raymond agreed. The two friends walked into her office and she printed out the email. He put on his reading glasses and slowly read it. After finishing, he removed his glasses and said, "Just when I think he's a total asshole, he goes and writes something as beautiful as this."

Raymond's eyes started to well up as did Rose's. "Rose, all I can say is it sounds as though he wants you to let him go. Maybe that's the message he gave me – I just don't remember. But I promise I'll look in my hospital emergency bag. Perhaps it's in there. I just haven't had the strength or the nerve to go through it – bad memories. However, I promise I will look when I get home."

Rose thanked him for reading the email and listening to her struggle with closure. "You're welcome Rose. You know I'd do anything to help you and Nadie."

He stopped for a second as if he'd remembered something then continued talking. "And, did I read correctly that Joe bought you the Villa in Italy where you spent your honeymoon?"

"Yes, Raymond he sure did – crazy huh?"

"Would you expect anything less from that unbalanced ferret?"

She told him no, and that she wouldn't have it any other way.

"He was the love of my life Raymond, and so is Paul. How did two men, two magnificent men, fall in love with me? Incredibly lucky I guess."

Raymond interrupted me. "Luck you say? I don't think so! Luck has nothing to do with it Rose. You were meant to meet these two men and to be the spirit of hope for this incredible Montana family. It is YOU who chose this family, not the other way around. The universe has a way of working out what is needed and who needs to supply it. You, my dear Rose, are that person for this family – if this makes sense."

I shook my head no. "None of this makes sense to me, but I trust your Native American wisdom even if it sounds like bullshit."

"Ha, you are becoming as wacky as Joe was – and I love it!"

"Now, how about we go back into the family room and enjoy ourselves. They're probably wondering if I had another heart attack and passed out in a closet thinking it was the bathroom."

"RAYMOND, that's not funny!" Rose scolded.

He laughed, "Yes, it is, and you know it!"

Jameson eventually came looking for Rose and Raymond.

"Where the heck have you two been? I was worried."

Jameson said Chinchilla called, and said her father was okay and to thank us for our hospitality. Mona sends her regards as well. She's on her way to Pago-Pago to visit Tucker's family and wanted to wish us a very Happy Holiday.

Rose could hear voices from the family room. "Charlotte is that you? Are you still up? It's Christmas Eve and almost 9:00 PM."

"Everyone else it still up Mama! The house is so noisy I couldn't go to sleep if an anvil fell on my head!"

Rose shook her head at her dramatic reasoning. "Okay another few minutes then off to your room. Santa won't leave you any gifts if you're still awake."

She rolled her eyes reminding her mother that she was too old to believe in Santa and she already knows what Kcough and Meryl are giving her." Rose stared over at Keough as if to say *you are joking, right?*

Kcough shrugged, "Now Rose, you know I've got a real soft spot for this precious little darlin'. She asked for a surf board so we got her one."

Rose glared at him as if he'd lost his mind. "Keough I think the soft spot is in your head!" Where the heck is she going to surf in MONTANA?"

Meryl saw that Rose was pissed about their wasting money on Charlotte. She pulled her aside and whispered, "She may not be able to surf in Montana, but she can learn in Hawaii. That's the second part of her present she doesn't know about. We're flying to Maui tomorrow night, so mum's the word, okay?"

"Okay Meryl, so it's you I need to holler at as well."

Meryl shrugged. "Oh Rose, for goodness sake, lighten up, you're only young once!"

Rose laughed at her developing sassy attitude. "It's Keough who's corrupting you, isn't it?"

She laughed and said, "I'll never tell." Rose gave her a hug and they wished each other a Merry Christmas.

Paul walked over to the two women and asked what they were rabbiting about. Rose told him about Charlotte's gift and her holiday travel plans. "Well that's brilliant. It'll give you some time to rest up. You're still looking a bit . . ."

Rose stopped him. "Poolie, yes I know I look a bit poolie!"

Paul calmly said, "I was going to say pale, but if you insist, I'll say poolie."

Cecilia motioned for everyone to gather in the family room because she had an announcement to make. *I wonder what's going on, please no more bad news,* Rose thought. She announced how much she loves being a part of such a unique and wonderful family and that there was going to be one more addition to the family.

Jannine elbowed Rose and whispered "OH MY GOD is she pregnant?"

Rose spit out her eggnog and laughed. "I don't think so Jannine, she's well into her sixties!" She called Raymond over. He kissed her on her cheek and they announced they were engaged. Jannine elbowed her again and said, "Now, THAT'S a great surprise!"

Everyone congratulated and toasted to their new life together. Rose asked Jameson if he knew about this and he nodded. "Yep, I did. It seems they've been secretly seeing each other for a while, but Raymond threatened to drive me to the Bitterroots and abandon me if I let it out. Sometimes I don't know whether he's kidding or being serious."

Rose told Jameson never to underestimate Raymond. He made a mock scary face and thanked her for the warning.

As Cecilia walked around the room giving hugs and getting hugs from everyone, Raymond walked over to Rose again and asked how she was feeling. She told him that she was fine, just worn out from all the current events.

"Rose, you know I'm okay so you needn't worry about me. Cecilia takes very good care of me, and by the way she won't be leaving until we're married next year. And, another surprise, Jameson has agreed to fill in as your new chef and housekeeper while we're on our honeymoon, if it's okay with you and Paul. To my surprise he took up gourmet cooking as part of his recovery." I'm very proud of him. He's become one heck of a decent fellow. To be honest Rose, I'm going to miss him but not enough to take him with us on our honeymoon."

"Raymond if you vouch for him then I'd be happy to have him in our home."

He was about to walk away when he came back. "Oh, I finally remembered what Joe wanted me to tell you.

"Do I want to know Raymond?" Rose asked. "Is it good or bad?"

Raymond shook his head. "It's from Joe, who the hell knows. Anyway, he said to tell you, Paul, Charlotte and the little one to move on.

"That's it, short and sweet Raymond – move on?"

"Yes Rose, that's what he said for me to tell you. He also whispered something else and for the life of me I can't remember. I asked the medic to write it down because I knew I'd forget. I gave it to Paul. I didn't even read it. It's horrifying enough to get one message from that gibbering lunatic. I didn't want to be haunted by him trying to remember another."

Rose laughed because I knew how much he truly loved Joe.

"Well, we'd better head back to the family room because it looks like our midnight dinner is ready."

Raymond kissed Rose on her forehead, and wished her, Paul and Charlotte a very Merry Christmas. "You are all such beautiful souls."

After dinner everyone was chatting about their resolutions for the New Year and Charlotte and Paul were singing the most horrible versions of Jingle Bells Rose had ever heard. She needed some fresh air so she went out on the kitchen deck to ponder Joe's message. Rose looked up at the star that Joe had named for her and said aloud,

"Joe, I will move on, however, I'll never ever forget you. And, as part of this moving on, it's time to give my husband his Christmas Eve gift."

She went inside to their bedroom. A few minutes later, Rose joined the rest of the family for the midnight tradition of lighting the tree. As always Charlotte ran over to join Rose and Paul. Being the youngest Montana she did the count-down then flicked the switch. The entire family room lit up with colorful twinkling lights.

"It's such a beautiful sight with the fireplace glowing, isn't it Paul?"

"Yes, it's brilliant Poppet."

Rose announced that the Montana tradition mandates everyone gets to open one gift on Christmas Eve. Paul handed her a small sterling silver box tied with a bow and white ribbon. Her hands were shaking so badly, she had to ask Paul to hold the bow.

"Oh Paul it's beautiful." Inside was a heart shaped diamond ring with two smaller diamonds on each side. The inscription inside the band read, *Love, Always & Forever Paul.* "It's magnificent Paul! When did you, how did you . . . I don't care, I LOVE it!" He leaned over and kissed Rose.

"And, I love you too my beautiful and brilliant wife." Rose winked and told him she'd give him his gift after everyone went to bed. He grinned and asked if he was going to get lucky?

"Darlin', you married Rose Montana. That already makes you the luckiest man alive."

One by one the living room emptied. Rose knew Charlotte would be up at the crack of dawn sorting through all her gifts. It was time she gave Paul his gift. They closed the bedroom door behind them and started to undress. Paul began to unbutton his shirt then stopped.

"Poppet, I know you said you had a gift for me and it might involve tremendous amounts of heavy breathing and lots of sweat, but I must tell you . . . you don't look well at all. You've been trying to hide it for days. I know you well, Amelia so please be honest with me, what's wrong? Is it me? Is it because I agreed that you should let Joe go and supporting you in your choice to delete all of his emails? Please, tell me Poppet? What can I do to help?"

Rose asked him to sit down as the news would be life changing.

"Okay, now I'm officially petrified."

"I'm just as nervous as you Paul, but first open your gift. I handed him a red silk Christmas stocking with BG embroidered on the top and a small card attached that read, *No Refunds/No Returns*.

"So who's BG?" Rose told him he'd know once he saw his gift. He reached into the stocking and removed a small box and ripped off the wrapping paper. For the first time since they had been married, Rose witnessed Paul cry. He hugged her so tight for a moment, she couldn't breathe, and then said, "This is the most wonderful gift I've ever received in my entire life." He held the test stick up and read the word aloud, *PREGNANT*. Paul's eyes widened. "We're having a BABY!"

Rose laughed and said yes. "Oh my God this is brilliant, absolutely brilliant!" He squatted down to stomach level and stared at Rose's not-so-round belly. He wiped his eyes again and asked how far into the pregnancy she was.

"I don't know yet hon—maybe five-six weeks. I won't know for sure until I see my doctor."

"And the BG stands for boy or girl I assume?" He asked

"It's too early to know – Merry Christmas Paul."

He kissed Rose and said, "And, a Merry Christmas to you too Amelia."

The two chatted about how this would change their lives in the way of travel, working, romance, and so on. "We'll have to hire a Nanny. Two kids with Montana and Saxton blood will be a handful for us."

"I agree Poppet. Double the trouble, huh?"

"Yep, I agree Paul but just think Charlotte will have someone to occupy her time, not to mention boss around."

"That's true Poppet." He leaned over and hugged her again.

A piece of paper protruding from the top of his shirt pocket caught his attention. "Oh, and before I forget, earlier this evening Raymond gave me this note. He said it was for you."

He took it from his shirt pocket and handed it to Rose. "With all the celebration I completely forgot all about it. He rambled on about something or other regarding Joe during his heart attack? He didn't want to forget what Joe told him so he asked the doctor to write it down. Being in the state he was in, he said he knew he wouldn't remember. .I don't know what he was on about or what it says. I didn't bother to look at it." Rose slowly read Raymond's note and then she had to read it again. Her jaw dropped. "How did Raymond know? How could Joe have known? Hell, I didn't even know until this evening?"

Rose gave the note back to Paul. The two let out a loud sigh and simultaneously fell backward on the bed. The note simply read, *CONGRATULATIONS – it's twins! Love Joe.*

Epilogue

On one of my many research trips I met up with an old timer who told me that writin' western novels is a huge undertaking, especially if you want the stories to be authentic. You can't imitate Zane Grey or Louie Lamoure. You've got to put yourself in a cowboy's boots, ride herd and camp under the stars to experience why cowboys are the way they are. If readers can't imagine themselves in the story they won't read pass the first chapter. You've got to physically rope them in with an attention-grabbing introduction. Starting with *it was a dark and stormy night* won't keep "em reading." If your opening line ain't right, you're just writin' another boring dime-store novel that no one will remember or even worse, they'll leave it at a restaurant or at a bus terminal for some other tenderfoot to read. There's nothin' sadder for an author than to see their book sittin' somewhere half read. That's a lot of time and work for nobody to enjoy. Western writers are like old prospectors. We dig and dig until we find the perfect hunk of silver or gold. The novelist becomes the forge that shapes the words into something believable and unique. It takes blood, sweat, nerves and a lot of long nights hoping that one of your characters will take the lead and guide you on your imaginary journey. So, when I or should I say Montana Joe chooses his characters they must be worthy of carrying an entire storyline and if they meet up with other characters that are willin' to help 'em, he or she will let them saddle up and tag along for the ride. I never know who's goin' to take over the lead in my westerns. Sometimes it's the main character, sometimes it's not. I let them decide the peckin' order.

There are times I'm not sure what century I'm in let alone where my characters are headed. I just let them ride hard and follow their lead. A cowboy's creed is a sacred vow – never give up on yourself.

A western author's life is long cattle drive full of droughts, dust storms, flooded rivers; but pard' when you're lucky, it's clear starry skies to sleep under, warm campfire and hot coffee in the morning.

At daybreak you're back in the saddle and by midday, when ya' finally drive all them ornery beasts across that river to level pasturelands, its cowboy heaven. Seein' your fans eyes light up when that novel is finished makes it all worthwhile. I tell ya', there ain't nothin' like it!

I could continue to ramble on about how much I love the old west and the Big Sky state of Montana, but instead I'll leave you with a couple of questions. If you could step back and re-live your life, would you do it? Would you take a different path? Would you keep ridin' through them thorn patches or would you follow your heart across the river into that lush pastureland and start anew? I've asked myself these questions dozens of times. But the truth be told, I wouldn't change one single part of my life. I created the nom de plume of Montana Joe because underneath all these fancy duds, university sheepskins, I'm just an Ol' Joe from Montana – nothing special. Now I reckon if I'd lived in Idaho I would have been an Ol' Joe from Idaho. Yep, that might sound better but there's nothin' like Montana. It's where my heart is. It's where I was born and probably where I'll die. Well, I best let you kind folks get goin'. Thank you for the interview. It's been one hell of a good ride!

And, if you haven't figured it out by now old cowboys never really die. They just *cowboy up* and keep on ridin'. Because there's always one more cattle drive on the horizon.

[Excerpt from Lash Jackson Montana's final Interview with *Big Sky Western Writers Magazine*]